OXFORD DOUBLE

KU-711-565

Veronica Stallwood

headline

First published in 2001
by HEADLINE BOOK PUBLISHING

First published in paperback in 2002
by HEADLINE BOOK PUBLISHING

10 9 8 7 6 5 4 3 2 1

ISBN 0 7472 6845 2

Typeset by Avon Dataset Ltd, Bidford-on-Avon, Warks

Printed and bound in Great Britain by
Clays Ltd, St Ives plc

HEADLINE BOOK PUBLISHING
A division of Hodder Headline
338 Euston Road
London NW1 3BH

www.headline.co.uk
www.hodderheadline.com

now lives near Oxford. In the past she has worked at the Bodleian Library and more recently in Lincoln College library. Her first crime novel, *Deathspell*, was published to great critical acclaim and became a local bestseller, as did the eight Oxford novels which followed, all of which feature Kate Ivory, and her most recent atmospheric suspense novel, *The Rainbow Sign*.

When she is not writing, Veronica Stallwood enjoys going for long walks, talking and eating with friends, and gazing out at the peaceful Oxfordshire countryside from the windows of her cottage.

Praise for Veronica Stallwood:

'*Oxford Shift* gives Colin Dexter a run for his money among the dreaming spires' *The Times*

'A deceptive and atmospheric tale' *Time Out*

'Not only plausible but absolutely compelling' *Scotsman*

'Stallwood is in the top rank of crime writers' *Daily Telegraph*

'One of the cleverest of the year's crop' *Observer*

'*The Rainbow Sign* is a thriller that can't be faulted . . . The plot, sensed rather than seen, unfolds page by page, alluring and tantalising' *Shots*

For Audrey Quinn
the perfect travelling companion

I should like to thank Clays of St Ives, Suffolk, and in particular Steve Jones, for showing me over the printing works and answering my questions about printing processes. Needless to say, none of the people in this story resembles anyone I met at Clays during my visit.

1

Why would a man wear a wig?

Kate Ivory was pondering this question as she listened to the protests of a small, shrill French child who was refusing to leave the plane without her toy rabbit. The child and her mother, who was also loud and shrill, were successfully blocking the narrow gangway. A stewardess had been dispatched to search the vacated seat, but meanwhile the rest of the passengers were waiting more or less patiently to disembark. Kate, jammed against a woman in a grey anorak, had been staring at a man a few yards ahead of her in the cabin and had come to the conclusion that his hair – a glossy chestnut brown – was definitely false. It was just too perfect and not quite the right shade for his pale skin. And it wasn't as though the back of his neck was that of an old man: more like someone in his twenties or thirties. She wished he would turn round so that she could see his face, but his attention was concentrated on the obnoxious child.

'On l'a trouvé!' called the stewardess, and the passengers stirred expectantly.

Of course, thought Kate, there might be a perfectly valid reason for the man to cover his bald cranium with someone else's hair. Illness, for example. Or vanity. Men, in her experience, were at least as vain as women. She had yet to meet a man who could pass a mirror without checking his appearance.

1

There was still no movement towards the exit. It was stuffy in the cabin, and the woman in the grey anorak was breathing out wine fumes that Kate was forced to breathe in. Wouldn't it be uncomfortably hot underneath a wig? She found that she was scratching her own head in sympathy. Her hair was short and all her own, and artfully streaked in silver-blonde and caramel shades. As she stared at the wig, the neck below it turned pink as though the man knew he was the object of her attention.

At last the queue shuffled towards the exit. Kate checked her watch. Seventeen and a half minutes remained before the coach left Gatwick for Oxford.

The recalcitrant child was stamping her feet and shouting in spite of being reunited with her rabbit. The chestnut wig had ducked sideways and managed to overtake child and mother. Kate lengthened her stride to keep up with him.

If it was a question of vanity, why had he chosen that particular colour? Kate, whose novelist's eye always noticed such things, saw that he wasn't badly dressed: he wore a pale raincoat over black trousers. The collar of a dark-blue shirt showed above the raincoat. And he was wearing brown leather gloves, although it was hardly cold enough for such things. *Burglar's gloves*, she thought. No, she was being ridiculous. Her imagination was running away with her. Perhaps he had something nasty wrong with his skin that caused his hair to fall out and scales to spread over his hands.

As his back view disappeared from sight she saw that he carried a case small enough to count as hand luggage. Doubtless he would catch whichever coach he was aiming for while she was left watching strangers' suitcases revolve on the carousel. She should have travelled with a small case, she told herself, showing her passport to a man in a blue suit. But then she would have had to leave her five favourite pairs of shoes at home, not to mention her cream silk jacket and the seven paperbacks she had taken with her to read on holiday.

The man in the wig had sensed that someone was staring at him as he waited to leave the plane. It was nothing specific, just a feeling in the back of his neck that he tried to dismiss as fantasy.

He began to worry. Had his wig slipped? Were there strands of his own undistinguished hair sticking out from underneath it and causing everyone to smile at his vanity? He tried to check his reflection in a window but the image was too dark and indistinct. Still, he couldn't see anything glaringly wrong. He tried to relax and at least appear to be calm, even if he didn't feel it.

He was aware that another set of footsteps echoed his own, briskly in step, as he walked up the ramp away from the plane. Could someone be following him? He didn't turn round when he took his place in line at Passport Control, and handed over his passport. The officer looked at it, glanced at him, ignoring the presence of the wig. He was through

The footsteps behind him, interrupted in their turn by the need to present a passport, speeded up until they were close behind again. Still he refused to turn round and see who it was. It was when she went to collect her suitcase from the carousel that he finally caught sight of her. She shouldn't have taken so many clothes abroad with her, he thought smugly. Blonde hair, cunningly streaked with a caramel colour, expensively cut and shining with good health. He wouldn't have noticed a woman's hair in such clinical detail a few months ago. But since acquiring his wig – was it the right colour? Should he have gone for something more discreet? – he had become fascinated by hair in general, and women's hair in particular.

She wasn't interested in him, of course. That had been his nerves. She didn't look at him as she watched for her case to appear from behind the screen, like a performer in a cabaret. She wore good clothes, practical for travelling but in a distinctive colour, and she had a good figure underneath them. Just a little over medium height, but not too tall. In other circumstances he might have made an excuse to speak to her.

He stopped himself. He really shouldn't be hanging around like this. If he wasn't careful, he'd miss his coach. And it was unwise to loiter in the airport, waiting an hour for the next one. That was how you bumped into old acquaintances or got into conversation with strangers who turned out to live just a few doors away from you.

He turned and walked swiftly away through Customs. He took the Green lane where no one stopped him or asked to look in his small case. He strode along the corridor to the coach stop. He was looking forward to taking off the wig. Could he risk doing so in the coach? It was as warm as a woollen cap pulled down over his head and he could feel drops of perspiration trickling down his neck. But at least he was through Passport Control and Customs. There was nothing to be frightened of now.

He enjoyed the coach ride. He could think over his problem in peace. There was something about the combination of solitude and motion through the gradually darkening countryside that was helpful to constructive thought, he found.

* * *

Kate had spotted her suitcase on the carousel at last and grabbed it by the handle. There was a slight chance that she would still catch the six o'clock coach: she was wearing jeans and trainers and was fit enough to run, even with a suitcase. She slowed down to a respectable pace through Customs, then speeded up again.

Someone was in her way: a large man with shaggy hair, a worried expression and three bulging sports bags that looked as though they were about to disgorge their contents all over the floor.

'Sam?'

'What? Oh, hallo, Kate. What are you doing here?'

'I've been on holiday. Are you all right, Sam? Do you need a hand?'

'No,' he said swiftly. 'Really, there's no need.'

But at that moment Sam dropped one of his bags. Kate tried to identify the sound it had made. Was it full of metallic objects? Or something solid, like books. There might have been a slight clanking noise, and then again, she could have imagined it.

'You look as though you need help,' Kate insisted. 'Let me take one of them for you.'

'Really,' said Sam, a sheen of sweat across his cheeks, 'I do not need any help, Kate.' He put down the remaining two bags and stood as though guarding them. It was difficult to read the mood of a man whose face was largely covered in beard and whiskers, but his voice was expressing irritation.

'Are you looking for the Oxford coach, too?' she asked.

'No. Yes. Well, not really.'

In another man this confusion might have appeared odd, but Kate recognised that in Sam's case it was normal behaviour. He depended on his wife to organise him and was patently lost without her.

'I think we've missed it by now, anyway,' said Kate. 'Would you like to go for a coffee or something?' Not that she really wanted Sam's company for the next hour. There was a slight awkwardness between them due to the fact that Kate had lived with Sam's brother for some months, but had left him and moved back to her own house a few weeks ago.

'I'm afraid I've got someone to . . . something to . . . well,' said Sam lamely.

'Have you just returned from a trip abroad?' said Kate doubtfully. 'Or are you just leaving for foreign parts?'

'. . . meeting someone . . .' mumbled Sam.

'That's all right then,' said Kate, letting him off the hook. 'I'll go and sit on a bench and read my book for an hour.' She allowed the words *all by myself* to hang in the air.

'Yes. Right,' said Sam, hoisting one bag over his shoulder and picking up the others.

Sam and Emma must be really miffed with her, she thought, as she watched him shamble off. That was a pity, since they were old friends of hers and she was really quite fond of them. Still, you couldn't go on living with a man just because his brother wanted you to.

She walked the long corridors to the coach stop, not bothering to hurry any more. When she reached the bay she could smell diesel fumes, as though a coach had just left. The bench was empty so she sat down, pulled out a paperback from her handbag and started to read. There was another coach due at seven o'clock. In three hours or so she'd be home.

* * *

The breeze that had buffeted the coach from Gatwick to Oxford had also blown away the clouds and left the sky clear for the stars. Lights had sprung up in houses all over the city and marched in golden lines around its perimeter. The High Street was deserted as the coach drove towards Carfax. Even the kebab vans were missing. In the colleges on either side of her the electric lights were rendered mellow by ancient windows and Oxford looked as it might have done a century or more ago. Then they left the town centre, passed by rows of modern buildings and came to a halt in a distinctly unhistoric coach bay. Kate retrieved her case and crossed the small square to find a taxi.

A few hours ago, in France, it had felt like summer; here in England, although September had not yet arrived, there was already a clammy chill in the air that reminded her of autumn. As the taxi turned the corner into Agatha Street, she told the driver to stop. 'I'll walk from here,' she said, counting out the fare. The coins felt heavy and reassuring after the flimsy foreign ones she had been using for the past fortnight. She could understand why so many of the English resisted the idea of changing their currency from sterling to Euros – though she didn't agree with them.

When the driver noted the size of the tip she had included he said, 'Thank you,' and added, 'You sure you can manage that case?'

Kate hauled her suitcase out of the cab and on to the pavement, then slung her large leather handbag over her shoulder. 'No problem,' she panted.

She watched the red tail lights disappear down the narrow street. No one else was about: she was alone in the August night. There was very little moon, and although the golden

7

haze from the city lights stained the sky to the east, she could see the major constellations, even if she didn't know their names. Ah! There was one she could identify: the Great Bear sprawled tipsily in his usual place above her house. She was home at last.

Number 10 Agatha Street was set in the middle of a terrace of identical small houses built somewhere at the end of the nineteenth century, or perhaps at the beginning of the twentieth. They were described by estate agents as 'period' – though *which* period was never specified.

After the months away from Fridesley she could survey the street with a stranger's eye. Its seedy character was disappearing as prices rose. Agatha Street was only fifteen minutes from the town centre (if you were a fit person with a brisk style of walking), and you needed to be a well-paid professional if you wished to buy one of its houses now. Kate missed the lively street life that used to fill the place with noisy children, skateboards, overflowing skips and rusting cars that someone was always 'working on', but nothing could stop Fridesley from going up in the world. Soon every child would carry a violin case and only be glimpsed for a second or two as it was shepherded from front door to four-by-four by its mother or *au pair*.

The house to the right of her own had lights blazing from every window. The Venns had moved away, which meant that Kate had new neighbours to get used to in number 12. No one had bothered to pull the curtains, so she was able to watch a figure enter the room downstairs and hear the sound of voices and laughter. These must be the people her mother had told her about. They were evidently enjoying life in their new period home. Roz had stayed in Kate's house while Kate herself had been living with George, and she had been a bit sniffy about these new neighbours – Kate remembered now that they were called Foster – but the brightly lit house and the sudden bursts of laughter struck her as cheerful and lively. In the week between leaving George and going on holiday, while she had shared the house with Roz, Kate hadn't really noticed any neighbours, but now she looked forward to making their acquaintance.

By contrast, in the house to the left, someone had fitted blinds to the windows and there was only a dim haze of light filtering through them downstairs, and no sound of voices or laughter at all. Old Mrs Arden's brown chintz curtains had been removed: this must be another new neighbour. Kate had never done more than pass the time of day with Mrs Arden, who had lived in the house since Kate had moved in, but the two of them had been on good terms in an understated, English way. She hoped the old lady had made a huge profit out of her ungentrified house and was now installed in a luxurious retirement home on the proceeds of the sale.

A light came on in the upstairs room. Kate just had time to see that the room appeared to be an office, with a desk and a computer set at right angles to the window and overshadowed by a large green plant, when someone pulled down that blind, too. Male, she noticed, neither particularly old nor very young, and then he was nothing but a darker blur against the light green blind.

Another burst of laughter came from the house on the right and she sensed the head behind the blind lift for a moment as though interrupted in its train of thought. On the other hand, it could be her imagination at work again. She really must set it on to something practical, like writing a novel.

She crossed the road, walking slowly to savour the moment, then pushed open the front gate. Time to face your empty house, she told herself. The holiday's over, Kate.

It was only about fifteen minutes later that the door bell pealed.

2

When Kate opened the door there was an unfamiliar figure standing before her.

'I'm Laura Foster. And I've come to welcome you home to Agatha Street.'

Kate saw a woman about her own height, and aged around sixty. She had a surprisingly small head, capped with short, smooth hair brushed to lie flat in a style that Kate associated with the Thirties, and she wore bright lipstick and a wide smile. Her eyes, opened very wide as though drinking in Kate's whole appearance, were blue, made huge by brighter blue colour applied to the lids, and mascara that fanned out her eyelashes like a doll's. She was wrapped in a black and scarlet shawl that dripped with beads, chips of mirror and fringing, and accentuated the fact that her waistless body broadened out from narrow shoulders to wide hips in a stiff, bell-shaped skirt. She reminded Kate of her bedside lamp. Laura Foster's skirt was even the same shade of blue. Kate realised it was her turn to say something.

'How kind of you,' she managed. It was, after all, the first time anyone had ever welcomed her back to her own house.

'Now, Edward and I are quite agreed,' said Laura. 'You must come straight round to us. We were longing to get to know you even before your holiday, but hardly had you arrived home when you whisked off again! And now we must all have a drink in celebration of your return.'

'Isn't it rather late?' asked Kate.

'It's hardly a quarter to ten,' said Laura. Her pointed face split into an even wider smile. 'The evening has only just started.'

Kate had been looking forward to making herself a cup of tea, curling up on her sofa and reading another chapter of her novel, but Laura's smile was catching, so she smiled in return and said, 'I'll just get my handbag. I don't want to lock myself out of the house on my first night home.'

'It must be hard for you, Kate, being on your own again after being one of a pair,' said Laura sympathetically, leading the way out of one gate and in through the next. She walked with a stiff-kneed gait that reminded Kate of a mechanical doll. And although Laura paused as if waiting for Kate to respond to the comment, Kate kept her thoughts on no longer being one of a pair to herself.

'This evening there will only be the four of us,' Laura was saying, 'but usually we keep open house for all our friends and neighbours. We like people to pop in, any evening.' Just as Kate was wondering how Laura could cater for so many, so frequently, she added, 'Of course, I'm always grateful if people bring a little offering with them: a few sausage rolls, a pot of hummus, even a packet or two of crisps.'

'I haven't—' Kate started to say.

'Oh, I don't expect you to bring anything this evening. This is *our* treat,' Laura interrupted. She had paused a few feet from her door and spoke in lowered tones. 'I'm so sorry that it all went wrong – or should I say "pear-shaped"? – between you and George Dolby.' She laughed at the expression. 'But we don't want you ever to sit at home feeling sad and lonely, dear. You just pop round to see us whenever you're feeling low.'

'So you've heard about George and me,' said Kate as Laura pushed the front door open.

'I hope you're not offended! You know what Fridesley is like – just a little village, really. We've only been here for a few months and already we know *everyone's* business. Mrs Clack's shop is quite the village pump.'

Actually, Kate had lived in Agatha Street for about seven years without learning anything about the other inhabitants, apart from her former neighbours, the Venns. And in their case she had heard most of their eventful lives unfolding through the party wall.

'I knew this house when the Venns lived here,' she said, stepping into the narrow hallway. Strong smells of cooking sausages and flaky pastry gusted over her, and something yeasty that she couldn't quite place. The hall seemed smaller and more crowded than when the Venns had lived there, which was surprising considering the many hours Tracey Venn had spent shouting at her children to put their belongings away. The impression of clutter was reinforced by the large number of pictures, hung edge to edge, that crowded the walls.

'Harley Venn was quite a friend of mine,' Kate added, trying to indicate that she, too, was a concerned and involved Fridesley resident.

'And doing so well with his GCSE courses,' said Laura. 'He's got a lovely young girlfriend, too.'

So she didn't even know the latest news about Harley.

As she looked around she was reminded that the house was just like her own, but its mirror image. And as she peered at the pictures, she saw that the walls, painted a deep gold colour, were covered in what appeared to be the artwork for dozens of picture books.

'Are these yours?' asked Kate, stopping to admire one of them: bright colours, strong shapes, humorous figures.

'Oh, yes! I've always kept very busy as a children's book illustrator,' replied Laura, standing beside her.

'They're lovely,' said Kate truthfully.

'Thank you. I like to think they gave pleasure to lots of children all over the world.'

'Did you have children of your own?'

'No. I'm afraid not. You know how it is: we thought we'd get round to it one day when our careers were properly established. For years we were too busy with our work and our house. Time slipped away. And then it was too late.'

Kate was silent.

'Be sure you don't make the same mistake,' said Laura sadly. Then she smiled with a visible effort and added, 'Of course, all the children who enjoy my illustrations and enter into the world I've created are *my* children in a sense. That's the way I think of them.'

'Do you still paint?'

'I still illustrate books. Edward was a teacher. He's retired now, but I don't think I can ever give up my work. In fact, I have a new commission on my desk at this very moment. I shall get started on it tomorrow. It's so exciting!'

Kate wondered when she had last felt as enthusiastic about her own work. Laura Foster could teach her a thing or two, she could see.

As Kate followed her into the sitting room she noticed that Laura had short, plump legs beneath the blue skirt, and was wearing green ankle socks and yellow clogs, rather like a character in one of the jolly pictures on her wall. Kate felt herself warm to her new neighbour. She'd just have to make sure that she kept some areas of her life to herself.

'Hallo, Kate!'

'This is my husband, Edward,' said Laura.

Edward was a couple of inches taller than his wife, with sparse grey hair, a pointed beard, very blue eyes and a florid complexion. He wore a multi-striped shirt and red cotton trousers. His smile was just as wide as Laura's. He reminded Kate of a gnome, but to be fair to him perhaps the image was suggested by the pictures in the hall rather than by the man himself. She said, 'Hallo, Edward.'

Edward shook her hand with both of his. The expression on his face was so warm and friendly, so *concerned*, that Kate felt she should produce a broken heart for him to mend on the spot. His hands were small and pale and plump, though, and it was difficult to imagine them mending anything at all.

'And this is another neighbour, Jeremy Wells.'

'I popped round to his house a little earlier and insisted he join us for a drink,' said Edward, at last releasing Kate's hand.

Jeremy Wells was somewhere in his thirties, Kate reckoned, and flimsy-looking. He rose to his feet when Kate approached and shook her hand in a well-brought-up way, politely asking her how she did. His hand was long and thin, and his handshake not quite as firm as Kate liked. She saw hair that was so fair it could be mistaken for grey, and eyes that were a light hazel with a spark of intelligence in them. He had surely been a very good-looking child with his slight build and delicate colouring, but his jawline was too soft for a man and his face oddly undefined for an adult. He wore the clean but faded jeans and dark-blue pullover that were the Fridesley uniform for off-duty professionals. He must have felt hot in the pullover, for the Fosters had lit a fire in the small fireplace.

'Why don't you two young ones sit here on the sofa,' said Laura, pressing a large glass of red wine into Kate's hand. 'Get this down you. I'm sure you need it after your journey. And are you hungry, dear? I've prepared a few little snacks, but I could make you a sandwich if you like.'

'No, really. I'm fine,' said Kate. The colours in this room were jewel-bright: sapphire and emerald, ruby and amethyst, and there were more of the picture book designs on the walls. The sofa where she and Jeremy were sitting was garnet red and very comfortable.

'Whereabouts do you live?' Kate enquired.

'On the other side of you, at number 8,' said Jeremy. 'We must have been neighbours for nearly six months, but somehow we haven't bumped into each other.'

'I've been away a lot,' said Kate, not wishing to be too precise about her months with George Dolby, when Roz was living in her house, and her return (minus George) three weeks previously. 'I think we've only overlapped for about a week.' And during that week she hadn't been in the mood for socialising. She just hoped that, like her, Jeremy didn't have the private lives of all the neighbours at his fingertips. She felt in need of some old-fashioned reticence after a few minutes with Laura and Edward. 'Perhaps you met my mother?' she said. 'She was staying at my place all this year, until she moved into her own house about a week ago.'

'Lots of auburn hair and a bright yellow car?'

'Yes. Though she's traded in the car for a newer model now.'

'We nodded in a friendly fashion once or twice.'

'All that kind of standoffishness is going to change now

we're here in Agatha Street!' said Laura, interrupting. 'We don't believe in these stuffy English manners, do we, Edward?'

'We certainly don't! We're all going to be the best of friends.' He smiled roguishly at Kate and his beard wagged up and down. 'That's what I say to all the young girls.'

There was something so friendly and open about Edward that Kate couldn't object, even to the reference to her as 'a girl'.

'I hear you've retired,' she said. 'Have you taken up any hobbies?' She wasn't much good at small talk, but in Laura and Edward's honour she was working particularly hard at the trivial conversation. She thought she saw a faint smile on Jeremy's face as though he had noticed the effort she was making.

'I like to potter around, you know. Making things, mending things,' said Edward.

'Any little job you need doing, just ask Edward,' said Laura gaily. 'He'll be round with his tool kit and his oil can.'

'I like to make myself useful,' said Edward, and his blue eyes twinkled above his rosy cheeks. Kate felt she would be letting him down if she didn't produce a gutter to clear or a chair leg to mend. And yet she didn't need a handyman. she was quite capable of looking after such things herself. What about the bookshelves she'd fitted into the alcove in her study only last year?

As though to compensate for her own competence, Jeremy said, 'I wish I had your skill, Edward. I've a pile of shelves and brackets just waiting to be put up, and they've been leaning against the wall for months.'

'You need an electric drill,' said Laura.

'It sounds too dangerous for someone with two left hands. I

wouldn't know how to use it,' said Jeremy.

'I can soon show you,' put in Edward, looking keen.

Jeremy just smiled as though he really preferred his shelves vertical rather than horizontal.

'Laura tells me you've just got back from holiday, Kate,' said Jeremy. His voice sounded light and cool compared to Edward's as he rescued them both from the attentions of the gnome.

'I've spent a wonderful fortnight in France.'

'Really? Which part?'

'Périgueux. It's a lovely old city, just a train ride from Bordeaux.' She was grateful he'd moved to an impersonal topic, but Jeremy, too, had apparently come to the end of his supply of sociable conversation and was concentrating on his glass of wine. She filled in the pause by chattering on by herself.

'I saw such a ridiculous thing as I was getting off the plane. There was this man ahead of me, wearing a red wig.' Chestnut, actually, but you had to tell a good story.

'I expect he was bald,' said Laura reasonably.

'But he was young. And the wig was such an unlikely colour, and so obviously false, and although it was quite warm he was wearing thick leather gloves . . .' Kate trailed off. Her amusing little story wasn't going down very well. Laura looked as though she was about to contribute a recipe for hair growth, Edward looked blank, and Jeremy was still gazing into his wine. She wished he would come up with another conversational opening. Being dragged out of his house late in the evening to meet a strange woman must have been unnerving for him. But Laura and Edward were emanating so much goodwill and bonhomie that it was a pity it was having so little effect on their guests.

'Poor Kate's had such a sad time,' said Laura, as though this explained the pointless wig story. She took her armchair and pulled it close to Jeremy. 'But we're not going to let her pine away, are we?'

Edward poured more wine into Kate's glass (although she had hardly started on it) in unspoken sympathy. For a moment Kate wondered how the Fosters, if retired, could afford to be so generous with their wine to relative strangers.

'What's been wrong?' asked Jeremy dutifully, looking up from his glass. He was frowning slightly. Kate didn't think he wanted to hear about her emotional problems.

She started to say 'Nothing', but Laura over-rode her. 'She needed the holiday. She was looking quite peaky that week before she left. She's been trying to forget, you see.'

'It wasn't quite—' began Kate.

'I'm sorry. I'm upsetting you. I'm a great one for bringing these things out into the open. But I can see that you don't want me to talk about it, do you, Kate?'

'No,' said Kate. But not for the reason that Laura had assumed.

'I hear you're a writer,' said Jeremy, changing the subject again, to Kate's relief. The way the Fosters were trying to draw her out was doubtless as embarrassing for him as it was for her.

'Yes. I'm a novelist. What do you do?' If they worked hard enough they could lead Laura right away from the subject of Kate's love life. There was nothing so very fascinating about it, anyway.

'I'm a minor academic,' Jeremy replied.

'Not as minor as he makes out!' put in Laura. 'He's a Fellow at one of the Oxford colleges. I call that pretty impressive, don't you? Which one is it, Jeremy?'

'I'm not a Fellow, just a college lecturer,' said Jeremy. 'And my college is Bartlemas. It's hardly one of the famous ones. Quite mediocre, in fact.'

'Jeremy! You shouldn't run yourself down like that. How can you say such things!'

Jeremy was smiling, as though he had just squeezed a lemon into an oily salad dressing.

'Bartlemas,' said Kate, trying to placate Laura. 'I did some work there once.'

'Teaching?' asked Jeremy.

'More administrative than teaching. And it was a summer course for visiting Americans. I don't remember seeing you there, though.'

'They don't allow humble lecturers into the college during the vacations. It's as though we don't exist until the week before term starts.'

Kate had met enough librarians who were bitter about their status to recognise a disappointed man when she met one.

'I can't believe that,' said Laura earnestly. 'You were at your college all day yesterday and again today.'

'What subject do you teach?' Kate asked, hoping to shift the conversation sideways.

'I'm an economist,' said Jeremy. 'I'm a research assistant at the European Institute.'

'That new building out near the bypass?'

'That's right. The Concrete Onion,' said Jeremy.

'It's not that bad,' protested Kate.

'I'm afraid it is,' said Jeremy. 'It was designed by a committee.'

Edward put in eagerly, 'You must tell Kate all about the work you've been doing on—'

But Jeremy's attention has been caught by the sick-looking

plant at Kate's elbow, and he had stopped listening to the Fosters.

'What have you done to your azalea?' he asked Laura.

'That brown thing? Well, I just water it and keep it warm,' she said vaguely. Kate was amused by the look of concern on Jeremy's face. Laura might as well have said that she neglected her child.

'You really mustn't use tap water on your azaleas,' he said seriously. 'They can't cope with the lime. You should give it rainwater if you can. And keep it away from the central heating. Not too much warmth, but plenty of light, though out of the direct sun. This one may be past saving, but a little care might revive it.'

'Really?' said Laura, looking bemused. 'I'm not very interested in house plants, I'm afraid. When they go brown I throw them away and buy a new set.' She laughed at Jeremy's horrified expression. 'You'll have to give me some lessons in their cultivation, I can see that. I'm afraid I've always had black thumbs.'

Jeremy looked as though he would like to begin the lesson then and there, but he merely said, 'I could lend you a book, if you like.'

'So kind of you,' murmured Laura. 'Now, you must have something to eat. Have you tried these little cheesy things?'

Jeremy took one from the bowl she held out to him, bit into it and promptly showered himself and the garnet sofa with flakes of pastry. Kate brushed at her trousers while Laura produced a miniature vacuum cleaner.

'I'm so sorry,' said Jeremy, licking his fingers.

'Don't worry about it, dear,' said Lorna. 'I'll fetch the

sausages. As long as you're careful with the mustard dip they shouldn't be too difficult.'

But Jeremy stood up and said, 'That's very kind of you, but I'm afraid I have an early start tomorrow, so I'll have to leave you now.'

Laura and Edward protested that the night was still young, but Jeremy, in his understated way, appeared quite determined. He hadn't relaxed in their company, Kate noticed, in spite of drinking two of Edward's generous glasses of wine. Yet the atmosphere, if a little strained at times, had been convivial. Had she said something to upset him? She couldn't imagine what.

But Jeremy smiled at Kate, and kept looking into her eyes as he said, 'We'll meet again, probably while putting out our dustbins.'

'And I'll nod in a friendly way,' said Kate. She thought there might even have been more warmth in his parting handshake than when they had first been introduced. So it couldn't have been something she'd said. He'd probably remembered that he had a deadline the next morning for an important piece of work. She knew only too well how deadlines could creep up on you when you were enjoying yourself.

When Jeremy had left, Laura said, 'I think he's a little shy. But quite a nice man underneath it all. You and he must get to know one another better, Kate.'

'I'll have to show him a few of my practical skills, for his own good,' said Edward, opening another bottle of wine. 'Do-it-yourself, repairs around the house, that sort of thing,' he added. He tilted the newly opened bottle in Kate's direction.

She covered the top of her glass, which was still nearly full. 'Really,' she said, 'I'll have to be leaving soon, too. I've so enjoyed the evening.' They were generous people, but the day had been a long one. The Fosters had cheered her up and stopped her from sitting alone in her house feeling sorry for herself, but now she felt more than ready to face the solitude.

But Laura was continuing, 'We'll just have to find you someone new. A nice young man who won't let you down.'

'George didn't let me down,' said Kate truthfully.

'You're so loyal,' said Laura. She placed a warm hand over Kate's. 'I do admire you for that. But I know how badly some men can behave. Edward and I will make sure we introduce you to all the eligible ones we know.'

'It's very kind of you,' said Kate. They were well meaning, but she could do without all this sympathy, let alone the introductions to eligible men. From the tone of Laura's voice you'd think Kate was about to be carried off by some fatal disease. 'But really, I'm quite happy on my own.' She was only telling the truth. She didn't want another man in her life just yet.

'Brave as well as loyal,' said Laura. 'Here, let me fill your glass up.'

'Really, it's still nearly full.'

'It's the genuine article: out of a bottle,' confided Laura. Kate raised her eyebrows. 'We make our own,' said Laura.

'How clever of you.' Kate thought the habit had died out years ago.

'But we ease our guests into drinking our home-made concoctions gradually. Some of them take a little getting used to. A friend brought us a few cases of Cab Sauv last time they were in Europe. So cheap! You wouldn't believe it! So we can afford to share them with you,' she added earnestly. 'Do you like it?'

'Very nice,' said Kate. Too much oak, too high in tannin for her taste, but she didn't want to hurt Laura's feelings. Shortly afterwards, she hid her half-full glass of wine behind the moribund azalea, thanked the Fosters profusely for their hospitality, and left.

They were, she thought as she walked the short distance to her own front door, the sort of people whose life and conversation were a constant performance. It was difficult to know who they really were behind the cheery smiles and the upbeat words. Perhaps they no longer knew themselves.

Back in number 8, Jeremy Wells was mulling over the events of the evening as he drank a tumbler of iced water to clear the alcohol out of his system.

He wouldn't want to hurt the Fosters' feelings, of course – they were harmless, if irritating – but he really couldn't allow Laura to take over control of his social life. He could see that many evenings spent in their company and in the company of every freeloader in the neighbourhood would very soon overwhelm him with boredom. He would have to think up some absorbing hobby, or demanding piece of work, that would give him a permanent excuse to absent himself from their little get-togethers.

He dug his fingers absentmindedly into the compost of his *Beloperone guttata*. It was a bit dry, he thought, and he filled the small watering can with tepid water and gave it a generous measure. He hated it when people spent good money on house plants and then neglected them, or treated them inappropriately. Perhaps he could write out a few instructions for Laura so that she didn't maltreat hers any longer.

And then there was Kate Ivory. He was glad they'd met and

been introduced properly like that. She wasn't really his type –
too restless, and although she'd been interesting to talk to he
suspected she might be a little waspish in her unguarded
moments. He had found that this was a general failing of
intelligent women, especially in the academic world. Not that
Kate Ivory came across in any way as an intellectual, but he
could imagine that she would give her unedited opinions on
any subject if given half a chance. This evening she must have
been tired after her journey, and she had had to undergo Laura's
hamfisted sympathy over the break-up of her relationship with
some man or other, but he was afraid she would be relentlessly
bright and vivacious when he met her again.

But she did have unusual eyes, he had to admit. Quite simply
grey, with not a hint of blue or green. The hair wasn't natural,
but it was cleverly done. Yes, she'd make a perfectly acceptable
neighbour.

But what about the story she'd told about the man in the
wig? The Fosters hadn't been very interested, luckily. Perhaps
she'd let it drop now. She wouldn't understand its significance,
even if she made the connection with her new neighbour – she
would put it down to the well-known eccentric behaviour of
Oxford academics and never mention it again. He went to
check on the *Ficus benjamina*. No, it wouldn't need watering
for another day or two.

On the other hand, he wondered, returning to his previous
train of thought, suppose the sharp-eyed woman brought the
subject up again? Maybe he should speak to her about it and
put her mind at rest. He could give her a ring.

Glad to be alone in her own house, Kate lay in bed, reading a
chapter of her paperback. It struck her that she was still only a

few feet away from her companions of the evening, with Laura and Edward on the other side of one wall, and Jeremy on the far side of the other.

She laid down her book and turned out the bedside lamp that reminded her of Laura, and smiled at the thought that Laura might be simultaneously switching off a slim, sophisticated lamp in black and gold that spoke to her of Kate Ivory.

She remembered how Laura had talked about the children who enjoyed her illustrations. Under the bright exterior Kate had sensed an intensity of feeling. She wondered whether she might come to regret her own childlessness. Is that what lay in wait for her in some future time? Regret for unborn children and an overwhelming interest in other people's lives? Oh, come on, Kate! You've got years before you have to start worrying about such things. *Not all that many years*, whispered a voice inside her head.

And then just as she was falling asleep an image of Sam Dolby with his bulging sports bags drifted into her mind. What on earth had the man been doing at Gatwick airport? She didn't think he ever went anywhere without his wife or one of his numerous children.

3

Next morning, after fortifying herself with a pint or two of coffee, Kate thrust a load of washing into the machine and then went downstairs to her study. She hadn't sat down to work in this room for more than nine months and she pushed the door open cautiously, as though she might find that a stranger had usurped her place.

It was all right, she thought as she closed the door behind her. It was familiar. It felt like home.

The room was in the basement of the house, with a view on to a scrubby patch of grass which rose up from a rectangle of concrete (she really couldn't call it a patio). The grass was long and ragged and she would have to deal with it. But not now. Later, she told herself. Tomorrow, perhaps. There were daisies and some late-flowering dandelions adding colour to the turf; a self-seeded buddleia leant its nodding purple cones over the right hand corner of the patio (well, she could call it that if she felt like it).

Her computer stood on the desk where she'd left it, the printer beside it, still with a stack of clean white paper in its tray. The table she used as a second desk, for writing longhand in a notebook or drawing complicated diagrams of her plots, was unusually tidy. In fact it was completely clear. She had finished the research for the new book before leaving George. She hadn't settled down to any work in the week she had then spent in

Agatha Street, sharing the house with her mother, but instead had accompanied Roz on trips to Ikea and John Lewis to equip her own newly purchased house. Roz had moved out to east Oxford while Kate was in France, taking Kate's cat with her.

'I'll bring her back when you're ready to look after her again,' she had said. Kate was mildly offended by this, but she had to admit that Susanna was getting more loving care than she was prepared to give her at the moment.

But now it was time to get on with her writing. She opened the top right-hand drawer of the writing desk and took out an A4 pad, picked up her favourite black fountain pen and weighed it experimentally in her hand.

She felt like a beginner. She couldn't believe she would ever again manage to write ninety thousand words. She traced a few oblique strokes on the top line of the pad, then wrote 'I can't think of anything to say' several times. Just a thousand words, she told herself. That's all you need write today. Or five hundred, maybe. Jot down a list of the characters' names. *Alfred. Winifred. Albert.* She crossed them out again and sat chewing the end of her pen.

It was the quality of the silence that was different, that made the room seem strange to her. She was not yet attuned to the lives of her new neighbours. Usually at this time in the morning there would be pandemonium in the Venn household, with Tracey trying to persuade her children to get off to school. But Tracey was no longer at number 12. The Fosters, Laura and Edward, were living in the house, and there was complete silence from their side of the party wall. They must be very quiet people, or late risers.

On the other side, in number 8, Mrs Arden had lived her life to a strict timetable which involved playing her radio very loudly when some programme she was fond of was on – the Archers and the morning service were among her favourites – and at other times being so quiet it was possible to forget she was there. Kate had heard Jeremy in his kitchen, probably making coffee, at the same time as her. He was presumably in his own study now, working at whatever it was that academics did. She tapped the end of her pen on the desk a few times. It didn't help.

Maybe another cup of coffee would start the creative juices flowing. As she turned towards the door, the phone began to ring in the room above. She tried not to feel too grateful for the interruption.

'Hallo?' she said, picking up the receiver.

But the single tone told her that the caller had already rung off. Oh, well, if it's important, they'll ring back, she thought.

She made the coffee then carried her mug into the sitting room on the first floor, overlooking Agatha Street. She stared idly out of the window. A metallic-blue car was drawing up outside the house. Perhaps she had a visitor. A young woman climbed out of the car. She was tall and had short crimson hair – definitely out of a bottle! – and was wearing a brief black dress that showed off the sort of legs that start at a narrow ankle and reach right to the shoulder. Her height was exaggerated by shoes with four-inch conical heels. She walked smartly through the gate of number 8, clanging it shut behind her, and up to Jeremy's front door. The red hair swung around her face so that Kate couldn't make out her features. So much for the Fosters' matchmaking yesterday evening – though she wouldn't have guessed that Jeremy was the type to attract such a babe. Maybe the girl was his sister. Without opening the window and hanging out of it in an inelegant fashion, she really couldn't see any more.

She sipped her coffee and hoped that the Agatha Street show would continue. Sure enough, in another minute or so she heard the front door of number 12 slam shut and Laura Foster appeared on the pavement. She was dressed in a fuchsia-pink tracksuit and white trainers and jogged past Kate's house. Kate lifted a hand in friendly greeting, but Laura didn't look up before going through the gate of number 8. Lucky old Jeremy was certainly having a sociable morning. Kate heard number 8's bell peal, but there was a considerable wait before the door was opened. She allowed her novelist's imagination to fill in the gap.

'Jeremy!' squealed Laura's voice, rising effortlessly to Kate's window.

A muttering noise sounded to Kate like a man attempting to rid himself of an unwanted visitor. But then the front door to number 8 clicked shut, apparently with Laura on the inside.

Nothing happened for about half a minute, then the door of number 12 slammed again and Edward appeared in front of Kate's house, dressed in blue-striped shirt and emerald-green trousers. He carried his tool kit in one hand and an electric drill in the other, and looked like a man about to commit a good deed. He, too, rang at number 8 and disappeared inside, crying, 'It's the handyman!'

Kate hoped Jeremy hadn't planned a serious morning at his computer, or even a heavy session with the redhead, because his house must be getting quite crowded by now. And noisy. She could hear the Fosters' voices ringing through the party wall, interspersed with short silences when, presumably, Jeremy was answering.

Just as Kate had started on her second mug of coffee the

door to number 8 opened again. The fuchsia-pink figure reappeared on the garden path.

'So lovely to meet your sweet young friend!' Laura was saying, then she waved gaily and jogged back to number 12. As she passed Kate's house she looked up, saw Kate at the window, waved again, and called out, 'Hallo, Katie!' so that Kate could hear her through the glass. Kate mimed 'Hallo' in a neighbourly fashion.

'Let's get together for another little chinwag this evening,' shouted back Laura, loudly enough for the whole of Agatha Street to hear her. But then, she might well have been inviting the whole street to one of her get-togethers. You could overdo the neighbourly thing, Kate thought repressively, as she returned a vaguely encouraging wave that she hoped didn't actually commit her to anything. Kind and caring as Laura doubtless was, socialising with her and Edward was perhaps something one should reserve for a once-weekly treat. And anyway, Laura should be getting on with her new commission, surely, just as Kate should be settling down to her new book. She continued to sip her coffee.

Laura had turned into her own gate and disappeared. A couple of minutes later, Edward reappeared, still with his tool kit and drill and, perhaps, a slightly less jaunty expression on his face. Maybe he'd been turned down for the job of erecting Jeremy's shelves. He disappeared from Kate's view and she heard the door of number 12 close behind him.

It wasn't more than five minutes after that that the young woman in the black dress emerged from number 8, sent a penetrating glare winging towards number 12, then opened her car door. Kate had a quick impression of large dark eyes, a wide mouth in a pale face, and a ferocious scowl, before she turned away. The sun caught her hair as she slid into the driver's seat so that it flashed scarlet. Maybe I should try that colour, thought Kate. Or maybe I should stick with something less traffic-stopping.

The car door slammed. The lady was definitely in a temper. Well, enough excitement for one morning, Kate told herself. Back to work! And she went downstairs to her study for the second time.

There was still silence from Jeremy's side, but the Fosters, stimulated perhaps by their visit to Jeremy, were having an animated conversation that was apparently taking place with one of them at the top of the house and the other at the bottom. Just as Kate had grown used to this level of noise, and was doodling on her A4 pad with a gold marker pen, they added a little staccato door-slamming and some very heavy-footed pounding up and down the stairs.

You can ignore this, Kate, she told herself firmly. You have powers of concentration that can rise above a little distracting noise. She quickly jotted down some more names for her story. *Dorothy. Arthur. Enid.* She – or, strictly speaking, her mother – had come up with a suggestion for a novel set during the Second World War. She had developed the idea with her agent, Estelle, while she had been living with George. Just because she had changed her mind about George didn't mean she had to ditch her book, too. The names she had thought of sounded authentically nineteen-forties, didn't they? She was going to be able to get going on *Spitfire Lovers* after all (though she was having second thoughts about the title and hoped she might come up with a better one before she was finished).

She wrote 'Chapter 1' across the top of a new page. She would start with a short piece of dialogue. This one could be between Dorothy and Enid. 'Hallo, Dorothy,' she wrote.

Someone had switched on the television in the adjoining room on the Fosters' side. She could hear gunshots and screaming tyres, then shouting voices. The racket drove the neat little piece of opening dialogue out of Kate's head. Bother. She'd never get the book written at this rate. In another part of number 12 an electric drill was being driven into a resistant brick. She sighed. There was only one thing for it.

She went up to the bathroom and opened the wall cabinet. She was sure there would be a pair of earplugs here somewhere. Yes. Yellow foam ones. She pushed them into her ears. She could still hear vague thudding noises through them. Perhaps it was the sound of blood pounding through her veins and arteries, but she thought not. She found the headphones that she used with her Walkman and put them on over the top.

That was better. Now she could hear nothing but her own thoughts. She returned to her desk.

She stared at the blank page with its stark 'Chapter 1' at the top. No ideas came into her head. What were those characters called again? Avril? Marjorie? The A4 pad was putting her off, she decided. She'd be able to work more effectively at her computer.

The machine flashed into life when she switched on the power. Thank goodness for that! She knew that Roz had been using it while she lived in Kate's house, so it shouldn't have died of neglect, or whatever it was that computers died of when you ignored them for months. The screen blinked twice and came up with her familiar desktop. Roz hadn't buggered it up for her, anyway. After a couple of minutes the screen saver she had put on last year – *last year!* – swam across and admonished her: JUST GET ON WITH IT, KATE. The tall yellow letters disappeared slowly into the left hand side of the screen and then reappeared at the top right edge. OK, OK. Stop nagging.

Dorothy. Enid. The names came back to her. They were two women in their forties talking about the difficulties of feeding their families on their meagre rations. And one of them had a flighty daughter – called Avril, of course.

She started to tap at the keyboard, hesitantly at first, then the story took over and she typed happily on. The short dialogue developed into three pages of conversation. Another couple of characters joined Dorothy and Enid. It was some time before she came to a halt. Exactly how much meat were you allowed on your ration in the summer of 1942? She couldn't remember offhand. And was it possible for Avril to telephone her mother? Or were telephones permanently out of order? She could check through her research notes.

She hadn't unpacked her notebooks and her index cards, she realised. They were still upstairs, in one of the cardboard boxes that she had brought back from Headington with her and had failed to unpack in that week before she left for France. She had been putting it off, not wanting to be reminded of what she had lost. Although it had been her own decision to leave George and return home, she sometimes felt a twinge of regret about the break-up of their relationship. There was nothing to look forward to at six o'clock when she left her study, no one to chat to, no one to exchange news of the day's work with.

No, she told herself firmly. It's no use regretting it, Kate. The Dolbys have different values from yours. You'd never fit in with them. *Think what they did to the children.*

She went upstairs. The kitchen clock informed her that it was well past time for her coffee break. She'd have a cup of coffee and then she'd set to work on her research material. She could sort it out and put it away in her filing cabinet and then she needn't think about George every time she looked at the boxes.

She was still wearing headphones, and although her ears were now getting hot under the layers of protective foam she didn't bother to remove them, or the earplugs. She might even put a gentle CD on the Walkman, she decided. What was it they said? Play Mozart to increase your concentration, or romantic music to enhance your creativity. She didn't feel like listening to anything romantic at the moment, in case it reminded her of what she was missing, but she thought she might have some Mozart somewhere, a relic of a former relationship in which she had tried hard to acquire highbrow tastes.

So 'Mozart's Greatest Hits' accompanied her downstairs to her study to aid her concentration as she sorted through her index cards. The neighbours could take up the trombone or detonate explosives now for all she cared. She was quite oblivious of anything except 'Eine kleine Nachtmusik' and the flirtation with a married GI that young Avril was about to embark upon.

At one o'clock she broke off briefly for a bowl of soup and an apple, grateful that Roz had left a few basic items of food behind when she moved out. They would soon run out, though, and she needed to undertake a major shopping trip in the next couple of days. She changed the CD for something less uplifting and went back to her study. If she went on working at this speed she would have the first draft finished by the end of the month. Just for once her agent would be delighted with her.

That evening, when she had eaten her supper, the phone rang.

'Hallo, Kate?'

'Yes?'

'It's Emma. Emma Dolby.' Her friend sounded apologetic.

'You're still the only Emma I know,' said Kate. 'And we don't need to let my break-up with George affect our friendship, do we?'

'No. Of course not.' Emma sounded relieved, but still not exactly relaxed and cheerful.

'What's up, Emma?'

'Do you have time to talk?'

'I've got all evening. How about you?' Emma usually had a dozen small children at her knee, all demanding her attention.

'I'm free for an hour or two. Sam's taken the older ones out to McDonald's for me, and the little ones are in bed and asleep.'

'Brilliant.' She didn't ask *why* Sam had taken the older children out. Emma didn't usually allow them to eat junk food. 'So. What do you want to chat about?'

'Well, Kate. I'm a bit worried about Sam.' She sounded as though she was telling Kate a state secret.

'In what way?'

'He's not himself.'

Which didn't get Kate much further. She let her friend talk on until matters became clear.

'I know I'm not much fun at the moment,' continued Emma. 'I get sick every morning and my skin has gone greasy and spotty and I can't do a thing with my hair, and now I can't get into any of my decent clothes again.'

'You mean you're pregnant,' said Kate, managing not to add 'again'.

'Yes.'

'Congratulations. I know you and Sam wanted another child.' Which was a bit of an exaggeration. It was Emma who wanted another, Sam who reckoned they had enough children already. And Kate couldn't help agreeing with Sam.

'Kate, I think he may be having an affair. He keeps disappearing without saying where he's going. And he's so *nice* to me when he is here. He brought me a bunch of flowers the other day, and now he's *volunteered* to take the children out so that I can have a bit of a rest.'

'Sam's a really kind person.'

'Well, yes, he is. But he doesn't usually *show* it like that. I think he's seeing someone else. What should I do about it, Kate?'

'It's probably the pregnancy, making you imagine things. I'm sure Sam would never look at another woman.'

'Pregnancy doesn't make you stupid. It's a physical state, not a mental one,' said Emma sharply.

'Of course you know more about it than I do,' said Kate hastily. 'But you might be feeling a little more sensitive and vulnerable than usual.'

'You think I should forget about it?'

'Go out tomorrow and cheer yourself up with a new haircut. Get Sam to pay for it,' said Kate. 'It's all in your imagination.'

But as she put the phone down an image of bumping into Sam at Gatwick came into her head. Sam, who didn't want to stop and have coffee with his wife's friend. Sam, dropping bags on the ground. Sam, looking guilty. But surely he didn't look like a man who was having an affair? Sam Dolby wouldn't do that to his family.

The next morning saw Kate again at her computer, filling pages of screen with another chapter of *Spitfire Sweethearts* (more nineteen-forties, surely, than '*Lovers*'?). And once more, at half past ten or eleven o'clock, the Fosters started enjoying their action-filled lives. Laura, upstairs, began an animated conversation with Edward, who was in the basement. Perhaps she needed to chat all the time she was painting. Perhaps it was her equivalent of listening to Mozart.

Edward was using a hammer today, stopping from time to time only to wield what sounded like a power saw. Kate resigned herself to living in earplugs and headphones until the book was completed. This morning she put some Scott Joplin on the Walkman. She was sure it would be as effective as Mozart at improving creativity.

She worked so well that she barely stopped for lunch, just grabbing an over-ripe banana and a glass of juice from the kitchen before returning to her chapter.

When she finally emerged from the study it was past five o'clock. She took off her headphones and pulled out the earplugs. Normal sounds seemed magnified suddenly. A helicopter snarled over her roof, sounding as though it were only a few feet away. Car engines growled in Agatha Street. She could hear many voices, calling to each other as though issuing orders. She shook her head to bring her hearing back to normal. This was what happened when you deprived yourself of all external sounds for six hours. She wished there were a simple volume control that she could turn down.

Upstairs in the sitting room her answering machine was blinking at her. It could well have been ringing all afternoon, she realised. She wouldn't have heard it. As she played back her messages she felt the quiet glow of someone who has worked all afternoon instead of chatting to her friends.

'Kate? It's Jeremy. Are you in?' A pause, then the click of the receiver being replaced. Three beeps, then the second message started.

'Kate? You've *got* to be in. I can see your car there. Can you pick up the phone? Please.' It was Jeremy's voice again, sounding agitated. Had she had such an effect on him that he couldn't wait to speak to her again? No, she didn't think so, really. She considered calling him back, but she didn't have his number and, remembering his limp handshake, didn't feel like dialling 1471 to get it. He'd probably knocked on the door, she thought, but she'd heard nothing, and he'd have to learn that when she was working she couldn't be disturbed. And was it really important, anyway? She sniffed at the air. There was no smell of smoke, so the house wasn't on fire. It couldn't be desperately urgent, although he had sounded, well, a bit put out, especially the second time. She'd make herself a cup of tea and then pop round to his house to see what it was all about.

Before going downstairs to switch on the kettle, she wandered over to the window and looked out on to Agatha Street.

Police cars. Vans. Men in blue uniforms. Men in white overalls. Helicopters, two of them, hovering overhead.

The loud noise hadn't been an illusion. It had been real.

She saw blue and white tape across pavement and road, keeping out onlookers, isolating number 12.

What?

Just for a moment she couldn't believe what she was seeing. It was as though the world of her imagination had translated itself into reality and come to life on Agatha Street.

And then, gradually, she attempted to make sense of what she saw. Had a bomb exploded? No crater. No debris. And even through her ear protectors she would have heard it, or felt the blast. Canvas screens had been erected, blocking the view of the Fosters' house from people at ground level, but from her vantage point on the first floor Kate could see down into their front garden. A photo bulb flashed and drew her attention to what was happening by the gate.

A heap of clothes spilled on to the garden path and pavement.

No. Her brain didn't want to acknowledge what she was seeing. A small brown bird alighted on the windowsill a few inches away from her, cocked his head, blinked, then flew off again. The sky was blue with puffs of white cloud turning pink at their edges. It was a normal day. It had to be. Then she looked down into the garden again.

Fuchsia-pink and scarlet track suit. White and scarlet trainers. Green and scarlet trousers. Stripes and splashes. Not just a heap of clothes, but two people, one in a blood-soaked pink tracksuit, the other in blood-soaked cotton trousers and striped shirt. It could only be the Fosters. Laura's white leather trainer was very clear against the dark ground. She had small feet, Kate noticed. With wide toes. One white lace trailed behind her foot, as though it had just that moment come undone.

Kate felt the blood leave her face and for a moment she stood there, frozen, unable to move. The cliché was true, she found. She felt cold, and a little sweaty, and *frozen*. It was as though she had stepped off a cliff and was falling, falling, with the air rushing past her face.

She tried to pull her gaze away from the scene of carnage beneath her window, but she couldn't stop staring at it. Somehow there seemed to be too many body parts for two people, as though pieces, once human and alive, had become detached, like lumps of meat. She felt bile rise into her mouth. She wished the bird would return, or a helicopter roar close and blot out her thoughts.

A man in police uniform looked up and saw her standing

there, then walked towards her front door. She went downstairs to meet him and opened the door before he could ring the bell.

'What's happened?' she asked.

'May I come in?' he said.

He was showing her some sort of identification, telling her his name, but it didn't seem important. They went into the kitchen and Kate switched on the kettle. Just for something to do, she thought. I don't give a damn about the tea, I just need to keep occupied.

'What's happened?' she asked again.

'Have you been in all day?' asked the policeman. What was he? A sergeant? A constable? She hadn't noticed when he showed his warrant card, and she didn't care.

'Yes. Yes. I haven't been out. I've been here.'

'Can you tell me what you saw and heard?'

'No. I mean I saw and heard nothing.'

'You must have noticed something. The whole street heard it.' He sounded disbelieving. In the background the kettle was humming as the water heated. She could hear that all right, now.

'Heard what? What did they notice?'

'If you could just tell me about the day's events, as you saw and heard them,' he said, reverting to his neutral tone.

'I was working,' she said. 'I was wearing earplugs as well as my headphones.'

'Both? At the same time?'

'Yes. It sounds stupid, but it's true.'

'And you didn't look out of the window. You didn't see anything unusual.'

'I was sitting at my computer in the study. That's downstairs. It has just the one window and it looks out on to the back garden.'

'Like the kitchen?' he said, looking at the yellow-curtained window.

'Yes.'

'So. You were in all day but you saw nothing and heard nothing. Do you mind making a statement?' He hadn't even bothered to take out his notebook, she noticed. But why should he when she could tell him nothing?

'If you think it will help.'

'You work at home, then?' he said, as Kate poured boiling water on to tea bags. 'What do you do?'

She paused. 'I'm a novelist,' she said.

'A close observer of human nature. A watcher of the world as it turns. Someone who makes a point of noticing things.' He managed to keep any sarcasm out of his voice, but Kate felt her cheeks turning pink.

She added milk to the tea. 'Sugar?' He shook his head. 'You could take my statement while we drink our tea,' she suggested, passing him a mug. 'It shouldn't take very long.'

'No. I don't suppose it will.'

He took out an A4 form and wrote down her name and noted her address. He asked her age.

'And you saw and heard nothing because you were engrossed in your work for the whole day, and were wearing earplugs?' It was less a question than a statement.

'That's right.'

'If you do think of anything,' he said unenthusiastically, 'just let us know, will you?' He sounded as though he doubted that Kate Ivory, self-employed novelist, of 10 Agatha Street, Fridesley, could ever come up with anything remotely interesting to the police. Almost as an afterthought he added, 'Have you seen anything unusual in the past few days? Have you noticed any strangers hanging about the place?'

'I've been away for a couple of weeks, on holiday,' said Kate. 'I only got back the night before last. And in fact that was the first time I'd met the Fosters. Laura came round to introduce herself just after I returned, and to invite me round for a drink with another of our neighbours.'

'It appears that Mrs Foster was a very friendly person,' agreed the policeman. 'Very well liked in the neighbourhood. And her husband, too. Funny you hadn't met them before.'

'I'd been living on the other side of Oxford since the beginning of the year,' said Kate briefly. She didn't want to go into her relationship with George Dolby.

'You left this house empty?'

'My mother was living here in my absence,' replied Kate, who had hoped to leave Roz out of it.

'And she is?'

So Kate gave him her mother's details and the address in east Oxford where she might be contacted. Roz had probably noticed what was going on in Fridesley these past months much better than Kate ever could.

'So you went round to the Fosters' the evening before last for a drink. What did you talk about?'

'I'm sorry, I've forgotten your name,' said Kate.

'Police Constable Mundy.'

'Yes. I was introduced to my neighbour from the other side, Jeremy Wells. He's new in the street, too. We drank a couple of glasses of wine and talked generally about our work. Laura Foster told me she illustrated children's books. She said she had a fresh commission on her desk at that very moment,' said Kate sadly. No more jolly, bright figures. No more menacing forests or mysterious lakes.

'And nothing struck you as strange or unusual? Nothing in their manner?'

'No. It was all very pleasant. They were very welcoming, very sociable.'

He stared at her as though doubting that anyone could have noticed so little.

'Can you tell me what this is about? What happened to the Fosters? It *was* the Fosters I could see lying on the ground, wasn't it?'

'By their front garden gate,' he confirmed. He had the sort of lugubrious voice that seemed designed to impart bad news.

'And they were dead,' said Kate.

'Yes.'

'How did it happen?'

'We're still investigating the circumstances,' said PC Mundy.

Kate wanted to tell him to stop being pompous. 'You must have some idea. All that blood . . .'

'They were shot.'

'And that's the sound I didn't hear.'

'Apparently so,' said PC Mundy.

Had there been shouts and screams? Did they die instantly? Or did they know what was going to happen to them? Kate tried to think back to the hours she'd spent in front of her monitor. Surely she'd have heard something? But nothing came to mind except the dialogue she had been writing.

'Why?' she asked.

'Why were they killed? That's one of the things we are trying to ascertain.'

Then he wrote a couple of sentences on the statement form and asked her to sign her name at the bottom of the page.

4

To tell the truth, Kate couldn't imagine wanting to eat anything at all that evening after PC Mundy had left. But the food supplies left by her mother were nearly depleted, the fridge was empty and there were only two tins of soup left in the cupboard. She might fancy some fruit later, she thought, or even a shot of malt whisky.

She drove to the all-night supermarket, avoiding the Fosters' taped-off section of the street. It was a relief to get away from the sights, sounds and smell of death, she realised guiltily as she pulled into the evening traffic and headed east. Would it help Laura and Edward now if she dwelt on their dreadful death? She didn't think so. But what about their families? They had no children, she remembered, as she waited to turn right at the traffic lights. But might there be brothers and sisters, or even elderly parents, grieving for them? She didn't know. She knew very little about them. She had glimpsed only a tiny corner of their life before it was snuffed out.

By whom? And why? It was easy to imagine that it must be a maniac, but were there really such people at large in a quiet suburb? And the killer had used a gun. Pools of blood filled her mind's eye as she turned into the supermarket car park. It must have been an automatic weapon, she thought. Or semi-automatic – whatever that might be. But a single shot wouldn't have resulted in so much gore; it must have taken dozens of them to have cut the bodies up like that. She remembered Laura's white shoe, not much larger than a child's, and had to sit in the car for a couple of minutes, taking deep breaths, before she felt composed enough to walk through the doors and decide what she wanted to eat for the next week.

She found she had halted in the aisle containing cleaning materials. Did she need a new mop? Another spray for her counter tops? No. It was the pictures inside her head that she wanted to scour away. Bleach them out. Destroy them for ever.

She would never be able to do that.

'Kate?' It was a woman's voice, from just behind her left shoulder. Kate pulled a clean tissue from her pocket, blew her nose quickly and turned to see who it was.

'Camilla.' Her voice sounded flat and dull, even to herself.

'Are you all right?'

'Yes. I think so.'

'I was going to ask you what was happening in Agatha Street. The entire Thames Valley police force seemed to be converging there.'

'Yes. There's been an accident.' What a stupid thing to say! How could the brutal slaying of two people be accidental? 'At least, it wasn't really an accident. It's my neighbours. They've been killed.' Such small words to encompass such an unthinkable act.

'You're *not* all right,' said Camilla. 'You're a dreadful colour and your hands are shaking. I think you should sit down, Kate.'

It was at times of emergency that Kate could forgive Camilla for being the headmistress of a posh girls' school. Camilla radiated calm and competence. Kate felt as though she had plunged into a warm bath. Camilla would cope. Camilla would deal with everything. Nothing nasty could happen when Camilla Rogers was in charge.

'Have you got everything you need in your trolley?' Camilla peered in at a pack of eight dusters, a spray kitchen cleaner and a bottle of malt whisky. 'No, I can see you haven't,' she said. 'Did you mean to shop for food?'

'I've just got back from holiday. The fridge is empty,' said Kate.

Camilla didn't bother to mention that it would stay that way with Kate in charge of the shopping. 'I'll make sure you can eat for the next few days,' she said, taking the trolley away from her friend.

And so Kate bought herself a cup of coffee and sat at a table while Camilla pushed both their trolleys around the store. There was nowhere quite as normal as a supermarket coffee shop, she thought. The clatter of cutlery, the buzz of voices, the constant beeping of barcode readers could fill her head and stop her thinking about anything else. From time to time she saw Camilla's solid shape steering the two trolleys – both small ones, luckily – across an aisle. Kate knew her friend wasn't an enthusiastic cook, so she would probably choose easy to prepare items: ready-made quiches and pizzas and a few tins of tuna. When Kate could face food again, she might be able to cope with items as simple as those.

Camilla joined her at the table in under ten minutes. Kate fetched her some coffee, paid her what she owed for the groceries, and then sat and looked at her across the table. Camilla's round, brown eyes gazed back at Kate and her mouth was slightly pursed. She had gained weight since her jogging days and had taken to dressing in a matronly way which, with the grey streaks in her hair, made her look older than the couple of years' difference in their ages warranted.

'I don't know what happened,' said Kate, before Camilla could ask. 'I'd been working in my study all day and I knew nothing about it until I looked out of my window at teatime and saw two figures sprawled on the ground, and the police swarming all over the place. I recognised Laura's tracksuit, so I knew it must be them.'

'They were new, weren't they? I think I saw her in the post office or Mrs Clack's a couple of times. Friendly little soul, chatting to everyone, and that dreadful old gossip, Mrs Clack, addressed her by name, so she must have been a regular.'

'She always asks my name when I ask for my copy of the *Bookseller*, as though she's never seen me before,' said Kate.

'Laura Foster looked to me as if she was far too innocent to survive alone in this wicked world,' said Camilla thoughtfully. 'I thought she'd wandered in from some older and simpler place.'

'Yes, that sounds like Laura. I felt she would be most at home in the land of her book illustrations. Edward was less chatty, but seemed very similar. Pleasant people. Ordinary. Not the sort you'd think would get themselves killed like that.'

'You're sure it wasn't an accident?'

'No, it couldn't have been,' said Kate and didn't elaborate.

'Have you heard anything about the investigation?'

'The police weren't telling any of us anything, possibly because they didn't know any more than we did. They sent a man round and I felt such a fool because I couldn't give him any help at all. I only got back two nights ago, and that was the first time I met the Fosters.'

'Was it a shooting?' asked Camilla, who could be insensitive as well as kind.

'Yes, that's what the policeman told me. There was a lot of blood.'

'It's odd, isn't it? It doesn't sound as though they'd disturbed a burglar in their house, not if the bodies were outside in the garden.'

'At the gate,' said Kate.

'Was the gate open or closed?'

Kate unwillingly brought the scene back into her mind. 'Open. They could have been walking out through it at the time they died.'

'One behind the other, I imagine. It's too narrow for them to walk side by side.'

'Do you have to discuss it like this?'

'You'll only go home and brood if we don't.'

'You're right about that,' admitted Kate.

'Drink your coffee. It's getting cold.'

Kate did as she was told. Reluctantly, she was starting to follow Camilla's line of thought. 'They couldn't have died at the same time, then. The killer must have shot the one in front, then the other. Laura would have been leading the way. She was like that.'

'It must have been very quick. And Edward wouldn't have had time to realise what was happening before it was too late.'

'I hope you're right.'

'It sounds like a contract killing to me,' said Camilla.

'Don't be ridiculous!'

'What other explanation is there? The gunman turned up in front of their house, attracted their attention in some way, then shot them and zoomed away from the scene. Are the police looking for a car?'

'I don't know. It could have been a motorbike or even a pedal cycle.'

'It must be more difficult to carry a gun on a bike, though you could escape through the traffic faster than in a car. The evening traffic jam must have been building up nicely in the Fridesley Road.'

'Perhaps you've missed your vocation. You should have been a detective.'

'I'm just applying logic to the problem.'

'Well, I think we should give the subject a rest.' Kate had finished her coffee and she watched as Camilla emptied her cup. 'I like the idea of a motorbike, though,' she added grudgingly. 'And you could wear a helmet with the visor down and no one would be able to offer a description of you. You couldn't even guess at gender unless the biker was particularly tall or small.'

'So who's not interested in the problem?'

'Shall we make a move?'

'That's the next problem,' said Camilla, staying where she was.

'What is?'

'You can't stay in your house.'

'Yes I can. I have no intention of leaving. I've been away on holiday for a fortnight and before that I was away for months.'

'Poor old George,' said Camilla, then grinned at Kate's furious face. 'Just teasing. I'm sure it was all his own fault and that you were your usual sweet and caring self.'

Kate made a face at this view of her relationship with George. 'The point is that I don't want to move out of Agatha Street again. It's my home and I want to be there.'

'Have you thought about the reporters?'

'What reporters?'

'The ones who'll be banging on your door and asking for your opinion of the Fosters and your theories as to why they were killed.'

'Oh. Now you mention it I did notice that the TV vans were turning up as I left. I hadn't thought about the press.'

'And they'll be phoning you, too.'

'The answering machine's on. It'll filter the calls.'

Camilla was looking into her handbag. It was a square, sensible, well-worn article and she had to look through several pockets before she found what she was looking for. 'Here, Kate. Take this.' She handed across a door key. 'It's the spare key to my house. I'm leaving very early tomorrow morning for the Lake District. It's my last chance of some time to myself before I have to deal with the start of the school year. I'll only be gone for ten days, but you're welcome to use my place if you need to.'

'I can see it might be necessary, after all. I have a book to get on with, so my agent tells me, and it could be difficult at home with all the interruptions. Thanks a lot, Millie. I'm really grateful.'

'You could water my plants for me, if you like.'

'I'll do that.'

Camilla lived only a quarter of a mile away from Kate, in a detached house with a fair-sized garden around it. As far as Kate remembered, Camilla had a small collection of pampered house plants and her garden design involved large areas of gravel with a few sparse, but exotic, shrubs. Apart from those, there was a thick hedge for deterring young vandals which was professionally clipped by a man in a green van, so she thought she could cope adequately with her duties.

'Now, you're sure you'll be all right this evening on your own?' said Camilla as they stowed Kate's shopping in the back of her car.

'With all those policemen about? I'm sure I will.'

'You know what I mean.'

'I'll be fine. Don't worry about me. Just concentrate on renewing your strength for dealing with your posh, delinquent girls next term. Are you going away with a friend?'

'I'm meeting someone there,' said Camilla in a tone which forbade Kate to ask any intrusive questions – which probably meant she'd found herself another unsuitable man. Lucky old Camilla.

As Kate drove back to Agatha Street she felt her spirits sinking. She'd been glib enough about living next door to a killing, but the nearer she approached to her house, the less she looked forward to going indoors.

Contract killing? she wondered as she turned off the Fridesley Road. But why on earth should anyone pay out thousands of pounds (and surely a contract killing would cost that much?) to kill the Fosters? But what do you really know about them, Kate? You only have their word for it that Edward was a retired teacher and Laura an illustrator. That could have been a front. They might have been jewel thieves, drug dealers, spies. They could have fallen out with their associates and double-crossed them. No, it was no good: Laura and Edward were hopelessly transparent and respectable. But there could have been murky areas in their lives that you can only guess at, Kate, she told herself.

When she had put away the groceries she poured herself a small glass of whisky and walked into the sitting room. She pulled the curtains shut so that she could forget what was happening outside: the floodlights in the garden next door, the men who were doubtless examining every hair, every speck of dust, every fingerprint in number 12. She ignored the television set in the corner, too. But when she saw that the answering machine light was blinking she pressed the Play button, hoping that Camilla was wrong about the reporters.

'Kate. It's Jeremy. Again. We have to talk.' There was a pause and she thought he was about to hang up, but then his voice continued. 'You recognised me, didn't you?' Another pause. 'Yes, you must have done. But I need to know whether you told the police about it.' Three beeps. The message was over.

Recognised him? When? What was he talking about?

She felt tired and drained. She thought about the food she had just stowed in her fridge and freezer. She couldn't imagine ever wanting to eat it, and turned back to her whisky.

It was impossible to think that after what had just happened Jeremy could be talking about anything but the Fosters' death. But she couldn't see how his questions related to that.

The phone rang and she picked it up instead of waiting for the answering machine to cut in. Maybe it was Jeremy ringing again.

'Kate? It's George.' Not Jeremy, but George Dolby, the man she had left less than a month before. He hurried on, as though afraid that she would put the phone down on him. 'I've just heard the news. Are you all right?'

Dear George.

'It's a bit of a shock,' she said.

'Shall I come round? Or would you like to come over to my place?' There was a pause as they both considered what he had said. Kate had an overwhelming desire to lean on somebody. To take her problems and fears and hand them over to a tall, strong man who would deal with everything for her and stop her feeling as though the world was cracking open around her.

'That's a very kind offer,' she said carefully.

'But you're going to turn it down,' said George.

'Once I start . . .'

'That's what I was hoping for.'

'I mean that if I start depending on other people I'll find it impossible to be strong and independent any more.'

George laughed.

'I don't see you as a clinging vine.'

'A tendril or two was escaping there for a moment,' said Kate.

'The invitation remains open,' said George, and rang off.

Kate sat sipping her whisky and wondering whether she'd done the right thing. It had been hard enough breaking with George the first time; she didn't feel like going through it again. *But you needn't break with him*, whispered the voice of temptation. She could call him back, invite him over for the evening. The continuing attraction between them being what it was, they would soon be back where they had left off.

A little later, when the fiery sparks had hit her stomach and started to circulate around her body, the phone rang again. She let it go a couple of times. Was it George? Was she in any fit state to be cool and decisive with him? Probably not. She let it ring on.

The answering machine cut in and she heard her mother's voice.

'Kate? It's Roz. Are you all right?'

She picked the phone up. 'Yes.' She watched the tremor of

her hand. 'On the other hand, maybe not.'

'Why don't you pack a bag and come straight over here?'

'I've only just got back from my holiday. I don't want to leave.'

'Would you like me to come round?'

'You could help me drink this rather pleasant single malt.'

'I'll be with you in ten minutes.'

Only if you break the speed limit, Mother, thought Kate as she replaced the receiver. But then, with so many congregated in Agatha Street, I doubt if there are many policemen at large in Oxford this evening to notice such an infringement of the traffic regulations.

It was only two minutes later that there was a ring at her door bell. Roz would have had to hitch a ride on a passing helicopter to make it in that time.

She opened the door gingerly a couple of inches and peered through the narrow gap.

'Jeremy.'

'May I come in?'

She pulled the door a little wider. Jeremy slipped in sideways like someone in a bad movie and she closed the door behind him.

'I need to talk to you. Are you on your own?' he asked, following her upstairs. He had certainly broken her mood of a few minutes ago. She tried to put George out of her mind and succeeded only partially.

'I'm here on my own. Would you like a whisky?'

'Yes, please.' He sounded like a drowning man offered a lifebelt.

Kate handed him the glass. Now that he was facing her she could see just how awful he was looking. His hair was standing up on one side of his head as though he'd been raking his fingers through it. There were bags under his eyes, which were slightly bloodshot, and his skin was a pallid grey. He hadn't shaved very thoroughly and his clothes looked as though he'd picked them out of the dirty linen basket. She didn't relish the thought of spending part of her evening with such an unprepossessing man.

'I'm expecting my mother in a few minutes,' she said.

'Roz? Oh, shit!'

Kate raised her eyebrows at the expletive. 'I thought the two of you got on.'

'We do. It's just that I hoped I could speak to you alone.'

'I listened to your phone messages,' said Kate drily. 'What the hell were you talking about? I saw and heard nothing of the Fosters' deaths, so I couldn't tell the police anything at all. But if you know something relevant, I think you should speak to them yourself.'

'When are you expecting Roz to get here?'

'In about three minutes. Five at the outside.'

'It will take longer than that to explain. Can I come round tomorrow morning?'

'I'll be working.'

'How about first thing? Seven thirty, say?'

'Make it eight o'clock.' It seemed the only way to end the conversation and persuade the man to leave.

Jeremy swallowed his whisky and turned towards the door. 'It's about the Fosters,' he said.

'I thought it might be.' She followed him downstairs. 'But I know nothing at all about them, or why they died.'

He looked at her as though he was going to say something, but at that moment the door bell rang.

'You can leave through the back door if you like,' said Kate. 'There's a gap in the fence about halfway down where you can get through into your garden.'

'Thanks,' said Jeremy and disappeared into the kitchen, closing the door behind him. From the way he was behaving, he seemed more likely than Laura and Edward to be involved in something shady, but it was difficult to see what heavy crime a minor academic might be mixed up in.

Just another strange Oxford man, thought Kate, as she opened the door for her mother.

'I had to park round the corner,' said Roz, coming into the house. 'And then I was stopped by a plump little man in a leather jacket who asked me for my opinion of Laura and Edward Foster. Except that he called them Lorna and Edmund. He must have been from one of the tabloids.'

The door bell rang again, insistently.

'Take no notice,' said Roz. 'It's bound to be another of them.'

Kate peered through the frosted glass at the side of the door. The outline on the doorstep did look like a reporter, she decided.

'I'll disconnect the bell,' she said. 'You go on upstairs. The whisky's already up there.'

'I've brought you back your cat,' said Roz. 'I thought you might need company if you didn't want to leave the house.'

With all the worry about reporters, Kate hadn't noticed that her mother was carrying a familiar wire basket with an orange-striped occupant crouched in the bottom.

'Susanna!' she cried.

Susanna gave her deepest, most ferocious growl.

'I'll let her out,' said Roz. She bent to undo the door. As soon as it was open, the cat streaked past her and disappeared up the stairs, back paws thudding, tail high, third eye glaring at Kate. 'I'm sure she's pleased to see you really, it's just that she hates being in her carrier,' said Roz diplomatically. 'I've brought all her paraphernalia, too. It's in the car, but let's allow the press pack to retreat before we venture outside again.'

'She can use one of my bowls for the time being, and I noticed you'd left a tin of cat food.' Kate was in the kitchen, opening cupboard doors, pulling out dishes.

'She's already been fed this evening.'

'Never mind. I expect she can do with a top-up.' Kate was anxiously spooning top-quality cat food into a green cereal bowl. She tapped the side of the tin with the spoon, but no slim marmalade cat appeared.

'Don't worry. She'll make friends with you again soon.'

'I'm sure you're right,' said Kate doubtfully. 'I'll pour you a drink and we can both go and sit down.'

'Are you quite sure you want to stay here?' asked Roz a few minutes later. 'It feels as though you're resisting a siege.' She was sitting in the most comfortable armchair and wearing a black top and trousers, presumably in deference to the recent tragedy, though she had added a blue and green silk dévoré scarf which was more her usual style.

'Camilla's given me her spare door key so that I can escape to her place while she's away for a week or so. I may need it. But surely this circus can't go on for much longer?' Kate took the pink sofa and sipped at the whisky she had poured before Jeremy arrived.

'The interest won't last more than two or three days, I should have thought,' Roz said. 'We'll just have to hope for a government scandal or some such excitement to send the press scuttling back to London. I don't think they like it out here in the sticks. The pubs are too full of students. It makes them feel old.'

Kate knew that Roz was only running on like that to cheer her up.

'Did you catch the television news? Was there anything about it?' she asked. 'I couldn't face watching it myself.'

'Yes. They showed pictures of Agatha Street, and photographs of Laura and Edward. The police must have provided them with the pictures from the Fosters' house. There was an interview with a policeman who gave away as little as possible while asking for any help the public could give. The Fosters were shot, apparently, from a passing vehicle. Then one or two local residents told the interviewer how shocked and surprised they were and gave various descriptions of the vehicle the killer used. It was either a van, a car or a motorbike, depending on which one you believed. No one seemed to know why they were shot. And the police weren't commenting on who might have done it.'

'Did they mention any family?'

'One of them had an older brother living in Australia. I don't suppose he knew anything useful, either. I don't think they'd seen each other for years.'

'There must have been something in their lives that was completely at odds with their appearance. I mean, they seemed so normal, so *bland*, so harmless. You saw more of them than I did, but you can't imagine they might have been drug dealers or gun runners in another life, can you?'

'No. Nor spies.'

'I wouldn't have thought there was much to spy on in Agatha Street.'

'Perhaps the Fosters were mistaken for two other people.

What about the family who lived at number 12 before? What were they called?'

'The Venns. It's no easier to imagine Tracey and Ken mixed up with vengeful criminal types than it is the Fosters. Tracey spent all her time shouting at the children and Ken wasn't there for months on end. And I knew most details of their life because it was lived at such a high volume. There might have been some minor vandalism by the children, but nothing more serious than that. I can't think someone would hire a contract killer to get their own back on the Venns.'

'Didn't Tracey have a boyfriend?'

'Jason. Or Jace, as he was known. He drove a pick-up truck, drank lager and enjoyed head-banger music.'

'No. It doesn't sound likely, I agree.' Roz rose to her feet. 'I bet you've eaten nothing since it happened.'

'I'm not hungry.'

'I'll go and rustle up a little something. You'll feel better when you've eaten.' And Roz disappeared into the kitchen.

Later, when they'd had a slice of quiche, chosen by Camilla, and a green salad, assembled by Roz, Kate had to admit that she did feel better.

'But you need to detach yourself from what's happened,' said Roz. 'You're taking it too personally.'

Between them was the unspoken memory of the near-fatal attack on Kate in the cathedral. That had taken her a long time to recover from, mentally as well as physically.

'What do you suggest I do?' Kate didn't like people intruding on her emotions, even her mother.

'Look at it this way,' said her mother. 'You were working and you heard and saw nothing. You met the Fosters once only. They were pleasant, they were kind, but you didn't get to know them. It's sad. It's a tragedy. It's horrible that it happened a few yards from your doorstep. But really, it has nothing to do with you, Kate. You are not involved. You've given your statement, such as it was, to the police, and now you've done your bit. You don't know anything that would help solve the crime. So cut yourself off from it as much as possible. I know you don't want to come back to my place this evening, but do think about escaping to Camilla's house tomorrow if you need to.'

'I told you. I want to stay here.'

'Camilla was thinking of your wellbeing when she gave you that key.'

'I'll try to see it that way.'

'But you're not going to leave.'

'That's right.'

'Have you got a lightweight novel to read?'

'I still have the one I was reading on the plane.'

'I suggest you pour yourself another whisky, read a couple of chapters of your book, renew your friendship with Susanna, and then have an early night.'

Roz left, closing the front door swiftly behind herself and pushing her way through the crowd of onlookers that loitered in the roadway, waiting for something to happen. She returned a couple of minutes later and pushed a bin liner full of cat accessories into Kate's hands, then left once more to shoulder her way out through the sightseers.

Kate was amazed. Roz had never before lectured her daughter like that. She rarely suggested that she knew better than Kate what she should do. If only for that reason, Kate followed her mother's instructions, but pools of blood kept obscuring the words on the pages of her novel. On top of everything, Susanna still hadn't emerged from whatever piece of furniture she was crouching underneath. Kate was relieved when the phone rang and distracted her from her dark thoughts.

She looked at the clock. It was past ten thirty. Then she picked up the phone.

'It's Estelle. Kate, I've just seen your street on the television news. What's happened?'

'There's been a murder. Two murders.'

'Yes, I saw that. Did you know them?'

'Not very well, but they lived next door.'

'Next door!'

Kate was surprised that Estelle was so concerned. She didn't usually get involved with her authors' feelings or any other aspect of their personal lives. The woman must have a heart, after all.

'It was rather dreadful,' Kate began, but Estelle interrupted her.

'Never mind about that! Why aren't you out there? There are television people there, and reporters. You should have brushed your hair and worn something dark and restrained but sexy, Kate, and told them everything you know. You'd have got your face in front of millions of potential readers!'

'But I don't know anything. I didn't even see or hear what happened.'

'That isn't the point. You're missing out on some precious publicity here. Get out there first thing tomorrow and speak to as many reporters as you can. You're not a bad-looking woman. You should make the front pages of the tabloids.'

'I'll think about it,' said Kate, having no intention of doing so. 'Good night, Estelle.'

So much for the new, caring face of her agent. She returned to her novel.

When she went to bed she lay in the lamplight remembering that only twenty-four hours ago the Fosters had slept on the other side of the party wall.

It was after midnight when she switched off the lamp that had once reminded her of Laura. And tomorrow morning Jeremy was calling round to talk it all over yet again and give her *his* ideas on what had happened.

Then, as she lay awake in the darkness, she heard the shuffling sounds of a cat nosing a bowl of food across a kitchen floor in its eagerness to catch the final morsel. A little later, there was a thud on the duvet, and Susanna settled herself into her favourite spot in the dead centre of Kate's bed. Kate shifted sideways to accommodate her. The last thing she heard that night was the comforting sound of Susanna, purring.

5

Kate woke the next morning with a headache and a feeling that something dreadful was about to happen. The alarm was still shrilling in her ear and she leant across to switch it off.

Then she remembered that the tragedy had already happened. She tried to push it out of her mind, but it sat there like a leaden weight. She tried to shake herself free of it and act on Roz's bracing advice. The Fontors hadn't been friends of hers. She had seen and heard nothing through the CD on her Walkman. There was nothing she could contribute to the investigation.

She pulled on a dressing gown and went downstairs to make coffee and feed the cat, though not necessarily in that order.

Jeremy was coming at eight. For such a harmless-looking man he had been unusually mysterious. She couldn't believe he had anything to do with the murders, though. Perhaps he was one of those people who needed to be at the centre of any dramatic event, to give their own dull lives some meaning. Maybe he just wanted to talk it over, analyse it, discuss his experience with another person who had been involved. It was possible that together they might be able to make sense of it and then start to forget.

On the other hand she wasn't sure that Jeremy would be her first choice of confidant. She would have to explain to him that she needed to get back to work. He'd have to leave before nine, she would tell him. Eight forty-five.

She had breakfasted, showered, dressed and read the front page of the newspaper ('Couple slain in quiet Oxford street') by the time Jeremy turned up.

'There's still no hint of a motive,' she said, indicating the article. 'Who on earth would want to kill them?'

'My paper says it must have been an accident. A case of mistaken identity.'

'Come into the kitchen,' she said. The chairs there weren't as comfortable as those in her sitting room, and she didn't want to encourage him to stay. 'Coffee?'

Jeremy had made more of an effort this morning. At least he had shaved and combed his hair, and dressed in fresh clothes. But when she handed him his coffee he slopped it on the table as he was putting it down. The bags under his eyes had been replaced by dark rings, as though he hadn't slept much the previous night. From the way he kept glancing round the room, she wondered whether he had stayed awake in order to make sure that no one was creeping up behind him to murder him, too.

'Did you know them well?' she asked. She had to start the conversation somewhere, or Jeremy would sit in her kitchen, silent and morose, all morning.

'Not very well. Not much better than you did, I imagine. I'd been invited round for a drink several times, and I'd accepted two, or maybe three, of the invitations.'

'Didn't you enjoy their company?' she asked. She didn't see what he would be able to add to their understanding of what had happened if he hardly knew them, either.

'They were pleasant enough, but we didn't have much in common. And I felt that Laura wanted to take over my life and organise it for me so that it suited her ideas of what I should be and do.' At least the man had started to talk, even if what he had to say was rather banal.

'I had a hint of the same thing.'

'On the other hand, she was a genuinely kind and concerned woman. Underneath the irritation I felt I knew she was someone I could always rely on. If I'd been in trouble, I would probably have gone to Laura. She would have listened. She might even have suggested a remedy, for she was a very practical person. Much more so than Edward in many ways.'

'Edward and his tool kit,' said Kate.

'Perhaps he wasn't quite as good at mending things as he thought he was,' said Jeremy, smiling slightly.

'But have you any idea why someone would want to kill them?' She had to bring him on to the subject or they'd wander around it all morning.

There was a pause. Jeremy ran his left hand through his hair, picked up his mug with his right, and drank some coffee. His face had drooped back into its worried lines.

'The other evening, you did know you'd seen me before, didn't you?' he said when he had put the mug down again. He was staring very hard at Kate.

'What? What on earth are you talking about? You said something similar in the phone message you left me.'

'At Gatwick.'

'The only person I saw at Gatwick was Sam Dolby, looking shifty.'

'Before that. On the plane,' insisted Jeremy. 'The day before yesterday. The flight from Bordeaux to Gatwick. You were standing a few places behind me while we waited for that dreadful child to find its stuffed rabbit.'

'That was you in the wig?' And Kate laughed without

thinking. 'You're really telling me that was *you*?'

'I could feel you staring at it and I knew you'd spotted that it wasn't my own hair. And then we met a few hours later at the Fosters and you started going on about it. I thought you were winding me up. You *did* recognise me, didn't you?'

'I hadn't seen your face while we were on the plane,' said Kate. She'd been too fascinated by the wig. She'd noticed his light-coloured raincoat and his brown leather gloves, she remembered. But that was all. It had never struck her that it might be Jeremy Wells when she was introduced to him later that evening. 'And then you walked away really fast, and you only had hand luggage with you so you didn't have to wait for your suitcase, so I lost sight of you. And then when I bumped into Sam Dolby I forgot all about the man in the wig.'

'Oh my God! This is all unnecessary.'

'The lights were on in your house when I got back,' continued Kate. 'So it never entered my head that we'd been on the same flight.'

'I caught the six o'clock coach back to Oxford.'

'I had to wait for the next one. I didn't even know you'd been away. Why should I? I just didn't associate you with France when we met at the Fosters. What were you doing in Bordeaux?'

'It was just a routine trip.'

She could hear that Jeremy was being evasive.

'And how did you hide it from Laura? I thought she kept a log book of all your comings and goings.'

He smiled weakly. 'I was only gone for twenty-four hours and my lights were on a timer.'

'So she thought you were in the Onion, working hard at whatever it is you do all day.'

'Could we forget this conversation? Forget it ever happened.

Pretend it was someone else in the wig.'

'No,' said Kate.

Jeremy drank some more of his coffee. 'Any chance of some toast?'

It was a relief to leave her seat and cut bread, push it under the grill, get out the marmalade and a plate and set them before her guest. The atmosphere in her kitchen had grown a little strained.

Jeremy placed both hands on the table, then held the left in the right, as though to still their trembling.

'I got involved in something stupid,' he said eventually. 'And now I'm trying to get myself out of it.' His teeth crunched down on the toast, and crumbs showered over the table to join the pool of coffee. Jeremy, she noticed, was a messy eater. Or maybe she should put it down to his obvious nerves.

'How's this connected to the Foster's death?'

Jeremy was silent.

'Surely that's what matters at the moment, not your stupid wig!'

'You're right. Of course it has nothing to do with the Fosters. How could it? But I was nervous you'd mention it to the police. It would look a bit odd, don't you think? They'd have me in for questioning, and then the college would hear about it, and they'd see me as even less of an asset to them than they do now.'

'So it has nothing to do with the murders? You're sure about that?'

'It was just a silly joke. It would only waste police time if you told them about it.'

Kate thought he was protesting too hard, but she didn't believe such a witless man – and an academic, at that – could have anything to do with violent crime. A little plagiarism, perhaps. Jealousy, envy and back-biting, maybe. But nothing serious.

'OK. I'll forget about it,' she said.

'Thanks. And now I need to ask you to do me another favour. Please.'

'Like what?'

'There's something I have to drop off on a friend at college. I'd like you to take it for me.'

'Why don't you take it yourself?' Kate poured herself another mug of coffee and absentmindedly picked up a spare slice of toast, then spread it thickly with butter and marmalade.

'I can't take it. I don't want to be seen.'

'Would anyone be any more interested in you than in me?' She assumed he was talking about the press.

'I don't know. But they might be.'

'This is getting ridiculous.' Kate bit into her toast and washed it down with coffee. 'What is it that needs to be delivered, anyway?'

'Just a disk.'

'A computer disk?'

Jeremy pulled a small padded envelope from his pocket. 'Look. Really, there's nothing to it.' He pushed the packet across the table to Kate, avoiding the coffee puddle as he did so. Kate picked it up and weighed it speculatively.

It seemed to her that it was heavier than a floppy disk would be, and a little thicker. Perhaps, she thought irreverently, it was only a CD after all. Maynard Keynes's Greatest Hits.

'What's on it?' she asked.

There was a short pause, then Jeremy said, 'It's the outline and sample chapters for a book I'm writing.'

'Why is it so important?'

Another pause. 'You know what academic jealousies are like,' he said.

Just as she'd thought, then! 'Who would I deliver it to?' she asked.

'A friend of mine,' said Jeremy. 'A man called Alec Malden.'

'At Bartlemas? I don't know him. Is he new?'

'He's been at the college a couple of years, I think. I can tell you how to find his rooms.'

'Why me?'

'Because you're here,' he said baldly. 'Because I don't want to go out. And because there's no reason for anyone to connect us. We hadn't met until a couple of days ago.'

'Why don't you ask your girlfriend?'

'What girlfriend?'

'The tall girl with the red hair.'

'I don't know anyone like that.'

'She visited you yesterday morning. I saw her.'

'No you didn't. You've never seen her. Promise me that, Kate. *You've never seen her.* And I haven't got a girlfriend.'

'If you say so.' The man was mad. She would have to humour him. 'Now, tell me how to find this Alec Malden.'

'Walk straight through the main gate, past the lodge, but don't stop there. Don't speak to the porter. If you look as though you know where you're going no one will take any notice of you. Alec's room is in Pesant Quad, Staircase 4, on the top floor.'

'Is there a password?'

'This isn't a game,' he said curtly. 'You're to give the packet to Alec and to no one else.'

'Into his hands only,' said Kate, feeling silly.

71

Jeremy looked at her expectantly.

'Very well. If it's that important to you, I'll go this afternoon.'

'This morning,' said Jeremy. 'I'd like to know that it's been delivered safely.'

'Right,' said Kate. 'And then I'll forget that I met Alec Malden, or that I ever went to Bartlemas for you.'

'You're getting the hang of it,' said Jeremy, sounding relieved.

'And I expect you'd like to leave now, through the back door, and use the gap in the fence.'

'Yes, please.'

'Would you like me to eat the Jiffy bag when I've delivered the disk?'

'I don't care if you think I'm mad,' said Jeremy. 'As long as you do *exactly* what I ask.'

Kate unbolted the door for him and watched his furtive progress into the next-door garden.

If she hadn't promised Jeremy that she'd tell no one, she'd have phoned Roz and told her about this crazy assignment. Roz would tell her to hand the packet back to Jeremy and forget all about it, that she would do better not to get involved. But, against her better judgement, she *was* getting involved. No, she told herself firmly. You're just acting as a postman. Once you've delivered the disk it will all be over and you can forget about it.

She went to fetch her jacket. She might as well get the thing over and done with.

6

Kate went on foot to Bartlemas College. It was a sultry morning
and she wore a light summer dress. She chose the black cotton
one with the full skirt because it had a deep, hidden pocket in
the side into which she could slip Jeremy's disk. She could
walk with her arms free and her hands empty and no one would
know she was carrying anything at all. Then she put on a pair
of sunglasses. This cloak-and-dagger stuff was catching.

She walked through the dwindling crowd of onlookers
outside number 12, ignoring the stares, and turned on to the
Fridesley Road, which looked quite normal. She headed into
town. Her route took her through the centre of the city and
down the High Street. She paused only to check out the clothes
in the windows of her two favourite shops, then turned into the
cobbled lane that led to Jeremy's college.

It was several years since she had been at Bartlemas, helping
Emma with her summer conference on Gender and Genre. The
porter in the lodge looked different from the one she remembered younger, perhaps, and less interested in the people
entering the college. She smiled slightly then strode through
the archway into the front quad, giving her best imitation of
someone who knows where they are going.

She walked past the magnolia tree, which stretched sixty
feet up the chapel wall and nearly as far sideways. It had long
ago shed its thousands of violet-flushed waxen cups and now

was covered in glossy leaves. Nature had gone mad when she had contrived that magnolia tree, outdoing herself in exuberance only when she had designed the peacock's tail.

The choir was practising in the room at the corner of the quad. She could hear the bright young voices, repeating a phrase until they had it to the satisfaction of the Master of Choristers. She passed through another archway, noted the sign on the oak door on her left that said 'Song Room – Silence Please' then paused for a moment.

That wasn't Bach, Vivaldi or even Pärt they were singing. No, it was something from *Cats*. Was this their latest CD? 'Bartlemas Choir Sings Andrew Lloyd Webber?' And Kate, who never attended a chapel service unless it was a wedding or a funeral, was duly horrified at the lowering of standards.

She turned to her right, past a dank medieval wall, through another small archway, then out into the sunshine of Pesant Quad. There was a square of turf, innocent of daisies, in the centre, and a door at each corner with a Roman numeral carved into the stone above it. Staircase 4, Kate reminded herself – no, Staircase IV – was just to her right.

The stairs were narrow and worn in the middle, apparently from the thousands of scholars' feet that had filed up and down them in their pursuit of learning. One of the present-day scholars passed her on his way down from the first floor. He was depressingly clean and tidy, to Kate's eye, and looked as though he was aiming for a career in accountancy. Perhaps he had a secret vice, but she suspected he would merely look shocked if you suggested such a thing.

As Kate reached the top of the stairs, she could hear voices from behind the door ahead of her. Did this mean that Alec Malden was not alone? Should she continue, or wait until she could find him on his own? The idea of loitering around Bartlemas College all morning, kicking her heels, didn't appeal so she decided to carry on. Maybe Alec Malden talked to himself in a loud and cheery voice. Maybe he was practising for the next speech he had to give. She knocked.

'Enter!' A quieter voice than the one she had heard on her way up the stairs. Not quite so jolly. And she did dislike it when people said 'Enter!' rather than 'Come in!' Nevertheless, she entered.

There were two men in the room. It was a very nice room, she saw, walking in: square, bright, painted a pale yellow, and with shelves full of books covering its walls. It wasn't untidy, or dusty, and didn't have that old-sock smell that she associated with the dens of academics.

'Yes?' It was the smaller of the men who spoke. He was about Kate's height, and spare, with receding grey hair and a thin, yellowish face. He was standing on her right as she entered, and had a narrow chest and the sort of collapsed diaphragm that made Kate want to tell him to sign up for the local gym. She desisted, however, from making any such suggestion.

'Hallo,' she said brightly. 'My name's Kate Ivory, and I was looking for Alec Malden.'

'You have found him,' said the same man. Dyspeptic, thought Kate. I don't know what it means, but I'm sure that's what he is. He had deep grooves running down the sides of his mouth which gave him a melancholy, rather waspish, air. 'What is it you want?' Alec Malden continued. She saw that at any moment he would glance at the watch on his wrist and ask her to hurry up, he hadn't got all day.

'I'm really just a postman,' said Kate breezily, wishing that the other man would decide he had urgent business elsewhere.

'I've brought you something from a friend of yours.'

'How mysterious!' said the other man. 'Why don't you tell us all about it? I like a good mystery. Did you say your name was Kate? How charming.'

Not at all the reaction Kate had intended.

'This is our Master,' said Alec Malden drily. 'Harry Joiner.'

There was something about the term 'Master' that always made Kate's hackles rise, particularly when the assumption was made that he was *her* master.

'I believe I met your predecessor,' she said coolly, searching her memory for a name and finding it just in time. 'Aidan Flint.'

'Dear old Aidan,' said Harry Joiner easily. 'You'll find I'm a very different kettle of fish.'

Harry Joiner was taller and bulkier than Alec Malden, and his face was redder. The lines on his face looked as though he smiled a lot. All in all, thought Kate, he didn't look much like an Oxford academic. Nor did he sound like one. His accent came from somewhere east of Romford and he hadn't bothered to modify it at all or lose any of his glottal stops.

'I'm one of the new breed,' he said, as though reading the expression on her face. 'I may not know much about Economics as a theoretical subject (eh, Alec?) but I do know how to run a company and show a profit.'

Alec looked as though he had swallowed a lemon, peel and all.

'Perhaps you'd better hand over whatever it is you've brought for me,' he said to Kate.

But as Kate still hesitated, Harry Joiner said, 'The young lady doesn't feel comfortable with me here, Alec. Can't you see, she's longing to be left alone with you.' And he laughed, his face redder than ever.

'That's all right,' said Kate stiffly, wishing that he would, in fact, go away. But it was his college, after all, even if this was Alec Malden's room.

'Why don't we sit down while she explains who she is and who sent her?' said Joiner easily.

And so the three of them sat on Alec Malden's comfortable chairs, Kate perched on the edge of hers, as though poised for flight.

'Are you going to tell me it's too early to force Alec to open his bottle of very dry sherry and offer you a glass?'

'I'm afraid so. I have work to do when I get home,' said Kate primly.

'Well, that's an attitude I can understand,' said Joiner. 'You can tell she doesn't work for Bartlemas, Alec!' Then, as though the thought had suddenly struck him, he added, 'You *don't* work for us, do you?'

Kate allowed him to worry about it for a couple of seconds before she said, 'No.'

'So who has sent you, and what have you brought for me?' asked Alec Malden.

'It's from Jeremy Wells – you know him, don't you? – and it's just a disk,' said Kate.

For a moment, Kate had the impression that she had completely dumbfounded her two hearers. Then Harry Joiner relaxed and asked, 'Are you talking about Jeremy Wells, one of our lecturers?'

Kate couldn't see any point in telling a fib. 'Yes.'

'A disk, you say?' asked Alec Malden. 'Do you know what's on it?'

'Jeremy said it had something to do with a book he was writing,' said Kate, hoping she wasn't breaking Jeremy's confidence. But then, all his secrecy seemed quite ridiculous now she was sitting in this elegant room in a respectable Oxford college.

'I think you should get out the sherry, after all, Alec,' said Harry Joiner. 'Pour us all a glass.'

Kate wondered about mentioning the fact that she would rather have whisky, if he had such a thing, but thought better of it. The atmosphere in the room had lightened considerably, but possibly not quite *that* far.

While Alec was busy with bottle and glasses, Harry Joiner leant towards Kate in a friendly way. 'And how is Jeremy? He must have been very upset by the murder. Wasn't it quite close to where he lives?'

'Two doors away. And yes, we're all upset by it,' said Kate briefly, not wishing to discuss the subject here.

'Just his usual self, though, apart from that?'

'I'm not sure what he's like usually,' said Kate, the memory of a chestnut-red wig fresh in her mind. 'We met for the first time a couple of nights ago.' No need to mention that they had met at the Fosters'.

'So it was particularly kind of you to run this errand for him,' said Joiner. 'On such a very short acquaintance.'

'He was most insistent. I really couldn't get out of it without being rude.' She looked at Joiner's friendly face and decided to take a chance. Alec Malden hovered behind Joiner's chair, apparently not wishing to interrupt their conversation. 'Actually, I'm a little worried about him.'

'Why would that be?'

'Now, admittedly I don't know him very well, so I don't

know what his normal behaviour is like,' she said carefully. 'And with a murder happening just two doors away, I suppose anyone could get a little worried. But . . .'

'Yes?'

'But do you think he might be suffering from paranoia? Delusions, hallucinations?' she asked in a rush.

Alec Malden joined them, handing a small glass of straw-coloured liquid to each. (Oh, goody! Really dry sherry! Kate tried not to pull a face.)

'He's done one or two odd things lately,' said Kate. No need to mention the wig. 'And he seems to think that people are *after* him. I mean, take this disk.' She took the small Jiffy bag out of her pocket. Joiner appeared to follow her movements avidly. 'It's just the manuscript of some academic work, he said.'

'Possibly the fruit of many years' labour,' said Joiner solemnly.

'But he was behaving as if it contained state secrets.'

'We don't have many of those left,' said Alec Malden, giggling.

'And as though the whole of the KGB, or whatever it's called nowadays, was after him.'

'I think we'll have to come clean with Kate,' said Joiner.

'Must we?' Malden sounded startled.

'Yes. It's only fair on her. Poor Jeremy,' continued Joiner, ignoring Malden. 'I think it may be the afterburn from that divorce of his. He took it very hard when Janice left him, you know,' he confided.

'What's that got to do with this disk?' asked Kate.

'It's just that you're right: he has been behaving strangely for the past few months. Perhaps he's been working too hard, or maybe it's some genetic weakness. Isn't his father in a home of some kind, Alec? I'm sorry that you've got involved in it, but don't worry, I expect the worst of it's over now. Just try to be kind to him, that's all.'

'You're probably hoping you won't have to see him again,' put in Malden. 'I expect you've had quite enough of his fancies by now, haven't you?'

'It is a bit much, especially when there's a *real* tragedy on our doorstep,' admitted Kate.

'You go home and stop worrying about it any longer,' said Joiner. 'You've done your bit – you've brought us the disk, haven't you – and you can leave it to us now. We look after our own here at Bartlemas.'

'Would you like more sherry?' asked Malden solicitously.

'*No*. Thank you.'

'Now, what about that disk?' asked Joiner.

Kate still had it in her hand.

'He did ask me to give it to Alec Malden and no one else,' she said apologetically.

'And here I am,' said Malden, standing close beside her. 'But don't worry. In any event, Harry and I are as one in this, aren't we, Harry?'

'Of course we are, Alec.'

And so Kate handed over the little packet that Jeremy had made such a fuss about to Alec Malden, while Harry Joiner smiled on them both.

'Don't you want to check it first?' she couldn't help asking as Malden took the envelope to his desk, placed it inside a drawer, and locked it away.

'No need. I'll look at it later, when I have the time,' said Malden.

'We're sure it's just what you said it was,' put in Joiner.

'I suppose we mustn't keep you any longer,' said Malden.

'But it has been such a pleasure having you here,' said Joiner. 'Thank you so much for coming.'

Kate had risen to her feet and turned towards the door.

'Why don't you see our guest as far as the lodge, Alec?'

'Really, I can find my own way out.' This effusiveness was a bit much, especially after their initial coolness.

As she reached the bottom of the staircase she thought she heard the two voices again, but this time raised in some kind of celebratory shout. She'd never understand academics: all this fuss about some boring economics text.

When she finally emerged into the sunlight of the High Street she rewarded herself for completing her chore by buying herself a particularly beautiful shirt in heavy dark green silk before returning to Agatha Street.

She went straight into her own house, ignoring Jeremy's, and after she had hung up the new shirt she went to her phone and left a message on Jeremy's machine.

'Mission accomplished!' she told him, and didn't mention her name. Wasn't that the sort of thing you were meant to say after delivering a mysterious package?

She was a bit miffed that Jeremy wasn't sitting by his phone, waiting for her call. If he wasn't at Bartlemas, either, where was he? She put him out of her mind and went downstairs to concentrate on the latest chapter of her book.

As she typed away in the peaceful silence, she tried not to feel relieved that she no longer needed to wear earplugs.

As it got close to lunchtime, she heard the phone ring upstairs. Was it Jeremy? It was time he returned her call. Then the machine picked up and from the quacking sound that carried all the way down the stairs, she knew it was her agent. She went upstairs to intercept.

'Kate? Any luck with the press?'

'I spoke to a few people, but I don't know whether they'll use what I said,' lied Kate.

'You probably left it too late. You should have been out there as soon as it happened.'

Estelle's brashness in relegating the Fosters' tragedy to a photo-opportunity was having a salutary effect on Kate.

'Was there anything else?' she asked.

'How are you getting on with the new book?'

'Really well,' said Kate, feeling virtuous from the hour's solid work she had just put in on it.

'Good. Nearly finished?'

'Not exactly. But coming along nicely,' said Kate judiciously. No need to be too specific about actual word counts, she had always found.

'I have some good news for you. We've had an offer for translation rights from Denmark.'

'Excellent.' Kate wondered what the population of Denmark might be and how many of them were interested in historical romances.

'They're taking two titles and they've offered an advance of—'

The sum meant little to Kate since she had no idea how many Danish kroner there were to the pound.

Estelle was continuing. 'Of course there's commission to come out of that, but you should clear nearly fifteen hundred.'

'Each?' asked Kate hopefully.

'For the two.'

'Oh, well. It's a good start,' said Kate.

'How much longer do you think you'll be on the new one?'

'*Spitfire Sweethearts*? At least another month. Maybe two. Will the Danes be interested in that, too, do you think?'

'They might well be. Let's call it six weeks, shall we?'

'Fine.' There was nothing like a deadline to get the creative juices flowing, Kate had always found.

'Oh, and another offer's come in for large-print rights for one of your earlier titles. *Spring Scene*, I believe.'

'Another huge cheque?'

'A few hundred. But these small sums do add up.'

'I feel it's all going to happen this year.'

'Perhaps.' Estelle didn't sound quite as confident as Kate would have liked. 'And because everything's going so well at the moment, I thought we might have a little outing to cheer you up.' It wasn't like Estelle to offer any sort of plum to her authors. Why was she doing this?

'You think I need cheering?'

'The little happening next door did look *very* messy on my television screen.'

'Where were you thinking of taking me?' I never knew you cared, Estelle!

'I was introduced to a perfectly lovely man last week. His name's Owen Grigg and it just happens that he lives and works quite near Oxford.' She paused, as though choosing her words carefully.

'Yes?'

'He runs a printing works,' said Estelle. 'Well, you could say he *owns* it, really.'

'A man of substance?'

'Exactly.' Estelle sounded relieved that Kate had picked up her meaning so neatly.

'A.L. Grigg and Nephew,' said Kate. 'Is that the company you're talking about?'

'I believe it is.'

'I had noticed that that's the company that usually prints *my* books,' said Kate.

'And they're about to print the new one,' said Estelle swiftly. 'The paperback edition that's coming out in October. So I wondered whether it wouldn't be a lovely idea for you to come and watch it roll off the press,' she ended in a rush.

'I'd really enjoy that,' said Kate, putting her out of her misery. 'When do you want to go? At least, I assume that you'd like to come with me,' she added slyly.

'Why don't I ring Mr Grigg . . . Owen . . . and fix a time when he can show us round himself. Personally,' she added, as though Kate couldn't grasp the point.

'Fine. Just let me know the day and time. I have nothing planned for the next few weeks, apart from some serious writing,' said Kate.

'I'll be in touch!' And Estelle rang off.

Dear Estelle! She was always falling for very rich, slightly overweight men. It never lasted more than a few months before she saw through to their sawdust souls, but she entered each new liaison with a wonderful spirit of optimism that Kate could only envy. It was, as far as she had learned, Estelle's only weak spot. When the Grigg affair ended she could introduce Estelle to Harry Joiner, perhaps. He would be just her type and she might be a match for him. And he was certainly rich. She couldn't imagine that Bartlemas College would have appointed him as Master for any other reason.

* * *

Much later that day it occurred to her that Jeremy still hadn't phoned her back. Surely it was the least he could do. She deserved one small thank you for the errand she had carried out for him.

But perhaps it was just one more symptom of his battiness.

7

It was nearly dark before she heard from Jeremy.

She was in the kitchen, peeling and slicing vegetables for her evening meal when there was a light tapping noise at the back door. For a moment she thought of Harley Venn, who used to come calling on Kate when he needed help with his homework, or a haven from the noisy life at home. But Harley had moved on, and now had a girlfriend his own age, by all accounts.

She opened the door, cautiously.

'Come in, Jeremy,' she said.

He wore black jeans and matching cotton polo-neck, with a black jacket over them. Nothing would have disguised his pale skin and even paler hair, though, if someone had really been looking for him.

'Where have you been?' she asked. And then, seeing him lift his nose towards the heap of chopped vegetables. 'Are you hungry?'

'I'm starving,' he said. Then, more politely, as Kate brought a pack of chicken breasts out of the fridge and started cutting them into strips, 'It's kind of you to take me in and feed me like this. I haven't eaten because I've been keeping out of sight,' he said.

'Of course you have,' said Kate, maintaining her policy of humouring a seriously dotty person. 'This is a stir fry, so you won't have long to wait. I'll put on some rice, and it'll be ready in about twelve minutes. Why don't you pour us both a glass of wine?' She indicated the wine box on the counter.

'I have to get away,' said Jeremy. 'The trouble is, I can't think where to go.'

Avoiding the question of why Jeremy needed to go into hiding, Kate asked brightly, 'Haven't you got any family? Couldn't you go back to your parents' place?' She remembered, too late, that Joiner had mentioned that Jeremy's father was in a 'home'.

'That would be the first place they'd think of when they came to look for me,' said Jeremy. 'I don't want to lead them back to my father: he's an old man. I have a couple of cousins, but they're older than me and rather set in their ways. I couldn't explain what's happening to them, they just wouldn't understand it.'

'Of course not,' said Kate soothingly, noticing that he seemed to think that she, on the other hand, could understand perfectly, as well as look after herself.

'Oh, I know you think I'm imagining it,' Jeremy said impatiently. 'But you can't deny what happened to the Fosters.'

'But that had nothing to do with you,' said Kate. 'It must have been the result of some murky episode in their past.'

'There were no episodes in their past that they didn't chat about endlessly at Mrs Clack's,' said Jeremy sharply. 'Even on your short acquaintance, you must have realised that.'

'People who lead blameless lives don't get killed by gunmen,' said Kate. 'Therefore—'

'They might have got involved in something by mistake. It could have been a mere accident. A case of being in the wrong place at the right time.'

'Well, yes. Mistaken identity. Isn't that your paper's favourite theory?' said Kate, flipping diced onion into the hot oil in her wok. 'And if you really want me to cook your supper, you'd better answer the question I've been longing to ask you all day.'

'What's that?' asked Jeremy warily. He placed a glass of Australian red by her right hand.

'Why were you wearing a wig? What's wrong with your own hair?' She added the strips of chicken to the pan.

'Nothing's wrong with it.' He ran his free hand through the inoffensive hair so that it stood up on his crown. 'It's just that I was using a, well, a false passport.'

Kate laughed. 'You're joking! What on earth for?' She stirred the sizzling meat in the hot oil.

'I was bringing something into the country that I shouldn't have had with me, and I didn't want to be caught.'

'But that red wig shouted out to be noticed!'

'It wasn't red. More a chestnut colour, I thought. And I'd worn it when I had the passport photo taken. I could have dyed my hair, but that might have been difficult to remove afterwards.'

'And what about the brown leather gloves?' *Burglar's gloves.* Better not say that, though.

'You'll think that was another silly idea. I didn't want to leave any traces. I was worried about fingerprints—'

'Fingerprints!'

'I must have been watching too many television detectives. I just wanted to hide as much of myself as possible.'

Kate giggled.

Jeremy relaxed and allowed himself a half-hearted laugh in return. 'You're right. I was being ridiculous. I'm not used to being in the world of smugglers and blackmailers. Any hint of criminality and I'm normally running like a startled rabbit.'

There was something about Jeremy's colouring and general air of anxiety that did inevitably remind Kate of a rabbit, and a startled one at that.

'I bet you never even ride your bike the wrong way down Queen Street,' she said.

Jeremy shook his head. 'I'd find it impossible to pass the "No Entry" sign,' he said ruefully. Kate thought she could at last see a glimmer of amusement at his own behaviour, perhaps even a hint of self-awareness. It was a start, if Jeremy wanted to rejoin the rest of the human race.

'It didn't occur to you, though, that the wig and gloves only drew people's attention to you?' she said.

'You were the only one who noticed me.' All the humour had left Jeremy's expression.

Kate stopped stirring the contents of her wok for a moment.

'Have you been working too hard, do you think, Jeremy?' She spoke kindly, remembering what Joiner and Malden had said.

'But I'm getting out of it,' said Jeremy, pacing across the kitchen and back again in a way designed to get on Kate's nerves. 'That's why I'm trying to get away from this place. They don't like it if you change your mind, you see.'

'Of course not.' Only half her mind was on Jeremy as she tipped the rice into a colander. 'It will do you good to have a holiday before term starts.'

'Hardly a holiday,' said Jeremy and didn't elaborate.

'Pour me some more wine, would you? Most of mine ended up in our stir fry.'

Jeremy did as he was told, while Kate tipped shredded vegetables into the mixture.

'I spent the day wandering around in museums, and then trying to persuade a couple of friends to put me up for a few days,' he said.

'No joy?'

'I couldn't explain why and so my story sounded rather weak.'

'Put us out a knife and fork each,' said Kate, draining the rice and dividing it into the two bowls that had been heating under the grill. 'We might as well eat here in the kitchen.'

She dished up the meal and they seated themselves at the table. Jeremy immediately attacked his food as though he hadn't eaten anything since the toast and marmalade that morning. Maybe the museums he had visited had lacked coffee shops.

'Had you forgotten about the disk, by the way? I did in fact deliver it to Alec Malden,' she said, forking in rice and vegetables.

'Thank God for that.'

'I take it that's a "thank you"?'

'Oh, yes, of course. Thank you, Kate.' Jeremy washed food down with a large gulp of wine.

'When I found his room, he wasn't alone, I'm afraid. The new Master, Harry Joiner, was with him.'

'The double-glazing billionaire.'

'I thought he must be rich.'

'And successful. The legendary self-made man. He wanted us to rename the college "Starglazer" after his company. Did you know that?'

'I've heard worse,' said Kate noncommittally. 'And it wouldn't be the first college to be named after its benefactor.'

'The Fellows gave one communal shudder and turned the idea down flat.' Then he returned to the subject that was still on his mind. 'But Alec didn't open the packet while he was there, did he?'

'No. He locked it away in a drawer without opening it.'

'Good.'

'You trust Alec completely?'

'He's a fine man. Reliable. You know where you are with Alec.'

So she could believe what Malden and Joiner had told her. Even Jeremy agreed that they were entirely reliable.

'He's not the most cheerful of companions, but you can trust him to do the right thing when they . . .' His voice faded as though he didn't want to face any more unpleasant possibilities.

Kate laid down her fork. 'Are you sure that "they" are really after you?'

'Yes. They must be.' He had his startled rabbit look on again, and Kate took pity on him.

'Then I've had an idea about where you could stay.'

Jeremy looked up, his face full of hope.

'My friend Camilla has just left for ten days in the Lake District. She thought I might like to stay in her house if I didn't like living so near to a murder scene. I have her spare key. Why don't you stay at her place?'

'Where does she live?'

'Only about four hundred yards away, in Waverley Lane. Is that far enough?'

'I don't think distance matters. It's the fact that no one can connect me to her. And they can't, since I don't even know her.'

'It should suit you. It's one of the detached houses hiding behind a thick hedge.'

'That would be ideal. Would she mind if I stayed there for a few days, do you think? Should you phone her to find out?'

'I haven't got her number, even if I wanted to ring her. And

I don't think she wishes to be disturbed. I'll have to do this on my own initiative. And if anyone ever asks, then we were staying there together. That's the sort of arrangement that Camilla would understand.'

'She sounds quite a goer.'

'She's a headmistress, and her pupils find her very stuffy, as a matter of fact.'

'Then she obviously has a secret life they know nothing of.'

'You could well be right,' said Kate, thinking of the 'someone' in the Lake District and the cheerful smile on Camilla's face. 'Do you want seconds? Yes? There's only fruit to follow. And you can make coffee for us both while I relax. Then I'll show you the way to Camilla's house.'

Jeremy's mood was catching, Kate found. She changed into black jeans and polo-necked top herself, then added a black sweatshirt. Should she cover her blonde hair? She pulled a beret down over one ear. It looked quite fetching, she thought, and applied another layer of eyeshadow.

'Front door or back?' she asked Jeremy when she went downstairs.

'They've taken the floodlights down. I think we can risk going out through the front,' he said seriously. He had a rucksack with him, filled, presumably, with a change of clothing and whatever else he needed for a night or two away. It clinked as he picked it up.

'I've brought food with me,' he said. 'Just a few tins of soup and some fruit. I can't very well live on the contents of your friend's fridge.'

'I expect you can creep out at midnight and stock up at the all-night supermarket,' said Kate cheerfully.

Jeremy hefted the rucksack over his shoulder. It, too, was black.

Kate couldn't believe he was in real danger, but she pretended to go along with his fantasy, slipping out through the front door and melting into the shadows as they walked back to the Fridesley Road, then turned off into the lane. It never ceased to surprise her that you could move so rapidly from town to country so close to the centre of Oxford. A few steps away from the main road and they were deep in rural gloom, their way lit only by the fitful light from the sky. A mournful lowing indicated that there were cattle nearby, and the scene was completed by the sudden too-wooing of an owl.

The way seemed further in the dark, especially as they were walking slowly, trying to avoid potholes and patches of mud. But at last they reached Camilla's house.

'I think she'd appreciate it if you watered her plants,' said Kate, letting him in.

Jeremy brightened. 'She has plants? Oh, yes. Those are interesting,' he enthused, while Kate saw only something green with very small white flowers.

'There are more green things out in the garden,' she said. 'I'm sure they'd appreciate your care, too. And don't bother about hiding behind the curtains and not showing any lights. I don't believe anyone except me knows that she's away, so they'll expect to see lights on and so forth.'

But Jeremy pulled the curtains before switching on the lights.

'Habit,' he said.

'Well, I'm sure you'll be safe here.'

'Thanks,' he said. The single word was obviously meant to cover everything from supper to the haven she had provided for him.

'Keep in touch if you can,' said Kate. 'I'm sure Camilla won't mind if you phone me occasionally.'

'Yes.' He looked as though he wanted her to leave.

'Look after yourself, now,' she said rather feebly.

He just nodded.

'I'll be going then,' she said, and slipped as invisibly as she could manage out of the door. As she walked back to Agatha Street she wondered just what would happen to Jeremy now. Had she done the right thing in playing along with his delusions? Should she suggest that he seek treatment?

She hoped that all he really needed was to rest, away from the horror of the Fosters' murder. It was all very well for her to help him to lie low for a few days, but Camilla would be back in just over a week, and he couldn't stay longer than that. And he would have to go to work, surely Term didn't start for another five or six weeks, but she imagined he had to make an appearance at the Concrete Onion at regular intervals. But Harry Joiner, Master of Bartlemas, was aware of the strain Jeremy had been under and it must be his problem, not hers. Jeremy was off her hands, for the moment. She could stop worrying about him. She just hoped that she wouldn't have to explain to Camilla in ten days' time that she had installed a man in her house to look after her plants. A strange man with stranger delusions. No, Jeremy would have found a better solution to his problems by then. Of course he would.

The moon was low on the horizon and glowing an angry orange colour, with a thin slice pared from one corner. As Kate watched, it moved further into the hazy cloud so that its outline blurred and she could hardly distinguish it from a distant streetlamp in the Fridesley Road.

* * *

Jeremy did ring her later that evening, just as she had settled down with a late-night news programme on the television.

'Kate?'

'Yes.' She was in no mood for a chat with Jeremy. Susanna had deigned to settle on her knees and was purring loudly. And Jeremy had accepted her help with hardly a thank you and no appreciation of how she had put herself out for him.

'I rang to apologise. I'm sorry. You went to so much trouble to find me a safe place to stay. You delivered the disk to Alec, when you had your own work to do, and then you even fed me this evening. And I was so wrapped up in my own worries that I didn't even thank you properly.' Jeremy's voice had reverted to the soft-spoken academic's, or even that of the polite little boy who had been his mother's pride. Kate felt her irritation begin to melt, and then wondered whether he was about to ask her for another favour.

'I'm glad you're feeling more yourself,' she said coolly, hoping to discourage him from taking her help for granted.

She was about to wish him good night when he put in quickly, 'I was just wondering whether you could do me one more favour?'

Aha. 'Yes?'

'I don't like to visit Mrs Clack's. You know what a gossip she is. And I was just wondering whether you could pick me up a newspaper tomorrow morning?'

'Any one in particular?'

He must have caught her tone. 'No, really. Any of the broadsheets will do. Whenever it's convenient for you to pop in.'

'Good night, Jeremy.'

8

Kate delivered Jeremy's newspaper first thing, using the excuse of her usual morning run to drop in at Camilla's place. Jeremy looked rested, but still wary, and was quite uncommunicative – but perhaps that was because it was barely seven thirty. She didn't stay to chat, but returned home to work on her book, making an effort to forget all about Jeremy and his problems.

News of the Fosters' death had disappeared from the front pages of the national press and retreated to the local papers. Mostly the articles consisted of speculation about how such a blameless couple could have found themselves the victims of what was assumed to be a contract killing. Edward's elderly brother in Australia was interviewed, but to little account: the brothers were on friendly terms but hadn't met for seven years. The gossip in Mrs Clack's shop continued unabated, but although it was more colourful and certainly more libellous than the press speculation it added little to Kate's understanding of the crime.

Later in the day Emma rang to ask Kate's opinion once more about Sam's behaviour. Her worries were centred, as far as Kate could tell, on his occasional unexplained disappearances and his general air of shiftiness. Kate could offer no explanation but made soothing noises down the telephone. She did see Sam, riding his bicycle, in town a couple of times over the next week. He appeared preoccupied and perhaps a little more worried than usual, but this she put down to his concern over Emma's latest pregnancy. He could well have been working out how to pay for a minibus to transport his ever-expanding family about their many activities. And as for his disappearances, they could easily be explained by a search for peace and quiet, away from the clamour of the house in Headington. Sam would never involve himself in anything immoral, let alone illegal, Kate was sure. He just wasn't that kind of person. She pushed out of her mind the observation that she had thought exactly the same about Laura and Edward Foster. And look how wrong she'd been!

Roz phoned from time to time to make sure that Kate was cheerful and occupied, but was more interested in her own affairs than her daughter's. Which was just as it should be, Kate told herself bracingly.

And Estelle phoned back with a date for their visit to Grigg's. It was for a day nearly two weeks in the future, but Estelle was already getting excited by the prospect.

'It's going to be such fun!' she gushed.

'Why don't you take the train from Paddington? I'll meet you at Oxford station and drive you out to the printing works,' said Kate.

'Thank you! I do so look forward to it.'

Love, Kate reflected, was a marvellous thing if it could transform the normally steely Ms Livingstone into such a gooey mess. She just hoped that Mr Grigg could live up to Estelle's expectations.

A few days later it occurred to Kate that she should check with Jeremy that he had remembered that it would soon be time to move out of Camilla's house. She ought to ensure that he hadn't left dirty mugs around the place, or dropped damp towels in heaps on the bathroom floor. After all, he had scattered enough crumbs over her own kitchen, and she couldn't rely on him to leave Camilla's house as immaculate as he found it.

She was about to phone him when the telephone rang.

'Kate? It's Jeremy.' He was speaking in a low voice and sounded nervous. Oh dear, he hadn't got over his conviction that wicked men with guns were hunting him all over Oxfordshire.

'It's time for me to move on,' he said.

'Yes. I'm glad you've remembered that.' She wouldn't ask him about the condition of the house. She had time before Camilla's return to do any housework and laundry that was necessary. She didn't usually volunteer to do such things, but it would be worth it if Jeremy could be persuaded to leave Camilla's and return to a normal life. And if he couldn't manage that, at least he might have the decency to disappear out of *her* life.

'Everything's been all right, has it?' she asked brightly.

'I'm not sure.'

'Well, at least you're still in one piece.' How could you take seriously the fears of a man who had walked through Customs in a chestnut-red wig, and believed that people were trying to steal his boring manuscript?

'Can you meet me this evening? I'd like to explain one or two things.'

Kate wasn't keen on the idea but, as it happened, she had a clear evening. And it was also true that her social life had not been very lively for the past week.

'How about a pub?' she suggested. 'That should be safe enough for you.'

'Why don't I see you at the fair?'

She had forgotten that it was the St Giles's Fair. For two days and nights in early September every year the centre of Oxford was brought to a standstill, buses and cars were diverted round side streets, while the whole of St Giles reverberated to the thump of generators and the blare of music, and the young of Oxford screamed their way round the various stomach-churning rides.

'I'll meet you on the corner of St Giles and Beaumont Street, by the Taylorian,' Jeremy was saying. 'At half past eight.'

'Fine,' said Kate, making mental notes.

She returned to her study wondering what she had let herself in for. Still, if she listened to Jeremy talking about his fears she might be able to calm him down and smooth them away. Alec Malden and Harry Joiner appeared to be used to Jeremy's funny little ways. Perhaps the whole of Oxford knew him for a lunatic with paranoid delusions. But there was a discrepancy in his story she would like to ask him about. It had been niggling at her all week.

And it might just mean that Jeremy wasn't batty after all, she thought, as she scrolled down to the bottom of the chapter she had been working on. There might be something in his story.

Although it was only the first week in September, it was misty and quite chilly when Kate left her house that evening. She was wearing jeans, trainers and a warm jacket, although she couldn't see Jeremy joining her in being hurled around the Oxford sky in the claws of a giant machine.

She walked up Beaumont Street, past the decorous façade of the Randolph Hotel and the elegant columns of the Ashmolean Museum. Ahead of her she could hear the noise of the fair and see the movement of the crowds. It's like a medieval nightmare, she thought. If you half closed your eyes so that you couldn't see the detail, you could imagine yourself back in time. The smell of massed humanity was similar, too, she guessed as she drew nearer: street food cooked in hot oil, taste disguised with strong spices. Here goes your novelist's imagination again, she thought happily. There were no modern vehicles in sight, and the backdrop of grey stone colleges, veiled by the foliage of plane trees, looked much as it must have done for hundreds of years. The figures wandering hand in hand, or queuing at the stalls for food, were garishly lit by the lights from the attractions so that details were lost and they might have come from any century. And music blared in every known key, from every direction, underscored by the thump of generators.

The smell of food served from mobile vans hit her as she reached the corner of St Giles. She turned to her left, and in the shadow of the Taylor Institute she saw a thin figure with pale hair. He lifted a hand in greeting and she recognised Jeremy.

Thudding noise filled her head and she could hardly hear what he was saying.

'Do we have to stay here?' she asked him, shouting to make herself heard.

'There's safety in crowds,' he said. 'And with the roads barred, there's nowhere for them to escape to.'

'Let's cross over the road,' she shouted back. 'It's quieter over there, if you want to talk.'

He took her hand as they moved through the throng. Shouting groups bumped into them and moved on again as though they were invisible.

'Can't we try that ride?' asked Kate, staring into the glowing green maw of a tunnel. This one at least had the advantage of staying at ground level instead of hurling itself into the sky. But Jeremy ignored the temptations of the thrill-packed rides as though they didn't exist. Around them young girls giggled and shrieked, attracting the attention of lager-swilling youths.

They pushed on through the mess of discarded food wrappers and empty plastic bottles until they found themselves in the relative peace of the eastern edge of the wide thoroughfare.

'What was it you wanted to tell me?' asked Kate. She was already tired of this evening's entertainment, since Jeremy couldn't even be persuaded to take her on the dodgems.

'You're right. We could risk going into the Lamb and Flag,' said Jeremy. 'We should be safe enough in there.'

The pub was hot and crowded and a thick layer of smoke hovered above the noisy, excited young faces. Jeremy pushed a way through, and then saw a couple leaving a corner table in the furthest section of the bar.

'I'll grab that table. You get the drinks,' he said to Kate, and edged his way to the free space.

Kate eventually caught the barman's eye and ordered a couple of pints of bitter. Then she bought them each a packet of crisps, for it looked as though they were unlikely to get anything else to eat that evening.

'You certainly know how to treat a girl,' she said, putting down the beer and offering Jeremy a small packet of salt and vinegar flavour.

'What?' Jeremy's mind was elsewhere. Then he said, 'Sorry,' and passed across a fiver.

'Keep it,' she said. She didn't add that she thought he might need every fiver he possessed if he continued to behave this way.

'Well?' she asked, when she had drunk some beer and crunched through a few crisps. She knew she didn't sound very sympathetic, but she was getting tired of Jeremy and his delusions.

'Where shall I begin?'

'I expect that is a rhetorical question,' answered Kate crisply. 'But nevertheless I should start at the beginning if I were you.'

The conversation around them was loud and would drown anything they might not wish to be overheard, but even so Jeremy dropped his voice.

'It's a long story.'

'And you'll have to speak up a bit because I can't hear you through this racket. Don't worry, no one's interested in us,' she assured him. To the nineteen-year-olds in the bar they must look positively middle-aged and very, very boring.

'I was born in a small town in the Midlands,' Jeremy began.

This, thought Kate, is going to take a *long* time. We must have at least another thirty-five years to get through before we get to the interesting part.

'My parents were older than average, just into their forties, and I was their only child. All their hopes rested on my narrow shoulders.' He smiled at the weak joke, but Kate willed him to get on with the story.

'I was a good child. Well behaved, polite, a credit to my parents. I think perhaps I lacked the imagination to be anything different. And Metford lacked scope for a would-be tearaway even if it had occurred to me to be such a thing.'

Kate noticed that, in returning to his roots, Jeremy returned also to the pernickety way of speaking that she imagined belonged to his father.

'Are you like your father?' she asked him.

'Yes. I must be. He's very old now, of course, and living in a retirement home.'

Gaga, thought Kate unkindly. 'And your mother?'

'She died five years ago.'

Kate drank more of her beer and wished he'd get on with the story. But Jeremy, in spite of his former nervousness, seemed to be in no hurry.

'Metford still had a grammar school in those days. Two in fact. One for boys, one for girls. I spent the first half of my childhood knowing that it was my duty to pass the eleven plus, and so that's what I did. There's a photo of me somewhere wearing my new school uniform and looking very proud. My mother stands beside me – looking old enough to be my grandmother, I have to say – looking even prouder.'

Kate rubbed her eyes. The cigarette smoke was making them sting and she was developing a strong desire to allow her lids to close so that she could drift away from Jeremy's story into her own, more exciting, thoughts.

'I did what was expected of me.' He spoke louder suddenly, so that Kate's eyes shot open and she listened to what he was saying. 'All through my school career I did the right thing. I played cricket, although I didn't enjoy it. I learned to play the violin, although I'm not musical. And I passed all my exams and came home at the end of every term with a glowing report of my progress and achievements.'

'Then why do you sound so unhappy about it?' asked Kate.

'It was all laid out for me: grammar school, A-levels, university. I even made it to head boy. Doubtless there's a photo of me somewhere wearing my badge. I came up to Oxford and the pattern continued. Until I took my Finals, that is.'

'You failed?' asked Kate – who had never been to university herself – sympathetically.

'Oh no. I didn't fail, not exactly. I took a Second.'

Second class. Second rate. That's what Jeremy would think, though most outsiders would think that any Oxford degree was an accolade.

'Was it such a disaster?'

'My father had been convinced I'd get a First. I knew somewhere in my second year that I hadn't got the right turn of mind for it.'

'But you *are* an academic. Loads of people would envy you that. It can't matter much now what class of degree you got, surely?' And what had all this to do with the fact that Jeremy thought he was being hunted by men with guns?

'But I'm not even a Fellow of my college,' said Jeremy.

'And that matters?'

He looked at her as though she was the one who was mad. 'Of course it does.'

'You mean it's about money? Status?'

'Both. I'm a college lecturer, you see. A very lowly species. They employ me to teach undergraduates the parts of the syllabus they know nothing about – and they only allow me on the premises during term time. And once a week they let me in to eat dinner with the Fellows.'

'Tough,' said Kate, who didn't admire self-pity.

'You think it doesn't matter?'

'In the grand design of the universe? No, I don't.'

'But this is Oxford. And it's the only world I know.'

Then it's about time you got out there into the big world and found out that no one owes you a living, thought Kate viciously. You're lucky to have a pleasant job in a beautiful city, and sufficient funds for a house, food and clothing. But she was kind enough, for once, not to say it aloud.

'You're doing all right, thought,' she said eventually. 'Haven't you got friends? They can make life bearable, I've found.'

'I don't think I have your gift for making easy friendships,' he said, sounding as though he disapproved of it. He probably did, at that.

'You're a member of a college. Doesn't that give you immediate access to congenial company whenever you need it?'

He looked at her pityingly. 'You don't know much about such places, do you? Alec Malden's the only man I trust there. He's a real friend. But the others . . .'

'Things aren't so bad,' said Kate bracingly. 'You live in a reasonable part of town. You've bought your own house. You travel abroad.'

'But I needed help,' said Jeremy. 'And that's where the story – the part of the story you're interested in – really begins.'

At this moment there was a commotion as two young women decided that they, too, could sit at Kate and Jeremy's table. They pulled over a couple of stools, they pushed the table so that beer slopped out of glasses, they giggled loudly and finally settled themselves down.

'We'd better have another drink,' said Jeremy. He passed across the same creased fiver. 'I'll pay this time, but I'd still be grateful if you could go to the bar. Better get me an orange juice.'

'And another packet of crisps, perhaps?' There was nothing like an extravagant evening out, thought Kate.

When she returned to their table she found that the two young women who had joined them were eyeing Jeremy up and down, trying to work out whether he was worth getting off with. Maybe he was an improvement on their usual men. A man with scalp stubble, black leathers and steel studs in unexpected places was staring hard at them. The two girls were dressed in black jeans, showing off broad thighs and the sort of hips that are developed after a lifetime's supply of burgers and chips. They had pale, pasty faces, lank dark hair and figures that spilled over the edges of their stools. Then she realised she must have been staring while taking this inventory – a bad habit of hers, but one she was unlikely to get rid of – for her stares were being returned, not in a friendly way. And I bet they're not making notes for their next novel, either, thought Kate.

'So, did you see him last night?' It was the fatter of the two, addressing her friend.

'He come round my place after the pub shut,' said her friend.

'Where had we got to?' Kate asked Jeremy, a little desperately.

'I was living in a furnished flat at the top of the Iffley Road, driving an E-reg Fiesta and knowing I'd never have anything better,' said Jeremy. 'I knew I'd get no further in my career.'

'He left before midnight,' said the girl opposite disgustedly. 'I was left sat in front of the telly on me own for the rest of the evening.'

'Did you watch that thing on Channel Five?'

'What was that?'

'Where they had these couples, right, and they were like doing it, right, with their bloke's mate, and they asked them—'

Kate managed with an effort to filter out this conversation and tune back in to what Jeremy was saying.

'It came to a head when I went to Brussels to deliver a paper at a conference on international currencies.'

Kate stifled a yawn.

'On the flight over they offered me an up-grade to Club Class, so I found myself sitting with men a lot better off than myself. Expensive suits. Shiny new luggage. The latest in laptops. It happened that the man sitting next to me was reading the same journal as me. And as a matter of fact, I had an article published in it. The only one of mine they'd published that year, but it just happened to be in that particular issue. We struck up a conversation.'

'And you "just happened" to mention that you'd written the article?'

'Possibly.'

'It must be a good feeling,' conceded Kate. 'I've always wanted to sit next to someone who was reading one of my books. It's never happened, though.'

'No.' Jeremy didn't sound surprised. 'Well, I was looking up some relevant information on my laptop, when it died.'

'Why did it do that?'

'I don't know. It always used to run really hot, and it just burned itself out. It was clapped-out, I knew, but I'd hoped it would last me a bit longer, until I could afford to buy a new one.

'Then, "Borrow mine," said the man sitting next to me – the one who'd been reading my article. And he said it so casually, as though he always had a computer or two going spare, that it really got to me.'

They were interrupted by a peal of laughter from the girls at the table. Jeremy looked across sharply, as though suspecting that they were laughing at him, but they were immersed in their own lives, or at least those of the characters they had been watching on television. The thickset man in biker gear seemed inclined to add himself to their table. Then he caught Kate watching him and turned away.

'What's wrong?' asked Jeremy anxiously.

'Nothing. I didn't want all those steel studs sitting next to me, that's all.'

'What?' Jeremy was back to his habit of glancing nervously around the bar. It made him look like a fugitive, thought Kate. Not at all the impression he was hoping to give.

'Don't worry. There's no one in here interested in you. Or us,' she added, to be fair. 'Go on with what you were saying.'

'When Janice and I divorced, she got half the house. It was only right, since she'd put a lot of money into it, but it did mean I couldn't afford my own place when we had to sell it and divide the proceeds. Property in Oxford is so bloody expensive.'

'I had noticed.'

'And they don't pay me enough to live decently. I should publish more, but academic authors get a lousy deal from their publishers.'

'So they all say.'

'Where was I?'

Feeling sorry for yourself again, thought Kate. 'Sitting on a plane bound for Brussels,' she said.

'Once we'd landed, we shared a taxi to the hotel. It turned out we were staying at the same place. The conference organisers had booked me in and paid the bill: it wasn't the sort of place I could normally afford for myself.'

The two girls had decided to leave. They stood up, slopping more beer on to the mess of crumbs and crumpled paper packets they had left on the table.

'He asked me to join him for a drink later that evening,' Jeremy was saying. 'There was someone I should meet, he said.' He was interrupted by the larger of the two girls who bent down towards him.

'If she won't give you what you're after, darling, you can come back to my place,' she said.

Jeremy winced and moved a few inches back against the wall.

The girls laughed again and pushed their way through to the door. A wave of music and screaming machinery blasted in as they opened it and went out into the fairground. Jeremy stared around the bar as though looking for someone.

'I've had enough of this,' he said. 'Shall we go?'

'What about the rest of the story?' He hadn't even got to the good bit. 'I need to know about the passport,' she said.

'Another time. I have to get going.' She could see that Jeremy had lost interest in baring his soul, even to someone as sympathetic as Kate Ivory. He picked up the rucksack which he'd brought in with him. 'I've hired a car,' he said. 'I'm leaving Oxford for a while.'

'But you'll have to come back. What about your job?'

'I'll work something out.'

'You'll be in touch?'

'Maybe.' He drew something from his pocket and handed it to her.

'Camilla's key?' she asked, taking it from him.

'Yes. Thanks for letting me stay there. And thank your friend, too. I think it probably saved my life.'

He had shouldered his rucksack and was pushing his way through the crowd, taking the same direction as the two girls. Just before he reached the door he turned to Kate again.

'Maybe you should take this, too.' He was offering her another key. She looked her query. 'It's the key to my house.

110

The plants must be parched by now. Do you think you could water them for me?'

Kate remembered his concern for Laura's azalea. She was glad to think there was something Jeremy cared about, apart from himself.

'Don't worry,' she said, taking the key. 'I'll treat them as my own.'

Jeremy smiled slightly. 'That's what I was afraid of.'

Other people were trying to leave the pub and they were blocking the exit, so they moved on. Outside, in the cobbled passageway, he said, 'I'm going now. Goodbye, Kate.' And he turned and strode away towards Parks Road. The man in the biker leathers pushed past Kate and paused to look around. He's wondering where those two girls went, thought Kate, watching his padded back disappear into the crowd.

Jeremy waited until he was out of Kate's sight before he dodged through a gate and into a doorway to see who, if anyone, was following him. Even away from the fairground crowds there were still plenty of people about. Groups of youngsters in dark clothing, indistinguishable in the pools of darkness between the streetlamps, drifted past. Giggles and high-pitched snatches of conversation reached him in the doorway, but he recognised no one. Did he even know who he was looking for? He hadn't known the biker in the black leather and studs, but somehow he had appeared like a figure from one of his nightmares – the sort of dream where you're chased down long, dark corridors and through deserted buildings by a faceless man with death on his mind. God! That kind of fantasy was worthy of dear Kate Ivory and her lurid imagination!

After five minutes or so, he slipped out of the doorway,

through the gate and into the street. Keeping close to the railings and as far from the street lights as possible, he made his way to the spot in Mansfield Road where he had left the hired car.

He'd have it out with the man, he thought, as he let himself into the driving seat. If he explained that he didn't want any more involvement in the affair – that things had gone too far, that he had never intended that the Fosters should become involved – the man ought to understand. He had seemed civilised enough when they'd met in that hotel room in Brussels. And the scheme had seemed so simple. Jeremy had the contacts, he was already travelling to France to meet people in the right field.

There had been the meeting in the café in Bordeaux where he'd sat with a cooling cup of black coffee, waiting for the Frenchman to appear and hand over the disk. He'd thought then that everyone was watching him, wondering what he was doing there. But it had all passed off smoothly enough in the end. It was quite banal, really, to anyone who had watched movies or TV dramas. And the money he had received already had come in more than handy. *There'll be a bonus in January 2002*, they'd told him. *That's when our investment begins to pay off.* He'd have to find a way to pay back some – not all, surely? – of the money they'd already given him, but he'd do that over time. He took a final look at the slip of paper with the man's name and address written on it. It wasn't his real name, of course, but the one they all called him by – 'Jester'. And the address consisted simply of the name of a house and the village somewhere in the wilds between Evesham and Redditch on whose outskirts it might be found. Clay House, Lower Grooms, Worcestershire.

As he made his way through the traffic diversions to the

bypass and the A40, he thought he heard the growl of a motorbike engine behind him. But there was no reason to think that it had anything to do with him.

I would like to have heard what happened next, thought Kate, turning to leave St Giles in the opposite direction from Parks Road. She wandered down through the middle of the fair, avoiding clusters of drunken youths, ignoring shouted invitations from a shaven-headed man with a beer belly to join in the fun.

You took so long to get your story started, Jeremy, and then we never reached the punchline. What happened in Brussels? Who was the man on the plane? Did you join him for a drink later that evening and meet his friend? And did he offer you a lot of money, and if so, what was it for? What did you possess that would be of interest to a man like that?

And what about the false passport? That's been worrying me all week. I know you can no longer get your hands on a passport in another name by using the birth certificate of a long-dead child. They closed that loophole after *The Day of the Jackal* tipped everyone off to the possibility. No. These days you need money, and criminal connections, to get hold of one. I thought you had neither, Jeremy, but I must have been wrong.

In Clay House, Fabian West poured himself a glass of brandy and settled back on the leather sofa to enjoy the new CD he had bought for himself: Verdi's *Falstaff* in an interesting new recording. He exhaled through pursed lips as he listened to the spirited opening chords. He had given up cigars, even after a good dinner, but he still missed the physical act of smoking – the way the smoke felt as it passed over the tongue and through the mouth – although he had found other means of obtaining the pleasure it had once given him.

An honest observer could only describe Fabian as a fat man. He would describe himself, however, as being well proportioned: if he was wide, he was also tall, and his voice was just the fruity baritone that one expected from a man with such a robust build. His hair was luxuriant, and still mainly black, and his feet and hands were large and square. But if it was true that Fabian's bulk had once been composed largely of muscle, it was no longer so. Fabian was now a soft man, with rolls of fat sitting on his shirt collar and above the waistband of his expensive, bespoke tweed trousers. Fabian was old-fashioned: he wore tweeds in the country, never in town. And his dark suits were worn for his business dealings in London and other capitals, not to frighten the Worcestershire county set.

But just because he was principally a businessman it didn't mean he didn't have his sensibilities, his finer feelings, he told himself as the scene at the Garter Inn unfolded. He didn't like any nastiness (as he put it to himself) to intrude on the civilised life that he had organised for himself. *I am a fastidious man*, he liked to say.

He had replaced the first disc of *Falstaff* with the second and was enjoying the amusing business with the laundry basket when the mobile phone, which he had placed ready before him on the mahogany table, rang. He checked the caller's identity, then replied.

'Stud?' he said. 'This is Jester. Yes?'

He listened to what Stud had to tell him. 'Excellent,' he said. 'The money will be in your account tomorrow morning.'

When he had rung off he picked up a slim, leather-bound notebook and a gold pen. He opened it to a page where he had written a list of names. He found 'Sancho' and crossed it through. 'Mr and Mrs Parker', at the end of the list, had already been deleted in the same way.

9

Kate was glad to leave the hectic lights and mind-numbing music of the fairground behind and return to the peace of her house in Agatha Street.

As she walked, she thought over what Jeremy had told her in the pub. It was the story of a man who had reached the ceiling of his career before he was forty, a man who would always be disappointed in his achievements even when an outsider might see them as considerable. But what else had she learned? That he went to Brussels and met a rich businessman who introduced him to another (whose name she hadn't asked) because Jeremy had some information that interested them. How long ago did this happen? She wished she'd asked him, but the heat and smoke in the pub had made her less attentive than usual. So, at some unspecified time after the meeting in Brussels he had returned from Bordeaux wearing a wig – because he was travelling under a false passport, and he had worn the red wig while sitting for the passport photo. Silly idiot.

She was still no nearer knowing where he had obtained that passport. He must have contacts in the criminal world. But if so, then everything – well, nearly everything – that Joiner and Malden had said to explain his behaviour was false. And they must have known it. The celebratory shout, the laughter, that followed her out of the college were for her: she had delivered something valuable into their hands, and she had swallowed their story. No wonder they were cheerful!

Go back a bit, Kate. If they weren't really interested in a manuscript on economics, if Jeremy wasn't scared that someone wanted to steal his work, then just what *was* on the disk you gave them? Something valuable, obviously. Something that had to be smuggled into the country by a courier using a false passport.

She considered the possibilities. Pornography? But would they need Jeremy for that? He hadn't struck her as a pornographer, but then she wasn't sure what one would look like. And he was solitary, as far as she could tell, and introverted, and he even owned a raincoat. Or what about industrial espionage? Suppose he had come across some secret that was going to revolutionise the world of economics, and had delivered it to Alec Malden on a disk. *Get real, Kate!*

Inside her house, Kate made herself a sandwich, poured a glass of wine and settled down in front of the television. She thought fleetingly of Jeremy's green plants, and decided to water them in the morning. If they'd survived this long they could manage for another few hours.

But the television series she was watching failed to keep her attention. She wandered back to the kitchen and chose some fruit from the bowl to take into the sitting room with her.

Halfway through the first apple, the phone rang.

'It's Emma.'

Kate was only too pleased to be interrupted. She turned the television off and settled down for a good gossip with her friend.

'How's it going, Emma? Have you started to feel better yet?'

'Kate, you're only *pretending* to care about my pregnancy. I know you're not much interested in children, let alone babies.'

'I quite like children,' said Kate, hurt.

'Really?' Emma didn't sound convinced.

'What's up?' It didn't sound as though Emma had rung for a cosy session of girlie gossip after all.

'I'm worried,' said Emma.

'Sam again?'

'How did you know?'

Because you've been rabbiting on about him for a couple of weeks now. But she said only, 'What's he done?' and tried to keep the 'again' out of her voice.

'I know you think we're really well off,' Emma began defensively.

'Comfortably off,' confirmed Kate.

'But we're not, really. I know we have this house, and no mortgage to pay, but we've only got Sam's salary and the oddments that I manage to earn.'

'And children are expensive little luxuries,' suggested Kate.

'They're not luxuries.'

'Of course not. Ignore my remarks.'

'But they *are* expensive, I agree.'

Especially when you have six, or perhaps seven, of them. 'Yes,' said Kate.

'And suddenly Sam says we need a new car, especially with the baby on the way, and we have to think of transporting all his or her gear, as well as Jack's and Tris's, and . . .'

'Yes,' said Kate, who knew that a recitation of Emma's children's names might well go on for a long time.

'He said we needed a people-transporter, or something like that. Something that we could pack all the children into.'

'Like a minibus.'

'But more expensive!' shrieked Emma.

'Surely not.'

'Sam *never* suggests spending money unless it's absolutely necessary.'

'He must think you really need a bus for the children,' said Kate.

'We have our bicycles,' said Emma primly.

'It might be a year or two before the new baby gets the hang of riding a bike.'

'Don't be silly. He or she will ride in the child's seat on the back of mine.'

A picture of Sam, followed by a string of children on bicycles in descending order of size, with Emma bringing up the rear with the newest baby strapped into its seat, popped into Kate's head. She tried not to giggle.

'I think Sam sounds very thoughtful,' she said. 'He has your interest at heart, Emma. And the children's,' she added.

'But how does he think we can possibly afford it?'

'Ah.' She didn't like to suggest that Sam, too, might have met a man on a plane to Brussels and found himself being offered a large sum of money. To do what, though? 'Maybe he knows someone who'll get him a discount on the price. Have you tried talking to him? Why don't you ask him straight out?'

'There never seems to be time,' said Emma. 'Whenever we're on our own, without the children that is, one or both of us is asleep.'

'You'll have to book yourself an appointment,' said Kate. 'Visit him at the office, or meet him for lunch.'

'Do you really think so?'

'It's the only way you'll find out what's happening.'

But it occurred to her after she had put the phone down that perhaps Emma didn't really want to know what was happening.

Sam had mumbled something about 'meeting someone' when she had bumped into him at Gatwick. At the time she had thought he was just making an excuse not to have coffee with her. But perhaps it had been true. And who would Sam have met? She had to admit that the most likely possibilities were one, a woman, and two, a man with a briefcase full of used tenners. She didn't like to think such things of Sam. She didn't blame Emma for avoiding the subject: sometimes it was easier to hide away from reality.

Kate returned to her apple.

Later that night, when she was in bed and drifting into sleep, she thought of another question she should have asked Jeremy. What was the subject of the article that he and his companion on the flight had been discussing? What, if it came to that, was Jeremy's particular area of expertise?

Next morning, when she had been out for a short run, and after she had eaten her breakfast, it occurred to Kate that she should check on Jeremy's plants before settling down to write the next chapter of her novel.

Of course, she told herself, letting herself out of her own house and in through Jeremy's front door, this has nothing to do with my uncertainty about the man. Absolutely not. But it was true that once inside number 8 she did look around with a certain degree of curiosity before filling the small watering can and going in search of thirsty green plants.

Very nice, she thought, pouring a pint of water into a tall plant with scented leaves that was winding its way up a bamboo cane. Sanded and polished wood floors. Old Mrs Arden didn't do that. Jeremy must have had it done professionally, by the look of it. And the sort of simple furniture that cost huge sums of money in understated shops off Sloane Square. That long sofa was covered in the very softest leather. I wouldn't mind a jacket in that stuff, she thought. The stereo carried the logo B&O and the TV was a wide-screen model.

Jeremy was doing all right for a man who had come badly out of a divorce and was a failure in his chosen career, she thought as she swamped some small spiky things on the windowsill. *Money and criminal contacts?*

She really ought to look upstairs, she told herself resolutely. She was sure she had seen something large and green by the computer up there. Yes, she had. There was also more good furniture. Halogen uplighters. The computer was a Pentium 3, she noted with a twinge of jealousy.

She had to remind herself that she was unlikely to find too many houseplants inside the cupboards or drawers, and leave them severely alone, but she did read the titles of Jeremy's books. *The Role of Monetary Policy in Economic Planning. Inflation Targeting and the ECB. Aspects of the Single Financial Market.* Not a decent plot among them, she guessed, let alone any interesting characters. They merely reminded her that he was an economist, however, and that didn't really get her any further forward.

She returned the watering can to the kitchen and took one last look around in case there was something she had missed. No. The place was so clean and tidy that there were no obvious hiding-places or even crannies where an important clue might be forgotten. It was time to get back to her own computer.

Computer.

She ran back upstairs and sat down in Jeremy's chair, in front of Jeremy's large, flat monitor, and switched on his computer. She waited impatiently while it went through its stately processes.

A dialogue box appeared. 'Username: Jeremy Wells.' Then it said 'Password?' and blinked its cursor in an empty space.

This was not something she had ever bothered with on her own machine since she was usually the only person to use it. So if Jeremy protected his files with a password it must be because there was something to hide.

What sort of password would the man use? She tried 'economics' and 'fiscal' and 'monetary', but the machine just repeated, 'The Windows password you typed is incorrect. OK?' Not OK, she thought. What would he be interested in, apart from monetary policy? She looked around at the neat, organised shelves, the spotless surfaces.

'Housework', she typed.

The machine rejected the suggestion.

What else? Oh yes, of course – house plants. She walked round, peering into pots, reading labels. *Beloperone guttata. Anthurium crystallinum. Ficus benjamina.* These were more likely candidates than 'inflation targeting', surely? She copied the names down on to the notepad that Jeremy kept by his telephone. (No useful notes scribbled here, unfortunately. No 'false passport' and a phone number, certainly.) Then she tried them out one by one.

When she reached 'benjamina', the computer capitulated and allowed her in.

Jeremy had been busy. There were dozens of files in the directories she searched. She didn't want to spend all day investigating them so she returned to the Desktop and looked to see what he had been working on most recently. She had to believe that if Jeremy had a file on his computer that would interest her, it had to be something he had been working on in the past week or two. And after all the effort she'd made to get into his computer she didn't like to think that there was nothing exciting there at all.

She studied the file names. Most of them looked to her as if they were to do with his work. But there was one that looked more promising. He had called it 'Jester', and it had last been edited just yesterday morning. She opened it to take a look. It was long and dense and she didn't think she could sit here in Jeremy's house and read it all the way through. Better to copy it to a floppy disk and take it back to her own house to examine at leisure. She checked its format and found that Jeremy used a more recent version of Word than she did. (*Face it, Kate, everybody does.*)

She placed a wodge of A4 in the printer and told the machine to print out two copies of the file. It was always best to have a second copy of a manuscript, she had always found, just in case of mishaps. And that was the good thing about tidy people, she thought as the pages began to spew out of the machine: you could lay your hands on reams of paper with no trouble at all. A place for everything and everything in its place, that was our Jeremy.

As the pages continued to emerge, Kate glanced at her watch. It was later than she thought. She'd spent more than an hour in Jeremy's house. And she'd promised to get back to Estelle to confirm the times of trains from Paddington to Oxford. She'd better return to her own place to make the call before Estelle disappeared on one of her extensive working lunches.

She left Jeremy's house. As she went down the stairs to her own study and switched on her own computer (a sturdy 486 with added memory) she wondered how Jeremy had managed to afford all that expensive gear.

First Sam, now Jeremy, she thought.

I wonder if they're connected?

And being an honest person, she noticed that she had managed to push to one side the question of the Fosters' murder. The pictures it brought to her mind were too horrific, and she had decided to leave it to the police. In spite of Jeremy's ridiculous behaviour, she was sure that the connection between him and the Fosters was too tenuous to have anything to do with their death. Even the local newspapers were beginning to concede that it had been a mistake, that the Fosters had been killed because they had been confused with two other people, probably implicated in drug manufacture or distribution. No one, however hard they tried, had managed to find anything at all criminal in the Fosters' background.

Jeremy was behaving as though the killer had been after him, but he looked nothing like Edward Foster, and even less like Laura, so he was surely wrong about that.

She logged on to the Thames Trains website and checked the timetable. Why couldn't Estelle have done this for herself, she wondered. But Estelle liked to think of herself as a technological idiot. Kate suspected that she considered it made her more feminine and attractive to men.

Armed with the information she needed, she rang her agent.

'Thank you so much, Kate. So efficient of you! I'll pass the information on to Crispen.'

'Crispen?' She could hear the 'e' quite plainly.

'He's your new publicity person at Fergussons. It's a good opportunity for the two of you to meet, and apparently the boy knows nothing about the printing side of the business.'

Kate just hoped that this wasn't another of Estelle's potential lovers, but surely she was concentrating on the financially fanciable Mr Grigg.

'Now, tell me how the book's coming along,' said Estelle firmly.

There was nothing fluffy about Estelle when it came to work, and Kate had to undergo a good fifteen minutes' grilling over plot and characters before she could escape. Then she went straight back to her computer to call up Chapter 8 and undertake a lengthy rewrite. When hunger reminded her it was well past her lunchtime she made a hasty cheese sandwich and took it downstairs with her, together with a mug of coffee. She typed on into the afternoon.

Meanwhile, next door in Jeremy's house, the pages of the 'Jester' file sat unheeded in the printer's out-tray.

It wasn't until the phone rang late that afternoon that Kate remembered that this was the day Camilla was due to return from the Lake District.

'Did you have a lovely time?' she asked.

'Perfectly satisfactory,' said Camilla, and Kate thought she heard a hint of smugness in her voice.

'And your plants are all looking healthy and thriving?'

'Yes. Shouldn't they be?'

'Oh, you know me and my ability to kill off house plants,' said Kate. How could she ask whether Jeremy had left Camilla's house as he had found it? She really should have popped round to make sure that all was clean and tidy before Camilla's return.

'Did you manage to escape from Agatha Street?' Camilla was asking.

'I did come round once or twice,' said Kate, not mentioning

that it was in order to visit Jeremy rather than to find a refuge for herself. 'Thanks, Camilla, it was very kind of you to suggest it.'

'It was useful to have someone keeping an eye on the place.'

'I have to call in at Mrs Clack's before she closes,' said Kate. 'I'll return your key on my way home, shall I?'

'I'll see you then,' said Camilla.

'Come in,' said Camilla an hour or so later when Kate arrived at her front door.

She was looking very fit, Kate noticed, and her colour had improved.

'You look as though you did plenty of walking,' she said.

'Would you like a cup of tea?' asked Camilla, ignoring the comment. 'Or is it time for a glass of wine?'.

'You'd better make it tea. I still have work to do when I get home.'

She followed Camilla into the kitchen, noticing with relief that the place seemed as clean and tidy as normal and there appeared to be no drifts of crumbs across the counter. Jeremy must have cleaned up after himself, thank goodness. Not that Camilla would have objected to his presence, Kate told herself, but life would be simpler if Camilla didn't know about it.

'Your plants are surviving, are they?'

'Beautifully,' said Camilla. 'If I didn't know it was you looking after them I'd say their condition had even improved.'

'Oh, well,' said Kate modestly.

'And thank you so much for your note,' said Camilla, pouring boiling water on to tea bags.

'Note?' Kate tried not to look too surprised.

'I hadn't realised you'd developed such an interest in gardening.'

'Oh, you know me – interested in everything.' She wondered how she could ask to see the note she was supposed to have written. Perhaps it was a disguised message from Jeremy for her.

'Milk? Sugar?' asked Camilla.

'Milk, please.'

'And we might as well eat some of the biscuits you so generously provided,' added Camilla, passing across the remains of a pack of milk chocolate digestives. 'Funny, I had you down for a dark chocolate person.'

'One's tastes change with age,' said Kate, biting into a biscuit and thinking how much she disliked milk chocolate.

Camilla ate a second biscuit, then went to fetch a sheet of paper from the other side of the room.

'There was just one word here I couldn't read,' she said, handing it across to Kate.

'Really?' said Kate, taking the paper and skimming rapidly through it. 'Surely it's quite clear.' Admirably clear, in fact, and in handwriting just a little neater than her own. How familiar was Camilla with her writing? Surely she'd never written her anything except a Christmas card?

She read the note aloud: 'I'm afraid the <u>Camellia japonica</u> by the back door is quite badly infested with scale insects. It is really too late in the season to attempt to control them with malathion, but you might manage to save your camellia if you remove the small brown limpet-like scales by hand. Many people recommend using the point of a knife, but I think a damp cotton bud is less traumatic for the leaves, and perhaps you could use a small brush for the stems. If you're not opposed to the use of insecticides you should apply something suitable just after the juvenile scale insects hatch, in early summer.'

'Malathion,' said Camilla thoughtfully. 'That was the word I couldn't read. What is it, exactly?'

Kate delved into her memory and came up with, 'It's a preparation for killing scale insects.'

'Really?'

Kate felt like one of her friend's fourth formers caught smoking in the cloakroom.

'Do you mind if I keep this note?' she asked, hoping they could leave the subject of pesticides.

'If you like. But why?'

Kate turned it over swiftly. 'I wrote it on the back of a flyer I was meaning to keep,' she said.

' "Learn office skills at home. Let the Jericho Corporation show you how." I thought you could type quite well already.'

'I need to brush up on my book-keeping,' said Kate, improvising.

'Isn't it easier to do it on your computer? I thought there were neat little software packages for dealing with all your financial affairs.'

'I like to leave my hard disk clear for my novel-writing.'

Camilla left the subject at last. 'More tea? Another biscuit?'

'I'd better be getting back home. I want to finish the chapter I'm working on before relaxing this evening.'

She folded Jeremy's note and put it in her jacket pocket. She had a feeling that she should remove this evidence of his occupation of Camilla's house. And maybe there was a secret message for her hidden inside the one for Camilla. Scale insects and malathion, indeed! She'd tell Jeremy what she thought of his green fingers next time she saw him.

Back in her own study, she took a good look at Jeremy's note. Neat handwriting of a kind common to many educated people. Written with a blue ballpoint pen. She read through the message again. It did seem as though it was only giving information on the eradication of scale insects from Camilla's lovely pink camellia.

She turned it over and took another look at the advertisement for the correspondence course. Why had Jeremy picked it up? It had probably come through his letterbox and every letterbox in the area. But then, she hadn't received one herself. She would have remembered that pale-green colour and the large logo which appeared to feature musical instruments locked in combat. Just scrap paper, she told herself. It has no significance whatsoever.

No, it wasn't important. There was no secret message there for her.

She pushed it into her in-tray and forgot all about it.

Next morning, collecting her weekly magazine from the newsagent's, she heard the news.

'Have you heard about Mr Wells?' asked Mrs Clack. Her hair was freshly tinted a striking damson colour and she was wearing matching lipstick and nail varnish. There was a hot, avid look in her eyes.

'Mr Wells? Oh, yes, you mean Jeremy.'

'*Guardian, Financial Times* and *Observer*,' confirmed Mrs Clack.

'No. I haven't seen him for a few days,' replied Kate, unwilling to encourage Mrs Clack's gossip, but wanting to know what had happened nevertheless.

'So sad,' said Mrs Clack, drawing out the suspense.

'How much do I owe you?' asked Kate.

'You want to pay up to date?' Mrs Clack had a red-covered

book on the counter in two seconds flat, turned to the right page. 'Five pounds twenty-seven,' she said. 'Including delivery charge.'

'But I collect my own.'

'That's your choice, dear. Young Nathan would be only too happy to deliver if you didn't call in.'

Kate knew she was going to lose this argument, although she felt herself to be in the right. 'Tell me about Jeremy Wells,' she said, giving in.

'Very nasty accident,' said Mrs Clack, taking Kate's money and handing over the change.

'How do you know?'

'It's in the paper, dear.'

'Let me see.'

'Twenty-five p,' said Mrs Clack.

'But that's yesterday's.'

Mrs Clack pursed damson lips and looked meaningfully at the gaggle of people who had just entered the shop. 'I've no time to chat, dear,' she said virtuously. 'Do you want the paper?'

'Yes,' said Kate, handing over more coins.

She left the shop, not giving Mrs Clack the satisfaction of seeing her tear the paper apart to find the news item she was looking for, but waiting until she was round the corner before opening it out.

'Oxford man dies in freak car accident.' And yes, it was Jeremy. Jeremy Wells, 39. She closed the paper, rolling it into a tight cylinder as though locking in the information, and walked home slowly, waiting until she was inside her own house before reading the details.

It had happened in the early hours of Tuesday morning. He was driving along a narrow country lane near a village called

Ab Lench. It was dark, of course, in a way that only the countryside can be dark and impenetrable. The road forked; there was a sharp bend. And, for no reason that anyone could see, he had come off the road and slammed into a tree. The description of what had happened wasn't clear. There were no witnesses, but since this was in the middle of the night on a lonely country road, that was hardly surprising.

Kate read the account again, trying to piece together what had happened. What time had they left the pub? It must have been around ten o'clock. Perhaps just a little later. Jeremy hadn't drunk much – just the one pint of bitter at the beginning of the evening before switching to orange juice. Maybe he'd walked away from her and found himself another pub and drunk himself stupid, but somehow she couldn't see him doing that. He wouldn't like the loss of control.

She took out her road atlas and looked up Ab Lench. A couple of dots in a network of white lanes, too unimportant to rate even B-numbers. She saw a fork in the road. Was that where it had happened? There was no way of knowing unless she got into her own car and drove over to look at it.

No. There was no point in doing that.

She looked again at the map. Where was Jeremy going?

The A44 slanted down the page to Oxford in the right hand corner. He must have turned off at Evesham and plunged into the web of lanes leading to villages with unlikely names. Had he a friend who lived thereabouts? She tried to think back to their few conversations, but she couldn't remember him talking about anyone by name except Alec Malden. She could ring Bartlemas and ask to speak to Mr (or Dr, perhaps?) Malden. And then what would she say? Alec Malden, she was sure now, had tricked her that day in his room at Bartlemas. There was no point in asking him about Jeremy's intentions since she wouldn't be able to trust his reply. And if Jeremy had wanted to see Alec Malden he would have gone to Bartlemas himself, not made off into the wilds of Worcestershire.

And what about the story he had been telling her? Jeremy thought his life was in danger. Malden and Joiner had persuaded her he was deluded. But now Jeremy was dead and she couldn't pretend that his death had nothing to do with the men he said were pursuing him. She could play down his fears while he was alive; now he was dead she was forced to take them seriously.

Maybe he'd done it on purpose. Maybe he had been so disillusioned with his life and his prospects that he had decided to do away with himself. But why drive to Worcester (or was it Hereford?) to do so? No, he hadn't been suicidal when she had seen him just a few hours before. He had hired the car and had it waiting ready somewhere near St Giles.

He had been on edge all evening, looking around him, wondering if he was being followed.

And what if he was right?

Someone followed him out of the pub and then to his car. Oh yes, Kate, and he just happened to have his own car parked somewhere nearby and followed Jeremy out of the city and into the country. Why on earth would he do that? If someone wanted to attack him they could do so in one of the alleyways behind St Giles. There was so much noise coming from the fair that no one would hear anything. The place was full of strangers, you wouldn't be recognised.

She was just letting her imagination run away with her again. There was nothing to say that Jeremy had been the victim of anything other than an accident. He had been going off to visit a friend, and after his single pint of beer, with his head full of fanciful stories and ungrounded suspicions, he had lost concentration, swerved off the road and slammed into a tree.

Which left, she had to admit, a fair number of questions unanswered.

10

She did ring Alec Malden, after all, just to tell him she was sorry to hear about the death of his friend and to enquire whether he knew anything about the funeral arrangements.

'There will be a service here in the college chapel,' said Alec Malden. 'He was one of the family, as it were, and the family will look after him now he is dead.'

I believe he saw himself as more of a distant cousin than a close family member, Kate thought but did not say. But she left her address so that she could be informed of the time and the day.

'Have you contacted his father?' she asked, just before ringing off.

'I understood he was suffering from dementia,' said Alec Malden. 'I believe that the journey and the unfamiliar surroundings would only confuse the old man. He is in his eighties, you know. Jeremy was a child of his parents' later years.'

'I believe Jeremy did mention that,' said Kate. 'Where is Mr Wells living, do you know? Perhaps I should write to him.' If the answer was somewhere near Evesham it would explain Jeremy's presence in that area.

'The nursing home is in Kent somewhere. I could find out and let you have the address, but I'm not sure that he will be able to make much sense of your letter.'

But Kate had found out what she had wanted to know.

She had thought for a little while that Jeremy might have been vising his elderly parent. But there was no way you would drive from Oxford to Kent via Evesham, she had to admit.

'I wonder why he was driving out past Evesham,' she said, switching to the direct approach. Perhaps there was some straightforward explanation.

'Oh, I don't think we'll ever know what was in the poor boy's mind that last evening,' said Alec Malden dismissively.

'I'll see you at the funeral,' said Kate.

She tried to put Jeremy out of her mind for the next week. After all, she had a book to write, the visit to Grigg's printing works looming, her mother to keep tabs on, her affair with George to recover from, and Emma to deal with.

'Couldn't you talk to him for me?' pleaded Emma on the phone yet again.

'I'm not sure that Sam and I have ever had a proper conversation,' said Kate dubiously.

'I'm sure he admires you,' said Emma.

'I'm just as sure he doesn't.' She didn't like to mention the fact that she had walked out on his younger brother.

'You could ring him up and ask him to join you for lunch. Or maybe for a drink after work.'

'I don't think so.' She could see any such invitation leading into a morass of misunderstandings from which her friendship with Emma might never recover. 'And what do you want me to say to him?' said Kate, realising too late that she was weakening her position.

'Just ask him what he's been doing this last couple of months,' said Emma.

'If he won't tell you he's hardly likely to confide in me, is he?'

'Well, actually, I haven't asked him, not really. Not straight out like that.'

Kate sighed. No wonder she hadn't married. She simply didn't understand the way married people behaved.

'I'll think about it,' she said weakly, since Emma was still waiting for a response.

'Oh, thank you!' said Emma and rang off before Kate could point out that she hadn't committed herself to anything.

Maybe, she thought brightly, she could get rid of two of her worries in one, simply by getting Roz to have the little talk with Sam. She was sure her mother would find out in a matter of seconds what it was he'd been up to. On the other hand, if it was at all illegal, she would probably join him and get herself arrested. Was she only storing up more trouble for herself if she got Roz interested in the Dolbys' affairs? That particular problem solved itself because when she dialled Roz's number she received no reply.

11

'I need your advice, Kate,' said Estelle. She was speaking
confidentially low.

'What!' Kate couldn't believe it. Estelle was always so sure
of herself. She was the one who told Kate what to do in any
situation. She had never asked Kate's advice on anything before.
'I mean, of course, Estelle. What is it?'

'I was wondering what I should wear,' murmured Estelle.
'Usually I wear a black suit, as you know, with a plain cream
silk top and pearl stud earrings.'

'Wholly appropriate, I should have thought,' said Kate.

'But don't you think it's a little too severe? I could wear red
lipstick, of course, and Jackson is resculpting my hair, and
Karyn is livening up the colour, but . . .'

Kate let her agent's voice wash over her. Estelle would make
her own decision, she was sure. She was tempted to say, 'But
it's only a visit to the printer's,' but that would be too unkind in
the circumstances.

'Yes,' she said soothingly. 'Yes, of course, Estelle.'

'And you'll remember to meet me at the station? You won't
be late?'

'I'll be there. Don't worry.'

'I've told Crispen to be sure to take the same train. We don't
want to be hanging around on a draughty station, do we?'

'I'm sure he'll be there. And so will I.'

139

She hoped that Estelle would remember all her care and concern when it came to negotiating contracts. She was sure she'd earned at least an extra couple of thousand on her next advance. But when she put the phone down she reminded herself that she was in no position to be critical of Estelle. She'd behaved just as stupidly herself when she and George had first met. She sighed. Those days were long gone.

The next phone call came as she was taking a break from writing, and it was from Alec Malden.

'Kate Ivory?'

'Yes.'

'I thought you'd like to know the arrangements for Jeremy's funeral.'

'Yes please.'

'The funeral service will be in the college chapel at eleven o'clock on Thursday morning. You are very welcome to attend, and to join us in the Lamb Room afterwards. Light refreshments, I believe, will be served. You know your way around the college, don't you?'

You've been checking up on me, thought Kate. 'I think so,' she said guardedly. 'I'm sure the porter in the lodge will be able to tell me where to go. Who told you my phone number, by the way?'

'You're in the book,' said Alec Malden mildly and hung up.

He was right: she was, but she still found the man a little creepy.

She was glad he had contacted her, however. What with the Fosters' deaths, and now Jeremy's, she needed some form of ceremony to bring herself back to normal. She had heard nothing about a funeral for the Fosters and wasn't even sure who would be organising it. The image of the two broken bodies lying on the path flashed into her mind yet again. She pushed it resolutely to one side.

Funeral, 11 o'clock, she wrote in her diary. She would wear the black suit she had bought back in the spring. She wondered about a hat, but decided that a black one would be overdoing it, while any other colour would appear frivolous. A black suit, impractical shoes and decorous earrings would be most appropriate. She and Jeremy had barely met, after all.

The third interruption came in the form of a phone call from Emma. Kate listened to the usual catalogue of mysterious behaviour by Sam (ho hum) and when Emma reached her wail of 'What shall I do, Kate?' she gave her considered reply.

'If you really want to find out, and you can't find a moment to ask him directly, you'll have to resort to subterfuge.'

'What?' Emma's usually keen mind was blunted by pregnancy, Kate feared.

'To be brutal,' said Kate, 'you'll just have to go through his pockets. See if there are any incriminating receipts or notes of unfamiliar phone numbers. Mobile numbers are really suspicious,' she added airily, getting into the spirit of the thing. And she had to admit she was getting a little curious herself as to what Sam was up to.

'I couldn't do that,' said Emma doubtfully.

'Of course you could,' said Kate bracingly.

'The children might see me and tell Sam about it.'

'Wait till the children are at school,' suggested Kate patiently. She wasn't clear about child development herself, but surely the little ones were too young to blab. Though she wouldn't put it past Emma's and Sam's infants to be articulate enough to give an accurate verbal report of any event they might have observed.

'Are you sure?'

'Take a look at his briefcase while you're about it, and those sports bags of his.'

'I might find something that explained his behaviour,' said Emma slowly.

'It will hardly be conclusive,' conceded Kate. 'And the most likely result is a big zero. No strange phone numbers, no unexplained receipts, no notes from attractive women.' That last suggestion was a mistake, she realised, as she heard Emma's wail of protest down the phone.

'I don't think you'll find anything,' she explained.

'He's too clever to leave any evidence,' said Emma gloomily.

'But it's more likely that there's nothing for him to hide.'

Kate wasn't sure whether she'd allayed Emma's fears to any appreciable degree, but she put the phone down and retired back to her own peaceful study, hoping for a quiet, uninterrupted hour on her work. When Estelle finally emerged from her pink, romantic haze she would expect a neatly printed manuscript from Kate to be sitting on her desk, awaiting her attention. She would not want to know about Kate's problems, whether they involved a distraught friend or an unexplained killing practically on her doorstep.

In fact, Emma left her in peace for a whole day before ringing back to report on the results of her search.

'I've found something in his sports bag,' she said, her voice dripping with tragedy.

'What is it?' asked Kate.

'I'm not entirely sure.'

'Would you care to describe it?'

'I don't think I would.'

They seemed to have reached an impasse.

'Do you want me to come over and examine it for you?'

'No.'

Kate tried again. 'Is it paper with writing on?'

'No.'

'Is it alive?'

'Not exactly.'

'You're not being very helpful, Emma. Give me some sort of clue, or I'll have to put the phone down and return to the serious business of writing a novel.'

'I've never actually seen one of these before,' said Emma carefully. 'Though I might once have read a magazine article about them. It would have been at the hairdresser's, or perhaps the dentist's, because I don't usually read women's magazines.'

'Emma!' She wanted to shout, 'Get to the point!' but was starting to have a glimmer of a clue what Emma was talking about.

'Why would he want something like that?' asked Emma, sounding hurt.

'Are we talking about adult toys, here?' asked Kate as delicately as she could. 'Sex toys, Emma?'

'You could call it that '

Kate decided not to ask for a detailed description. Emma had a prudish side that Kate found strange in someone who must have engaged in a certain amount of sexual activity in order to produce quite so many children.

'It's a particularly vulgar shade of purple,' said Emma at last.

'Your objection is aesthetic?'

'No! I object to the whole principle of the things,' said Emma.

'Have you decided what to do next?'

'No. How can I possibly speak to Sam about it? I wish I'd never found the thing.'

By which Kate gathered that she was to be blamed for the whole fiasco.

'You're probably right, Emma,' she said. 'It would be better to forget about the whole business. Just look on it as a brief phase that Sam's going through, like nail-biting or acne.'

'You do talk rubbish,' said Emma. But she sounded just a little mollified. Since diplomatic silence appeared to be the prevailing dynamic of their marriage, Kate imagined that Emma and Sam would survive this little hiccup without ever referring to it, whatever the purple 'it' was.

She couldn't, however, resist the temptation to pass the story on to Roz when she spoke to her that evening. She was expecting to have a giggle over it with her mother, but Roz seemed distracted and was hardly paying attention to anything her daughter said.

12

When Kata looked out of her bedroom window on Thursday morning the sky was filled with low, dark clouds, pregnant with rain. The wind was rattling the branches of the flowering cherry trees in Agatha Street and threatening to bring the first of the autumn leaves on to the pavements. In other words, it was proper weather for Jeremy's funeral.

She dressed in her black suit, as planned, chose a pair of long gold earrings, and slid her feet into impractical black shoes. By this time the rain was coming down nearly horizontally, driven by the brisk wind. A substantial umbrella would ruin the effect she was aiming for so she splurged out on a taxi to take her to Bartlemas, achieving the transfer from taxi to chapel door without noticeable damage to her appearance.

She had been in Bartlemas chapel a couple of times before. In fact, she had been to a memorial service for a staff member when she had been working in the Development Office. But on that occasion she had never met the man being formally remembered, and this time she felt quite different.

As she walked in she saw that the coffin was already there, resting on trestles in the aisle, a solid-looking affair that might even have been made from mahogany. A crown of white and yellow flowers, tormented into formal shape by the impersonal hands of florists, surmounted it. It was difficult to imagine the narrow body of Jeremy Wells lying inside so much conventional opulence. Another stiff floral display in the same yellow and white stood near the altar. Bartlemas were doing their best for the dead Jeremy, even if they hadn't much appreciated him while he was alive.

Kate took a place at the back. The pews were ranged parallel to the aisle and from here she had a good view of the congregation as it arrived and seated itself. She was in good time – one of the first, in fact – and also one of the best-dressed, she noted with satisfaction.

Bartlemas chapel was built in the usual Oxford T-shape, she had been told, and was particularly noted for its painted ceiling. Kate had dutifully learned such facts when she had been working there. Now she looked up at the ceiling and admired the painted angels, doubtless praising the Almighty, carrying large and unlikely musical instruments. They spouted banners that floated around their heads, rather like the bubbles in a strip cartoon. Kate craned her neck to try to read their inscriptions, but the ceiling was too dimmed by the candle smoke of centuries to allow her to do so.

As she straightened up again she heard the clicking of female heels on the stone slabs of the floor. A tall, slim figure in black was entering, her head hidden in a hat of the same colour. She walked as elegantly – and as self-consciously – as a model. She made her way directly, with long, swift strides, to the front of the chapel. A figure trotted behind her as though anxious to catch up with her. As he passed, Kate recognised him as the Master of Bartlemas, Harry Joiner. Even at a funeral he had the same jaunty air she had noticed in Alec Malden's room, and in his black suit and tie he gave the impression of the manager of a superior grocer's shop eager to show an esteemed customer to the cheese counter. Certainly he looked as though he would be

146

more at home in the world of commerce than discussing an abstruse point of transcription with a colleague.

But who was the woman? Was this Jeremy's girlfriend, the one who drove the blue car? She had only glimpsed her for a few seconds that morning in Agatha Street, but this young woman was certainly the same type. It was impossible to see her face under the hat, let alone her hair, but she thought it was the same person. But Jeremy had been adamant that she wasn't his girlfriend, now she came to think about it. And although he had mentioned his divorce, and his ex-wife, there had been no reference to any other woman in his life.

Meanwhile, the chapel was filling up. Kate recognised one or two of the Fellows and also some members of the Development Office and the Bursary, though she was cynical enough to think that the latter were there because they wanted an hour away from their desks rather than to pay their respects to an obscure lecturer. She rather hoped that none of them noticed her. They hadn't been very fond of her while she worked there, and there was no reason to believe they'd changed their opinion in the years that had passed since then.

The organ had begun to play softly in the background, something comfortingly religious. She looked up and down the pews but she couldn't tell if there were any of Jeremy's family there. These people looked more like his colleagues from the Concrete Onion, she would have thought, and in addition there were one or two men who looked like the duller kind of professional: bank manager, accountant, dentist, perhaps. Expensive suits. Maybe they were economists, or whatever it was that Jeremy had been.

The organ was playing more forcefully now, but there was no choir. Jeremy's funeral was not important enough to call the choristers away from their recording, apparently, and since term was still some three or four weeks away the students who might have taken their place wouldn't be back in Oxford until then. Kate looked down at her Order of Service. The music grew more solemn and rose in volume. The chaplain, a young, earnest-looking man, entered, greeted the congregation, and the ceremony began.

It was very much what she might have expected. The hymns and readings were conventional, the address by Harry Joiner was bland and given in tones of deepest sincerity. The singing was ragged, as though the members of the congregation hadn't sung these hymns since their schooldays. Kate heard Harry Joiner's voice above the rest, booming out the words with his usual confidence.

The service ended at last and the organ encouraged them outside. As they made their way to the Lamb Room for their 'light refreshments', Kate felt that the experience had been slightly unsatisfactory, but in no way that she could pin down.

The rain had dwindled to a light drizzle when they came out into Pesant Quad, but there was still a gusting wind that ruffled the women's skirts and blew well-brushed greying hair around well-fed academic faces. The hum of conversation grew louder as the mourners turned their backs on the chapel and started to look forward to wine and food. There, that's over, their voices seemed to say. Now we can forget Jeremy Wells (was that his name?) and get on with our own lives again.

The Lamb Room was in that part of the college which had been built during the eighteenth century. It was well proportioned, as one might expect, and had large windows giving a view of wind-battered, fading hardy annuals and a menacing cloud cover. Trays of red and white wine were circulating, handed round by women in black dresses and men in white jackets. The glasses were small, as though not to encourage the guests to linger too long. Conversation was carried on in a low murmur, to underline the fact that this was a funeral, with the occasional burst of laughter, quickly subdued, when someone forgot the solemnity of the occasion.

'*I*'ve always thought that funerals were jollier than weddings, haven't you?'

It was Alec Malden, who had approached unseen and was standing at her left elbow.

'Less jolly when the deceased hasn't even reached his fortieth birthday, *I*'ve always thought,' Kate replied.

'I thought you were barely acquainted with Jeremy,' he said.

'True. But he lived next door to me,' said Kate. 'I was worried about his odd state of mind these last few weeks and feel a little guilty at not taking more notice of him. And there don't seem to be many people here who aren't connected in some way with his work.'

'That's the nature of academics: dry people who live only for their scholarship,' said Alec, ignoring her other remarks.

Kate thought, *You could have fooled me!*, but managed not to say it out loud.

'A good turnout, nevertheless,' said Alec.

'Yes.' The standard college turnout, she thought, with just one or two extra.

'I must go and speak to—' Malden was saying.

'Just a minute.' Kate was staring across the room at the elegant figure in the face-obscuring black hat. 'Who's she?' she asked baldly, since Alec Malden looked keen to escape from her company.

'I've no idea,' he replied. 'Why are you interested in her?'

'Just curiosity,' said Kate truthfully.

'I thought as much. It appears to be your main character trait, but it must be a necessary one for a novelist,' said Alec Malden, smiling to remove the sting from his words, and he drifted away.

Kate, left alone, was free to stare at the woman in the black hat. It had a deep brim that swept across one eye and obscured half her face, which was pale, with heavily made-up eyes. Yes, it could be the girl from Agatha Street. Could she somehow ask her whether she owned a metallic blue car? Kate sipped her red wine (too cold, too acid, and she didn't enjoy drinking so early in the day, but she had to say her goodbyes to Jeremy) and watched what was happening on the other side of the room.

The woman – perhaps she was younger than Kate had at first thought – certainly had a piercing voice. Kate couldn't quite hear what she was saying through the crush of guests, but the two or three people who were near her were moving backwards, as though blown by the force of her vocal chords. Kate edged closer, skilfully avoiding eye contact with Sadie James from the Development Office, who looked as though she found Kate's face familiar, but couldn't quite place her.

'I think you should leave.' A man was addressing the woman in the hat. Kate was surprised to see that the speaker was Harry Joiner.

'Look, I don't need this,' the woman in the hat was saying. 'Not right now.'

'Hot sausage roll?' asked a waitress at Kate's right elbow.

'No!' she answered fiercely, afraid that she might miss more of the conversation.

'You and Malden have reached an agreement so I can't think why you're still here.' Harry Joiner looked quite different from his former jolly self. The whites of his eyes were suffused with blood and the pores on his cheeks looked like orange peel.

Dear, oh dear, thought Kate. *These people are not happy.*

She placed herself behind a group of suited male backs, at an angle to Joiner and the woman, with her ear pointed in their direction. She buried her face in her glass, in case someone tried to engage her in conversation.

'I don't think you really need another glass of wine,' Harry Joiner was saying, turning from bluster to persuasion. 'Why don't you have an orange juice, instead?' *You're trying to put one over on her the way you did over me*, thought Kate. *I hear it in the tone of your voice.*

'I'm not drunk, if that's what you think. I haven't had time yet, anyway.' But her voice had the truculence of one who had downed several large gins before attending the funeral, and she swayed slightly on her high heels. 'And that's no good for you, that juice. I only drink the organic sort.'

'And it would be better if you could lower your voice. This is a funeral, after all.'

'I knew him. He was my friend,' said the woman in the hat, defensively.

'He never mentioned you.'

'You're being really aggressive, you know that?'

'I haven't even started.' Mr Nice Guy hadn't lasted long, Kate noticed.

'I have to do what's right for me, you know? I've been thinking about the criteria for this funeral, right? And it's right for me to be here. You can't prevent me. I have the right.'

'God preserve me—'

'But such interesting uses of the term "right". Nothing wrong, is there, Harry?'

Kate looked up. Alec Malden had joined the two of them. He had laid an apparently friendly hand on the woman's arm.

'Miss Hailey – Sooz – it was very good of you to attend the funeral this morning – wasn't it, Harry? – but I'm sure it's been a great strain for you, and so I've called you a taxi. I'm sure you have to get back to your own work.'

'You shouldn't speak to me like—'

'The taxi will be waiting for you at the lodge in about four minutes' time and will drive you to wherever it is you've left your car.'

'High Wycombe,' said Sooz spitefully.

'Then it will take you to Oxford station,' said Alec smoothly. 'At our expense,' he added graciously.

'Yes, that's right.' Harry Joiner was taking control again, Kate noticed. His high colour was receding. 'Very good of you to have made the effort, Sooz. Especially since you can't have known Jeremy very well.'

'I knew Sancho all right,' protested Sooz. 'And I know—' But Alec had her arm firmly in his grip and had turned her towards the door.

'Not here!' he said sternly. 'I'll see you to the lodge.'

Kate turned away quickly. She didn't want Malden or Joiner to notice that she had been listening to their conversation. Sooz and Malden were trapped by a knot of mourners and she ducked her head again to catch more of their exchange if she could.

'Well,' Malden was saying. 'We agreed terms, and now you've said farewell to Jeremy, so there's no need for you to stay here any longer.'

'I needed to be sure you had it. Now I am, you'll hear soon enough,' answered Sooz. She sounded less drunk than before, thought Kate with surprise. Maybe it was the talk of money that sobered her up.

'From you?' queried Malden.

She laughed. 'You've been moved up a level. Didn't you know?'

At that moment Malden persuaded the people impeding their progress to move, and they pushed their way out of Kate's hearing range.

'Fascinating, wasn't it?'

The voice came from behind Kate's left shoulder.

'I think the young woman must have visited the pub before coming to the funeral,' said Kate.

'And had she attended the right funeral, one asks oneself. She didn't even get his name right. And hardly Jeremy's type, I'd have thought. I think they'd probably never met.'

'The Master and Dr Malden were a little hard on her, though.'

'Oh, you can't blame Alec and Harry for escorting her from the premises. The woman was drunk.'

The speaker moved at last so that Kate could see her properly. She found herself face to face with a sturdily built woman in a burgundy-red dress and jacket. Her eyes were bright blue and her hair an improbable shade of yellow that shone harshly against the dark red of her clothing.

'Really, the hair colour is all my own,' she said.

Kate had the grace to look discomfited. She lowered her gaze to the woman's face, which was square and free of cosmetics except for matching burgundy lipstick. 'Kate Ivory,' she said, holding out a hand.

'Goldy Silverman,' said the other woman. 'I'm the librarian here at Bartelmas.'

'You must have taken over quite recently.'

'Eighteen months ago. Do you know the library?'

'I worked here a while back, helping out with a summer school. The students weren't allowed into the library, but I used to sneak in occasionally.'

'But I believe you're a novelist in real life.'

'How clever of you to know.'

'We librarians are trained to know things like that.'

'Were you a friend of Jeremy's?' This might be a chance to find out more about her neighbour.

'A little. I don't think anyone knew him very well.'

'He seemed to be close to Alec Malden.'

'Oh, well.'

'You don't like him?'

'You hardly expect me to talk about my bosses when I'm on their territory.'

Goldy Silverman was very approachable, and probably quite indiscreet. Kate decided to encourage her to gossip. She could see that Rob Grailing, the bursar, had recognised her at last and was pushing his way through the crowd to get to her side. His unnaturally white teeth were bared in an aggressive smile and the summer had refreshed his tan. He still reminded her of a ferret, however, and she had no desire to renew their acquaintance. She made a swift decision.

'Would you like to get some lunch?'

'Good idea. Shall we go for a sandwich at Blackwell's?'

'And a latte,' agreed Kate. She did like a woman who could make her mind up just as rapidly as she could.

They said their goodbyes to Harry Joiner, and Kate smiled vaguely at the people she knew but didn't wish to speak to.

'Very good,' said Goldy, as they stood at last in Bartlemas

Lane. 'I can see you've perfected the vague smile and unfocused stare. I used to get cornered by every bore in the place before I managed that look of belonging to an alien planet.'

'I like to think they believe my mind is on higher, more serious matters,' said Kate, as they made their way across the High Street and into Radcliffe Square. She was starting to regret her impractical shoes by the time they reached Blackwell's, but at least the rain had held off and her hair was as elegant as ever.

Once they had chosen their sandwiches and collected their coffees, they found a table near the window and a comfortable sofa to sit on.

'I didn't ask you what you were doing at Jeremy's funeral,' said Kate, removing the plastic container from her chicken on granary.

'I was about to say exactly the same thing,' said Goldy, unwrapping a vegetarian equivalent. 'Were you a friend of his?'

'He lives – lived – next door to me.'

'So you knew him well.' Goldy bit into her sandwich.

'Not really. I've been away for a while.'

Goldy raised her eyebrows, unable to speak with her mouth stuffed full.

Kate had no intention of elaborating on her recent history. 'As a matter of fact, we met for the first time just two or three weeks ago.'

Goldy looked disappointed, swallowed her mouthful with an effort, and said, 'I was hoping you could tell me more about him.'

'Ah. That's just what I was hoping about you.'

They both drank coffee.

'We have met before, you know,' said Goldy eventually. 'But I can see you don't remember me.'

'Where did we meet?'

'I was working at the Bodleian, and you worked briefly in the Cataloguing Department.'

'I'm sorry,' said Kate. 'I was rather preoccupied at the time and you're right. I don't remember you.'

'I believe you were working for that odd outfit in St Giles, tracking down a gang that were stealing books to order.'

'That sounds like a much more exciting version of the story than the one I was living.' Kate returned to her chicken.

'Because,' persevered Goldy, 'I think there's something odd happening at Bartlemas.'

'Oh no!' said Kate quickly. 'I don't believe it! There was something odd happening at Bartlemas when I worked there before. And nobody was grateful when I worked out what was going on.'

'That's what I mean.' Goldy had finished her sandwich and was free to talk. 'You're just the person who can find out what's happening. You enjoy looking into mysteries and solving other people's problems, don't you?'

'No.'

Goldy took no notice. 'Not that I think it's anything to do with the college *per se*. It's more the people, or some of the people, who work there. I don't believe there's any kind of conspiracy.' She tipped up her coffee cup and looked inside. 'Shall I get us both another cup?'

'Yes please,' said Kate, and then knew that she would have to listen to Goldy Silverman's theories. She was getting a little tired of the brilliant blue eyes shining with what Kate now recognised as malice. Oh well, she'd wanted to find out more about Jeremy, hadn't she? And she'd imagined she could do it without getting involved, which was quite stupid of her, really. She wasn't sure how much of Goldy's story she could trust and wondered whether to say that she had to get back to work, after all. She could always suggest that she would happily investigate, but only for a hefty fee. No, that would be too unkind. And anyway, librarians didn't earn that kind of money.

'Shall I get chocolate fudge brownies to go with the coffee?'
'Good idea.'

13

'You recognised me straight away, didn't you?' said Kate when Goldy returned with the coffee.

'Yes.'

'And that's why you agreed to come out to lunch?'

'I was getting a little tired of the company in the Lamb Room. And I did wonder whether you would put your mind to working out what was going on at Bartlemas. You found the man who killed Jenna Coates, didn't you? And you weren't taken in by Chris Townsend's apparent suicide. You seem to have the right sort of brain for these things.'

Kate tried to look modest and unassuming about her gifts, but couldn't help smiling with pleasure at the compliments. 'You'd better tell me all you know about Jeremy, and what you think is going on at Bartlemas,' she said, digging a fork into her chocolate cake.

'Since he wasn't a Fellow, Jeremy was only around during term time, and even then he spent most of his time over at the Onion. But he did use the library – not for his own work so much as for his students'. He was very good at checking that we had up-to-date editions of the books they'd need, and he gave me a list in September every year so that we could get the books on the shelves before term started. Librarians appreciate little things like that.'

Kate drank coffee and didn't interrupt. She hadn't heard

anything very extraordinary so far, but perhaps Goldy would get to the point eventually.

'Like I said, I've been at the college for about eighteen months, and that's how long I've known Jeremy. He always struck me as a bit sad.'

'In what way? I thought he was rather self-contained.'

'I'm talking about eighteen months ago, when I first met him. He looked down-at-heel. You know that slightly seedy look that some academics get? Uncared-for. In need of a haircut. Clothes bought at Oxfam. You wouldn't want them to take their shoes off in case you caught a whiff of their socks.'

'I do, unfortunately, know just what you mean.'

'And then, early this year, things changed. He changed, I mean. He started to look, well, sleeker. Better dressed. Better fed. Less haunted. If it had been anyone other than Jeremy, you would have said he was acquiring a swagger.'

Kate wanted to say, *And you should see the expensive gear in his house*, but thought better of it. Goldy Silverman might think that she knew Kate Ivory, but Kate Ivory knew nothing at all about Goldy apart from what she had told her.

'Maybe he met a woman. The right woman can alter a man beyond recognition,' suggested Kate. But Goldy's comments were confirming the story Jeremy had given her, so this lunch wasn't entirely wasted.

'I asked him.'

'Yes?'

'Oh, in a joking way, of course.'

'I bet he loved that.'

'Really, I brought the subject up very lightheartedly. But he denied it. He said that since he'd broken up with his wife he had steered well clear of women. He said something about preferring his house plants.'

'*Ficus benjamina*,' said Kate.

'I'm sorry?'

'Nothing. It's just that he spoke the truth. He was devoted to his plants. But what about Sooz Hailey? Maybe he'd just met her and changed his image to impress her. She doesn't look as though she'd enjoy going out with a man who bought his clothes at Oxfam.'

'She's the one with the expensive black suit and hat and the loud voice?'

'Yes. Looking like the chief mourner. I wondered at first if it could be his ex-wife.'

'He was married to a schoolteacher from South Croydon, or so he told me once. And *her* name was something like Jane, or Janice.'

'And Sooz looked cross rather than emotionally devastated,' said Kate. 'I'd like to believe they were having a passionate affair, but I can't.' Actually she found it difficult to believe that Jeremy had ever had a passionate affair with anyone, but she didn't say so.

'So we're left with the puzzle of Jeremy's sudden change of mood and style, with no explanation,' said Goldy.

'And if Sooz wasn't his girlfriend, what was their relationship? Colleague? Student?'

'Neither, as far as I know.'

'Which leaves us with the thought that they had some business dealings together.' Kate was thinking about Sooz's visit to Agatha Street, but she didn't want to tell Goldy about that.

'We didn't find out what business she was in, unfortunately.'

'Harry Joiner had her cornered and Alec Malden whisked her away. We didn't have much chance,' said Kate regretfully. 'Could you ask Alec Malden next time you see him?'

'He doesn't come to the library, I'm afraid.'

'She'd left her car at High Wycombe, or so she said, so she can't be local.'

'You're suggesting that whatever money-making deal he was involved in, it wasn't here in Oxford?'

'Has his work always involved travelling?' asked Kate, following a line of her own.

'Yes. But only in Europe. I don't think he often went anywhere exciting.'

Kate wanted to say, 'What about Brussels, or Bordeaux?', but she didn't think Goldy would know the answers anyway. Instead, she said, 'And what do you believe his sudden prosperity has got to do with Bartlemas?'

'Officially I know nothing, of course. Across in the library we can get cut off from the rest of the life of the college. We get invited to lunch by the Fellows during the week before Christmas. The Middle Common Room asks us to dinner in the New Year. The students treat us to white wine and strawberries in the month of June. But we hardly *belong*, do we?'

'Don't we?' said Kate, who had never stayed in one library for long enough to find out. 'What are you trying to tell me?' It sounded as though this was yet another disappointed employee whingeing about her job.

'But we do hear things, nevertheless. People speak in our presence as though we don't exist. The library assistant and I usually have our lunch with the Master's secretary, the house-keeper and the college accountant. These are all people who know what's really going on in college.'

'If you say so,' said Kate, and tried not to yawn. Goldy wasn't being nearly as informative as she'd hoped. What was she going to pass on? Just a little college gossip?

'When Harry Joiner was elected Master, there was a lot of unkind comment,' said Goldy.

There she goes, off on a tangent again, thought Kate, glancing at her watch, thinking she would make an excuse and leave in a minute or two.

'Unkind?' she said, hoping to move Goldy along a bit.

'Well, he's not exactly an intellectual, is he? He was chosen, so the talk went, because he was a good businessman and would bring funds into the college, and he'd know how to look after the property and investments we had accumulated over the centuries.'

'Yes.' Kate stifled a yawn.

'And I'm sure he did all that,' Goldy continued earnestly. 'But he started to get close to Alec Malden, and to Jeremy, in spite of what he says, *after* Jeremy came into whatever it was he came into.'

Kate worked out what she was saying. 'So you mean that Malden and Joiner noticed that Jeremy was in funds and then found they had something in common with him, after all. They weren't interested while he was a poverty-stricken junior lecturer. Now they thought he might be worth a bob or two and they might profit from it.'

'That's what I think,' said Goldy, taking a small mirror out of her handbag and re-applying a fresh layer of burgundy lipstick. 'But I still wonder where Jeremy got his money from.'

'Maybe he had an uncle who died,' said Kate. 'Perhaps he used to bet on the horses and it was his lucky day.'

'I'll have to get back to the library,' said Goldy. 'I still

163

haven't extracted reading lists from all the tutors yet.'

'Before you go, tell me what your interest is in this,' said Kate urgently.

'What did you think of the funeral and the reception afterwards?'

'Very proper. Very nice,' said Kate non-committally.

'Did you see anyone who cared a fig for Jeremy Wells? Did you hear one of his colleagues speak about him with affection, or even with respect?'

'No.'

'Neither did I. I sensed a . . . well, a feeling of relief,' said Goldy.

'Another problem solved in a neat fashion,' suggested Kate.

'Exactly. And that's not good enough, is it? There has to be more to someone's life than that. I believe they were using Jeremy in some way that wasn't quite ethical or honourable, and now they're thankful that he's died so they needn't feel guilty about him.'

'And you'd like to get your own back?' said Kate, hearing the bitterness in Goldy's voice. The librarian had her own reasons for resenting the governing body, she felt.

'*Jeremy*'s own back, if you have to put it like that. You lived next door to him. You met him. You want to give him a better memorial than the one we attended this morning, don't you?'

'I'll think about it.'

'Keep in touch,' said Goldy earnestly.

'I expect we'll bump into one another again,' said Kate, picking up her bag and following Goldy downstairs.

'Perhaps you'll manage to find out where the money came from,' said Goldy, and dodged expertly through the traffic in Broad Street, leaving Kate on the pavement wondering where you could start with a man who cared only for his *Ficus benjamina*.

Which was the moment she remembered the file she had printed out from Jeremy's computer. She ran as fast as her stupid shoes would allow her to the cab rank in St Giles. Suppose someone had got to it before she did?

Fabian West had enjoyed an excellent lunch, but had denied himself the brandy afterwards. He liked to drink after he had concluded his business, not before. He checked the wafer-thin gold watch on his wrist. Yes, this should be the right time. He picked up his mobile phone and dialled.

'Alec Malden,' said the voice at the other end.

'Mr Malden, we haven't yet met, but my name is Jester.' His voice, even in his own ears, was mellifluous and tender.

'Yes.' Malden, he was pleased to note, sounded tense, his voice pushed out through his nose and pitched a little too high.

'If you check the balance of your current account I believe you will find that we have deposited half the sum you agreed with Tara for the property of ours which you are currently holding.'

There was a pause. 'And?'

'So now we can proceed to the transfer of this property from your hands to ours. The second half of your fee will be credited to your account as soon as this has been completed. We are men of our word, Mr Malden.'

'You don't want to come here, to my house, do you?' Malden was sounding more confident now.

'I think not. And you and I will not meet, Mr Malden, in any case. No, an employee of mine, whom I shall call only "Stud" – forgive the melodrama, please, Mr Malden – will meet you later today and effect the transaction.'

'Where and when?' asked Malden.

'Don't worry. *He* will find *you*. Just make sure that you have our property on your person from now until your bedtime. And take your usual evening stroll in the direction of Port Meadow.'

He broke the connection and smiled at the phone. It hadn't taken any very difficult detective work to find out Malden's routine: the man was a creature of habit.

Fabian rang the bell to call his manservant.

'I'll have that brandy now, I think.'

14

Kate paused in her own house only long enough to change her shoes for something more comfortable, then took Jeremy's key and let herself into number 8. She raced upstairs to the office. The copies of the file were still there, sitting in the printer's out-tray.

She switched off the machines, then unplugged them from the wall sockets. She picked up the printout and was about to return to her own house when the phone rang.

The sound was startling. Unexpected. For a moment she simply stared at the phone without attempting to answer it. *Don't be ridiculous, Kate. This is not a voice from beyond the grave.* She picked up the receiver.

'Hallo?'

'Oh, hallo. Mrs Wells?' A female voice, probably a clerk or a secretary.

'Er, not—'

The voice continued smoothly, uninterested in Kate's identity or her relationship to Jeremy, apparently. 'This is Deyton Infirmary here. We have the effects of Mr Jeremy Wells and were wondering whether it would be convenient for you to collect them.'

'Oh, yes, of course,' said Kate, thinking quickly.

'Today would be good for us. We have already been holding them for over a week.'

'Whereabouts are you?'

'At Deyton.'

'Silly of me.'

'The hospital is signposted from the A435,' said the efficient voice. 'You'll find us quite easily. Just ask for me at Reception.'

'What time do you go home?' asked Kate, checking her watch.

'My shift ends at five.'

'And who shall I ask for?'

'Mrs Chess.'

'It will take me a couple of hours or so to get to you,' said Kate, eyeing the pages of the Jester file.

'As long as you're here before four forty-five. We do dispose of effects if they are not collected within a reasonable time scale.' She had one of those voices that place the emphasis on the least appropriate words.

'I'll do my best not to inconvenience you,' said Kate.

She replaced the phone and returned to number 10, taking the file with her. She put the second copy away in the bottom drawer of her desk where she kept the spare copies of the disks containing her novels. She was torn between reading the file and collecting Jeremy's belongings. Either might provide the answer to her questions about him.

She checked her road map and calculated that she had time for a swift cup of coffee before leaving for Deyton. She'd have to hope that the traffic was light.

She sat on her pink sofa with her coffee cooling on the table at her side and Jeremy's file on her knee. She could allow herself ten minutes. She must just glance through it to see if it was going to contain anything interesting. *Jester*, she wondered. What did that refer to?

Notes on my relationship with Jester and others, she read at the top of the first page. So Jester was a man. Or a woman.

I first encountered Jester in a room in the Hotel Médon in Brussels in early February 2000. We were introduced by Red Pale, the man I had met on the plane from London.

They're using pseudonyms, thought Kate. And since they are hardly likely to be literary people, why would that be? The only answer that came to her was that they were criminals – which might explain why Jeremy had been wearing a wig. She could see that as a criminal, dear Jeremy might well have been inept, or second class as he would probably have put it.

Skimming down the page, she realised that even when writing notes Jeremy's style was a touch ponderous, and it was going to take her quite a while to get to the end of the file. One or two phrases leapt to her eye: *We gather your expertise is in monetary policy, and that you've written papers on the advisability of Britain's joining the Euro.* And further on: *They asked me about my contacts in France and Belgium and seemed very interested when I mentioned a couple in the ECB.*

ECB? What was that? She should pay more attention to the serious bits in the newspaper. Kate swallowed her coffee. She'd have to leave. After all, there might be some even more useful information among Jeremy's 'effects' and she didn't want the bossy-sounding Mrs Chess to dispose of them in an incinerator, most likely! – before she got there.

She slipped the pages of the Jester file into a manila folder, scribbled 'Jester' on the outside and wondered for a moment if she should hide it in her filing cabinet among a hundred similar folders. No, she was being melodramatic. She left it with Jeremy's key on the coffee table in the sitting room. She could continue reading it when she returned home.

Just before she got into the car she looked back at her house. It sat between the two darkened, silent ones that had once belonged to Jeremy and the Fosters. On one side a contract killing. On the other an unexplained fatal accident. For the first time since the Fosters' death she felt afraid for her own safety. What if Jeremy's death was in some way connected to theirs? On a sudden impulse she got out of the car, let herself into her house and switched on a light in the sitting room. That was better. It would be waiting to greet her when she returned this evening. She didn't like to think of *three* darkened, untenanted houses.

She placed the open road map on the seat next to her and aimed her car at the bypass. She had filled up with petrol only yesterday, so she had no need to stop before she reached Deyton.

It was twenty to five when she drew into the visitors' car park of the Deyton Infirmary. One pound fifty to park her car and she swore mildly as she scrabbled in her purse for the correct change, obtained a ticket and stuck it to her windscreen. The minute hand of the clock in Reception was just clicking into the three-quarters position as she reached the desk.

'Mrs Chess?'

'I'll see if she's in. Who shall I say wants her?' This young woman had the same mechanical voice as Mrs Chess.

'I've come for Jeremy Wells's effects,' said Kate, avoiding the question of her identity.

Mrs Chess, fortyish, grey-suited, with regimented hair and a professional smile, emerged from a back room and presented Kate with a neat, plastic-wrapped parcel labelled 'Jeremy Wells, Decd.'

'If you wouldn't mind signing. *Here*, and *here*.'

Kate signed her name as illegibly as she could manage.

'And printing your name, address and relationship to the deceased *here*,' concluded Mrs Chess.

Kate hesitated for a moment before describing herself as 'friend and neighbour'.

'I have the key to his house. I'll put these with the rest of his belongings as soon as I get back,' she said.

'Hmm,' said Mrs Chess. But she didn't argue.

And I will, I will, thought Kate. Just as soon as I've looked through them to see if they contain anything interesting, she conceded. Perhaps it was just as well she had turned up so close to the end of Mrs Chess's shift. Any earlier and the woman might have been inclined to dispute her qualifications as next of kin.

She couldn't wait to get home. She didn't bother to open the package, which wasn't much larger than a shoe box, to explore the contents immediately, but swung the car back on to the main road and turned left towards Oxford. The roads were filling up with commuters and it took her longer to get home than to drive to Deyton, so that it was well past seven o'clock when she finally arrived back in Agatha Street.

She unlocked the front door, glad that she'd left the light on, and went straight up to the sitting room. There was someone there, sitting on her pink sofa.

'Roz.'

'Hallo,' said her mother. 'I was about to give up and go home again. Would you like me to pour you a glass of wine? I've brought a rather nice sauvignon with me.'

'Thanks,' said Kate feebly. 'How did you get in?' Taking the wineglass from her mother, she glanced across to where she had left the Jester folder. Luckily it didn't look very interesting and it appeared to be just as she had left it, with Jeremy's house key next to it.

'Harley Venn used to leave a spare key to your house under a flower pot in his back garden.'

'But that was ages ago. I'd forgotten all about it.'

'I thought so,' said her mother. 'Harley must have forgotten about it, too. But it was still there, and it worked.'

'So I see.'

'You're not offended, are you?'

'Of course not. Just a little surprised, that's all.'

'And what's in the mysterious package?' Roz had seated herself back on the pink sofa and was well into her own glass of wine.

'Nothing very interesting. The Deyton Infirmary asked me if I would pick up Jeremy's effects. He must have been taken there after the accident.'

'I wonder how they knew how to get hold of you.'

'Actually, I just happened to be next door when they phoned. They must have assumed I was a relative, and it would have taken too long to contradict them.'

'So I'm not the only one who knows where Agatha Street keeps its spare door keys,' said Roz smugly.

'Jeremy gave me his, just before he left. He wanted me to look after his house plants.'

'I can tell he didn't know you very well.'

'They're still alive, aren't they?'

'Well, and what did you find when you were going through his belongings? Anything interesting?'

'Nothing. I mean I didn't.'

'So let's look inside the plastic bag, shall we?'

Kate was strangely loth to undo Mrs Chess's neatly taped parcel, and while she hesitated she found that Roz had picked it up and was ripping away the fastenings.

The infirmary had spared them Jeremy's clothing, at least. Probably it had been cut away by the nursing staff when he was first brought in, and then incinerated afterwards. Kate hoped so. His belt, an ordinary leather one, was there, and his shoes – brown leather deck shoes.

Kate watched while Roz sifted through the meagre contents of the package. Finally she came to a clear plastic bag containing a wallet, keys and other oddments. She tipped them out.

The wallet contained only what might have been expected by way of money – about fifty pounds – and credit cards, driving licence, university card. Among the oddments was a scrap of paper with writing that Kate recognised as Jeremy's. It was soaked with blood – Jeremy's blood, she reminded herself – and she could only make out a few letters. *Jes . . . Cla . . . Lowe . . . Worc . . .*

The first word could be Jester. The last must be Worcestershire. It didn't look much like an address – there was no house number or town. It would have to be one of those classy addresses, composed only of house name, village, county. If so, it seemed likely that this was Jester's address, but she couldn't read enough of it to be sure where he lived. But it meant that Jeremy must have been on his way to see Jester when he – what? – came off the road? Or was driven off the road, perhaps?

'What should we do with them?' asked Roz.

'I'll take them next door. I don't know who's in charge of his affairs. I don't even know if he made a will, or appointed an executor, but someone must surely turn up sooner or later and deal with things.'

'Don't be long,' said Roz, watching as her daughter left the room. 'I was going to tell you about someone I've met recently, but I'll have to go soon.'

Kate reappeared in the doorway.

'What sort of someone?'

'A man. A rather nice man.'

Kate wondered why she felt a sense of foreboding. Was it because her mother had such awful taste in men?

'As a matter of fact, he came with me because he wanted to meet you, too. But he couldn't stay long and he left before you got here.'

'He sounds very mysterious.'

'Not at all. Are you going next door with Jeremy's belongings or are you just going to stand there and look at me in that suspicious manner?'

'I'll be back in a couple of minutes,' said Kate.

As she let herself into Jeremy's house she wondered about the Jester folder and the key left on the coffee table. What if Roz's mysterious friend had helped himself to both while he was there in her house? Roz could easily have left him alone in the sitting room while she found the corkscrew and opened the bottle of wine.

No. Jeremy's house felt exactly the same as it had done when she had last been there, only a matter of hours previously. She decided to leave the package on the kitchen table, having first replaced the adhesive strips that had fastened it. She filled the small watering can and gave the nearest plants a hasty dousing before returning to number 10.

She meant to offer to cook supper for her mother and then ask her a lot of pointed questions while she ate, but she was too late. Roz, too, had left.

The sandwich she had eaten with Goldy Silverman seemed

a very long time ago. She pulled out the chopping board and started to attack onions and peppers. She felt like a really large bowl of stir-fry.

She was happily munching her way through health-giving, crisp vegetables when the phone rang. It should be an apologetic Roz, she thought.

'Kate? It's Estelle here.'

'Is everything all right?' Estelle didn't usually ring so late in the evening.

'You'll think I'm silly, but I just thought I'd check that you haven't forgotten about our trip tomorrow.'

'Of course not!' Trip? Oh, yes. To Grigg's printing works. 'I'm looking forward to it.'

'Yes, well, I'll see you at the station.'

Kate returned to her bowl of vegetables. Estelle must be psychic. The events surrounding Jeremy's death had put everything else out of her mind for the moment. Estelle might well have been waiting a very long time at Oxford station tomorrow morning if she hadn't rung to remind Kate about their appointment.

Roz had thoughtfully left the remains of the bottle of sauvignon in the fridge for her. She poured herself another glass and returned to the sitting room. She could spend a further half-hour on Jeremy's Jester file before giving up and settling down to some undemanding television programme, she thought.

They were clever, she read, picking up from where she had left off.

They were clever, or maybe I was just easily flattered. But they seemed so interested in my answers to their questions that I couldn't wait to tell them everything I knew, and to give them the names of my influential friends. They were particularly interested when I told them I knew Disque Bleu. Their habit of secrecy is catching, but they impressed on me that I must never use anyone's real name, not in writing nor on the phone. Who on earth would want to tap *my* phone, I wondered, but they take everything very seriously and expect me to do the same. I'm not sure I like being called Sancho. Does Jester see me as a simple rustic, a follower, a servant? If I am honest, yes, he probably does.

When was I next meeting Disque Bleu? they asked, and seemed delighted by my reply. (They pronounced his name 'Blue', of course.) How had we met? they wanted to know. How well did I know him? I explained how my work brought me into contact with members of the ECB and that we had been introduced by a colleague on one of my visits to France. We went out clubbing together one Saturday evening, though the entertainment was hardly to my taste, but the others seemed to enjoy it. I was to make sure that Blue and I kept on friendly terms, they said. We were to keep in touch by e-mail, or by letter, whatever seemed most natural. I was to find out as much about him as I could. No detail of his life was too small, too insignificant.

It wasn't difficult. Blue and I had a lot in common and regularly exchanged news and opinions. The academic world is a gossipy one, I've always found, and although in the past I had kept myself somewhat aloof, this time I followed instructions and gossiped with the best.

For I am being well paid for my co-operation – though I can imagine that I would have done what they asked just for the feeling they gave me of being *wanted*. Since Janice left I have felt that no one really notices whether I'm there or not, let alone cares about it.

They didn't tell me what I was a part of, and I made little effort to find out. I didn't think it was criminal – the people involved seemed too eminent and too prosperous for that. But as the months went on, they became more specific in their requests for information about Blue. Was he faithful to his wife? What were his sexual preferences? Did he enjoy any *unusual* sexual practices?

I have to say that I don't normally go in for this kind of conversation, even with my friends. But I was anxious to provide Jester and his colleagues with what they asked for. The reason was simple: since meeting him I'd received the money to replace my ailing computer, I'd indulged in more new clothes than I had previously bought over the past twenty years – and I had my eye on a nice little property in west Oxford that was well beyond my means as an employee of the university. And there was nothing vulgar about it. The money came in from Jester, discreetly, in modest sums paid into various accounts in two or three different countries. Never enough to alert any suspicious official to the possibility of money laundering or any such criminality. I couldn't see that I was doing any wrong. All I was doing was passing on gossip, providing a little innocent information here and there as it was required. It seemed to me that I was being exceptionally well paid for such services, but I was in no mood to question it. And if Blue had laid himself open to blackmail, that was his own fault. It wasn't as though I'd had a hand in corrupting him.

I found out what they wanted me to about the man eventually. As I said, this is a gossipy world and I had picked up a small hint while I was in Stockholm one day. Next time he and I got together I bought a few rounds of drinks, asked some judicious questions and listened hard to the answers. It involved women with very large breasts and buttocks, and wet mud, and a perverted form of sexual congress that I am not prepared to go into here. The thought of the mess, and the unlikely orifices, makes me feel quite ill.

Why did Jester and his friends want to know? Blue's work involved him in travel around France, and in liaison between his department at the Bank and various printing works. This must be about blackmail, I thought. But surely they're going to do nothing as crude as demanding money with the threat of exposure? Blue's appetites were unusual – and ridiculous – enough in the world of finance and banking for it to do him some harm if the facts were made public. But would it lead to his sacking, or even resignation? I doubt it. The worst outcome would be that people would laugh at him, I should have thought. I imagine that they did the same with him as with me – blackmail wasn't necessary in my case, was it? No, they had found his weakness and they doubtless offered him more of the same to persuade him to co-operate with them. Larger women. Bigger and splashier mud baths. It's like an addiction. You can't get free of it. That's what I found.

I asked Red (as he was called for short) next time I saw him, but he told me it was better if I knew as little as possible. I had the feeling he might pass me over a sheaf of ten pound notes to keep me quiet. I saw the intention cross his mind, and the contempt, but luckily he thought better of it. I did receive a note a few days later to tell me that a further sum had been paid into my Dublin account, but that's a different matter altogether.

And then, early in August, I received a message from Jester. The tone was different from his previous communications. I could feel the suppressed excitement, a quickening of pace as though at last their plans were coming to fruition. Blue would be travelling from Chamalières. I would come to Bordeaux, where I had colleagues I could visit. (Would they be available in August? Jester didn't care.) Blue and I would meet, as though by chance, in a café in the town and he would give me a small but very valuable package which I would bring back to England with me and hand over to Red.

I wanted to know more. I needed to know whether the object, whatever it was, that I was bringing back to England was stolen, or illegal in some way. I didn't want to be arrested for bringing drugs into the country, and this was what I thought I was being asked to do. The argument that I didn't know what was in the package seemed feeble to me and I didn't think a Customs officer, or a jury, would be impressed by it.

Jester was curt. He did not wish to explain. In the end he agreed that it was true that I wouldn't want to be stopped by Customs and have the item inspected. Some unpleasantness might result from this. After some mild argument on my part he agreed to provide me with a passport in another name. In the event of my arrest I might be afforded some anonymity, I believed – perhaps foolishly – by this device. At this point Jester stopped dealing with me directly. I was put in touch with another man – 'Stoker' – who would acquire the new passport for me. I furnished him with photographs, and this is when I conceived the rather silly idea of wearing a wig to disguise myself. My hair is one of my most distinguishing features – perhaps my only one, if I am honest about it – and I thought it a good idea to hide it.

Jester's manner had made me wonder just how long this lucrative supply of funds was going to continue. Would they have any further use for me once I had delivered the package back to England? Things weren't as simple as they had been at the beginning of the affair, but I couldn't tell Jester about that. However civilised the man appeared on the surface, I knew there was a ruthlessness behind his urbane manner, and it frightened me. I had better put down here that I didn't, of course, ever again, after the time in the hotel in Brussels, meet Jester face to face. We spoke on the telephone, and in his case it was a mobile one. I had the impression that he knew who was calling before I announced myself, so I assume he had one of those machines that flashes up the name and number of the caller. I must get myself one of those.

At this point, Kate found that her concentration was wavering. Discussion of the relative merits of mobile phones tended to have that effect on her. It was time to put the folder away and watch some undemanding television programme. She wondered for a moment what nickname the gang would choose for her if she came to their notice. Something derogatory, no doubt. Sherlock, perhaps? But for the moment she put Jeremy and his involvement in the criminal world to the back of her mind. She had to be up early tomorrow to be ready for Estelle and her girlish enthusiasm for the owner of the printing works.

15

As Estelle walked from the train to join her, Kate had time to take in the details of her appearance. She looked stunning, if a little out of character. Estelle's natural style was tall, thin, angular and elegant. She was mistress of a dozen little black suits, two dozen silk shirts in various shades of cream, and an array of Italian shoes that made Kate's eyes water.

'Hallo, Kate!' she called.

Today she wore a gently draped dress and jacket – silk, Kate saw as she got nearer – in a soft turquoise shade. There was a suggestion of ruffles, even a hint of cleavage. Her earrings dangled. Her bracelets jingled. Her shoes had heels and straps and would be killing her long before the morning was over. She wore pink lipstick and had fluffed out her hair.

'Hallo, Estelle! You look wonderful.'

'Do you really think so?'

'Stunning,' said Kate, meaning it. A curvier woman would have looked vulgar, but Estelle managed to make the feminine outfit look elegant. Kate herself had decided not to compete and was wearing lightweight black trousers and jacket with a plain top in a smoky red.

'And this is Crispen,' said Estelle dismissively.

A young man with floppy fair hair, blue eyes and an eager-to-please expression followed Estelle a respectful couple of paces behind.

'Hallo, Kate,' he said in an old-fashioned public school accent that he was unsuccessfully attempting to cover with estuary English. She suspected he had perfect manners and well-off, county parents. 'So kind of you to meet us from the train like this.'

'Hallo, Crispen,' she said, and shook hands. He should practise a firmer handshake, she thought, but then he looked as though he had only recently left school and was probably shy. She hoped he was boning up on important aspects of his job. She was hoping for plenty of publicity when *Spitfire Sweethearts* was finally published.

'I've brought my camera with me,' he told Kate. 'I thought I could take a few shots of you watching your book come hot off the press. We might manage to get it into one of the trades, or perhaps the local Oxford paper might take it.'

Kate smiled at him in a friendly way. At least he was going to try to justify his existence, she noted silently.

As they walked to the car park she was only sorry that she couldn't offer Estelle a lift in a classier car. Her cream Peugeot was showing its age and the front passenger seat left Estelle's long legs cramped for space. Estelle, however, was relentlessly cheerful about everything, obviously determined to enjoy every minute of their trip. Crispen closed the passenger's door for her and then climbed into the back seat, maintaining a polite silence for the whole of the journey.

A.L. Grigg and Nephew's printing works lay some six or seven miles from the station, on a small industrial site to the south of the city. Kate wasn't sure what she had been expecting – something small, perhaps old-fashioned, with men in shirt-sleeves and green eyeshades tending chuntering machines; boxes of type, the smell of hot metal, white-overalled girls packing printed sheets into cartons to send to the bindery. She wouldn't have been surprised to find that Owen Grigg was a man in blue overalls with oily hands and black fingernails. Failing all that, she was expecting a larger version of her corner duplicating shop.

Of course, Grigg's was nothing like that.

For a start, it was big. About ten times bigger than Kate had been expecting, and modern.

She parked in the visitors' car park, let Crispen out of the car to assist Estelle to unfold herself from the front seat, then followed them through the tall glass doors into the reception area. Half an acre of carefully designed welcome, calculated Kate. Low-key, of course. Nothing overwhelming. Shades of silver and anthracite, enlivened with vermilion and burnt sienna. The receptionist had an even more expensive haircut than Kate's, and a well-tutored smile.

Murmuring into a telephone, another reassuring smile, and the receptionist urged them to sit on the anthracite sofa and look through the latest in glossy magazines while they waited for the lift to bring Owen Grigg himself into their presence.

'Our Mr Grigg isn't short of a bob or two, then,' said Kate. So much understated good taste always brought out the worst in her.

'What?' Estelle was paying no attention to her, Kate saw, but from the look of concentration on her face was working out how to rise from the low sofa in the most youthful way she could. She tucked her feet back as far as they would go, leaned forward with an admirably straight back and prepared to rise in one flexible movement to her feet. Good luck, thought Kate, who was glad she wasn't aiming at such a high standard of deportment herself. Crispen had immersed himself in an article about motor cars.

The lift sighed to a halt; the doors whispered open. Owen Grigg strode towards them.

Estelle rose to her feet without a wobble and, lifting her arms a little away from her sides in a gesture of restrained greeting, glided towards him. Kate hoped that he appreciated the artistry of Estelle's performance. She and Crispen left them to it and waited for the introductions.

'Estelle!' Owen managed a two-handed clasp that expressed warmth and intimacy without being too forward. 'And you must be Kate Ivory.' He injected just the right amount of warmth into his greeting to her, too, Kate noticed. She saw treacle-dark eyes, with laughter creases at their corners. A younger man than she had been expecting, a little stockily built for her own taste, but he moved well and was wearing an excellent, and quite fashionable, suit. She could see why Estelle was smitten, and was only glad that he wasn't her own type. The last thing she wanted was to be in competition for his favours with her agent.

'Crispen Southmore? So glad you could join us.' A manly handshake and some sincere eye contact put Crispen at his ease.

'I believe they've put out coffee for us in the small conference room,' Owen was saying. 'How was your journey down from London?' – this to Estelle. And, 'We've had the privilege of printing all your novels,' to Kate.

Estelle took a few minutes to visit the ladies' room and came out smelling even more expensive than when she went in, with a fresh sheen on her excellent complexion.

They drank coffee, they nibbled biscuits, they discussed what they wished to see. Estelle came near to simpering, Kate saw. She wasn't entirely sure what effect her agent was having on Owen, though he leant towards her in an attentive fashion and smiled at her witticisms.

Then they left the rosewood panelling of the conference room and ventured into the world of printing.

'It's very kind of you to take the time to show us round yourself,' said Kate. Perhaps she was wrong. Perhaps Owen was as keen on Estelle as she was on him, or why would he take them on a guided tour when one of his junior staff could have done it just as well?

'I love showing off to visitors,' he said with a boyish smile. 'Don't try to take my simple pleasures away from me!'

Then someone must have switched on a machine, for the noise level rose suddenly and they could no longer indulge in small talk.

'I'll take you to the area where Kate's book will be produced,' he bellowed in Estelle's ear. She nodded vigorously to show her acquiescence.

Once they reached the next section of the works the noise level abated again. A stately conveyor belt transported sheaves of concertinaed printed paper from one side to the other. To their right stood huge rolls of paper, and beyond those a small area was contained in glass and fibreboard to form an office, insulated from the noise of the machines. Inside stood half a dozen people, all male except for one tall, slim, female figure who looked familiar to Kate. She moved behind Crispen so that she could get a better view and caught a flash of scarlet hair.

It was definitely the young woman who had called on Jeremy the day before the Fosters were killed.

'Who's that?' She had raised her voice to cut into the conversation ahead of her.

'What?' It was Estelle who turned to see what she wanted. She looked less than pleased.

Kate addressed Owen Grigg. 'I wondered if you knew who

the woman with the amazing red hair is.'

'Where?' He saw where Kate was looking, then. 'Oh, that's Sooz Hailey,' he said.

So she hadn't been mistaken. Sooz Hailey *was* the woman who had called on Jeremy in Agatha Street and she'd been at his funeral, too. She'd been fairly certain before, but now she knew. 'Does she work here?'

'No. She's a paper rep. She works for one of the biggest companies. She may look like an airhead but she's very good at her job. 'Why?' he added. 'Do you know her?'

'No. She was at a friend's funeral yesterday. It was just a surprise to see her here.'

'Do you want to speak to her?'

Kate might have answered 'Yes' but she remembered that Sooz had known Jeremy, and Jeremy was involved with dangerous people.

'No,' she said.

'Really? I thought you might want to ask her the name of her hairdresser!' And Owen laughed.

Crispen and Estelle were looking restive, as though eager to continue the tour. Crispen was fiddling with the settings on his camera.

'She's certainly popular,' said Kate, watching the animated group in the little office. From here she couldn't hear the strident voice, and Sooz was a striking-looking woman.

'Perhaps we should move on,' suggested Estelle. 'We don't want to miss the printing of your book, Kate.'

'Modern printing methods are very fast,' said Owen. He turned his attention back to Estelle, who was mollified now Owen was concentrating entirely on her rather than on Kate, though he turned to her to explain the different processes as they walked through the plant.

'The plates are produced by computer now, of course, from disks sent by the publisher,' he said as they passed a rack of transparent plates, rather like window panes, covered with pages of print. 'Your book is black on white, naturally, but we use several plates if we're producing something in colour.' And he showed her how the pages were placed in a seemingly strange order so that when printed, folded and collated they came out in the correct numerical sequence.

A man walked by, holding another plate carefully upright.

'Inman!' said Owen sharply. 'What are you doing with that?'

'Your friends were interested to see how we were getting on with their project,' said Inman. He nodded towards the animated group in the corner office behind them.

'No. I told you. That job is to be kept in the room over there. It is not to be paraded through the whole works like that.' He sounded suddenly like the boss and much less like the smooth businessman of a few minutes ago.

'I'll take it back then, squire,' said Inman, sounding not at all repentant.

'You're not going to allow him to get away with rudeness, are you?' asked Estelle.

Owen shrugged. 'He's a good worker. And a specialist in his trade.'

Inman meanwhile was walking back the way he had come; he turned right and disappeared through another door into yet another section of the works.

Owen Grigg made an effort to put the friendly smile back on his face and soften his voice. 'We're nearly there, Kate. There's the area where we'll be printing your book. What was it called again?' he asked apologetically.

Kate glanced at Estelle, but she had obviously forgotten the title, too.

'*Escape to Freedom*,' she said. 'The hardback came out last September.'

'Good reviews?' asked Owen.

'You got quite a nice one in the *Leicester Evening Gazette*, didn't you, Kate?' put in Crispen helpfully.

'Probably,' she said as nonchalantly as she could. That review must have run to all of two column centimetres.

'Well, here we are,' said Owen.

They had stopped in front of another conveyor belt, apparently trapped inside a metal cage. Once the machinery was switched on, the belt began to move. Little pleated clusters, in concertina form again, were persuaded to join together, were glued and taped and made to sit firmly and squarely in the form, at last, of a real book. Their pages were cut, their edges were trimmed.

'Oh, look!' said Kate, fascinated. 'They're books!'

'Excellent,' said Owen. 'It's nice to think we got that much right, anyway.' She started to warm to Owen Grigg after all. She was no longer quite so sure that he and Estelle deserved one another. Still, he was a big, grown-up lad and could doubtless look after himself.

'We can follow the process over here,' he said, leading the way. And now the bare wads were glued along their spines, and a bright, colourful cover was zapped into place.

'Here they come!' cried Estelle, excited in her turn. 'Get the camera ready, Crispen. Kate, get in close to the books.'

And they did as they were told, and Kate smiled, and the camera flashed. And then Owen handed her a finished book, warm to the touch, and the camera flashed again.

'It really is hot off the press, isn't it?' said Kate, feeling the brand new copy of *Escape to Freedom*. 'I hadn't realised that the phrase represented a simple fact.'

'Here, take a couple with you as a souvenir,' said Owen, handing two copies to her.

'Thank you.' She tucked them into her bag. Then she lingered for a few minutes, watching the paperbacks weave their shining way on to a platform, to be wrapped into packages ready to stack on pallets.

'They'll be in the warehouse tomorrow and in the bookshops in about six weeks' time,' said Owen, as at last they tore Kate away from the comforting sight of her own works, ready at last for sale to eager readers, and made their way back to the conference room. As they passed the entrance to yet another room, Kate paused.

'What's that?' she asked.

'Which one?'

'The one that looks like a creature from outer space, with arms and legs and brass antennae.'

Owen laughed. 'Not quite an extra-terrestrial. It's a Heidelberg press. A lovely old machine.'

'It certainly is,' said Kate, admiring its shining protuberances. 'What does it do?'

'It's for embossing – the covers of your paperbacks, for example. We don't use it so much these days. We have more modern machines, but I don't want to get rid of it, for obvious reasons, and it's still in use, even today.'

They moved on and arrived back in the rosewood conference room.

'Shall I order more coffee?' asked Owen, but Kate saw him glance at his watch.

'Shouldn't we be getting back to Oxford?' she said. 'What time's your train, Estelle?'

'Not for ages yet,' said Estelle firmly. 'And we'd love more coffee, Owen.'

Owen Grigg lifted a phone and coffee appeared a few minutes later. Estelle had just managed to engage him in a bantering conversation when there was a quick knock at the door and a young man opened it and entered the room.

'Yes, Ryan?' Owen sounded irritated by the interruption.

'I've just come to pick up the order for—'

'Of course. It's waiting for you in my office. See my secretary and she'll give it to you.'

'You don't mind if I check it over?'

'You'll find it's all correct, I believe.'

The man disappeared again.

'Sorry about this,' said Owen. 'You'll have to excuse me in a few minutes. I really will have to get back to work or the place will fall to pieces around our ears.' They laughed politely. 'Oh, and Kate, I hope you'll send me an invitation to your next launch party.'

Kate, who was rarely treated to such a thing, smiled warmly at Owen Grigg. 'Why don't you write your home address down for me?' she said, without seeing what effect of this piece of forwardness was having on Estelle.

Owen scribbled something down on a sheet of scrap paper. 'Here,' he said, handing it over. 'I shall definitely expect an invitation now.'

Kate smiled again at the ambiguity.

He had written, 'Owen Grigg. 18 Somers Close, Wootton, Oxfordshire.'

'Thanks.' She folded it in half and was about to slip it into her handbag when she noticed that Owen had written the note on the back of a flyer advertising a correspondence college. She recognised the florid logo with the aggressive musical instruments. 'I've seen this before,' she said idly. 'We've had these flyers stuffed through our letterboxes. Did you print them?'

'We must have done. But you won't have seen one before,' said Owen. 'If we're using these for scrap it's because they were just samples which were rejected. The college must have settled for something different in the end. I really can't remember.'

'Stop making a fuss about nothing, Kate,' said Estelle, piqued because Owen's attention was no longer on her.

Kate tucked the note into her bag.

'We really should be leaving,' went on Estelle, taking the hint at last. 'It has been so kind of you to show us round your lovely printing works, Owen. If *ever* you're interested in seeing how a literary agent operates, just give me a ring.' And she handed over her business card, pausing to write her home telephone number on the back. 'Give me a call any time,' she said.

Kate could only marvel at the way a strong woman could be putty in the hands of a personable man.

Then she, Estelle and Crispen said their goodbyes and left.

'Well, I think that was very satisfactory,' said Estelle as they walked towards Kate's car. Once she left the printing works she regained her usual brisk stride and her voice took on its customary sharp tone. If Owen Grigg liked the soft and fluffy type it was just as well he couldn't see her now.

'If I put my foot down we'll get back to the station in time for the two o'clock train,' said Kate.

'Don't you want to join us for a spot of lunch?' asked Estelle. 'Isn't there a cosy country pub we could go to?'

'Not on this industrial estate. And I'd better get back,' said Kate. 'You'll be telling me I should be getting on with *Spitfire Sweethearts*.'

'Yes, of course,' said Estelle, to Kate's relief now completely restored to her normal persona. 'Crispen and I will find a sandwich or something to eat on the train. Come along, Crispen!'

As Kate drove them back to Oxford she wondered how Jeremy had met the sales rep for a paper manufacturer. Oh well, where did people usually meet? In a club or a pub, or at a party. She couldn't see Jeremy enjoying any of those places, but then she hadn't known him very well. Perhaps he was just a wild child at heart after all.

She parked in the short-stay car park and walked with Estelle and Crispen to the station entrance.

'Thank you for acting as our chauffeur,' said Crispen.

'It was no trouble,' said Kate.

'Goodbye, Kate,' said Estelle.

'Goodbye,' said Kate.

'Come along, Crispen!' said Estelle in her bossiest tones.

'Just a moment,' said Crispen bravely. 'Kate, I wonder whether I could possibly ask you for one of the copies of *Escape to Freedom*? I haven't read it yet, and I'm really looking forward to doing so.'

Now there was a way for a publicity person to endear himself to an author! Kate could tell that she and Crispen were going to get on really well together. She took a copy out of her bag and handed it to him.

'Would you sign it for me?'

She found a pen, signed the title page with a flourish, then added a warm personal message for Crispen.

'Enjoy!' she said.

'You can read it on the train,' said Estelle sourly. 'While I'm getting on with some proper work.'

Kate sent Crispen a friendly smile. He didn't have to be frightened of Estelle since he didn't work for her.

'I'll be in touch,' he said. 'Soon,' he added.

Kate waved goodbye. What a pity Crispen was so young. He was a man of such good taste, after all.

Owen Grigg stood at the window of his office and watched the three of them disappear round the corner of the building into the car park.

He noted Estelle's change of posture and smiled. She didn't fool him, but she might be amusing for an evening or two's entertainment next time he was at a loose end in London. He wasn't sure he could stand the flirtatious manner for longer than that, and he knew she would change back to the bossy woman he detected under the blue silk dress once she 'had her man', as she would doubtless put it.

Crispen Southmore he dismissed as an irrelevance. But what about Kate Ivory? She had struck him as an observant woman – perhaps novelists had to be, even those who wrote the kind of historical schlock that she did – and he just hoped for her sake that she hadn't taken in more than she was intended to. It was a pity that Stoker and Feet had been around. And then there was Tara, of course. The stupid woman had to contact Malden and Joiner, but she shouldn't have insisted on going to Sancho's funeral afterwards. That was a piece of pointless theatricality. And unless Sooz had been to two funerals yesterday – which he doubted – that's where Ivory must have seen her before. Did it matter? Probably not, but he'd report it to Jester just in case. What name should he give Ivory? He thought for a moment and then grinned. Big Ears.

There was a knock at the door and Ryan Ashe came straight in without waiting for a reply.

'You've seen the samples?' Owen said.

'Very impressive.'

'Here's the first tranche.' And Owen passed across a machine-wrapped white package, the same size and shape as the parcels of Kate's books that were on their way to the distributor.

'Jester's well pleased,' said Owen, holding the door open for Ashe to leave. 'There could be a bonus for everyone soon.'

'Cheers, Red,' said Ryan.

'Cheers, Feet,' said Grigg.

As Kate turned to leave the station concourse she saw that the *Oxford Mail* was on the newsstand. She might as well buy a copy to read with her own sandwich and coffee when she reached home.

'Man Drowned in Canal,' she read on the front page. She read on. 'The man found drowned in the Oxford Canal yesterday evening has been identified as a tutor from Bartlemas College.'

Alec Malden.

16

Kate sat at her desk in her study with the two flyers in front of her. Both pale green, both with the same logo, both advertising the services of the Jericho Corporation.

Owen had said it was just a sample, never used. So why did Jeremy have one, too?

Owen could have been mistaken. Why should a man like that know the details of every little print job that passed through his works? But what he had said was, 'If we're using these for scrap it's because they were just samples which were rejected'.

Jeremy. Owen Grigg. Laura and Edward Foster. Sooz Hailey. Were they connected? And if so, how? She might as well add Kate Ivory, Crispen Southmore and Estelle Livingstone, she thought. She couldn't see anything that they all might have in common.

Think, Kate.

Printing. Publishing. That linked Kate, Estelle, Crispen, Owen and, peripherally, Sooz. What about Jeremy? He must have published books, or papers, at least. And Laura Foster was an illustrator of children's books.

Where did that get her? Nowhere, she had to admit.

And now Alec Malden.

The drowning was an accident, the newspaper account said. The police were not looking for anyone in connection with the death. Alec Malden, who lived, she found, in Polstead Road,

North Oxford, was in the habit of taking a walk in the evening, often in Port Meadow, or along the canal bank. He had slipped into the water and drowned.

There were no more details.

Kate looked at the byline at the head of the article. It was written by an old, if not close, friend of hers who worked on the paper. She looked up his phone number and called him.

'Bill? Kate here. I was just wondering if you could tell me any more about the drowning. Alec Malden,' she added.

'In the canal?'

'That's the one.'

'Hang on. I've got my full report here. Would you like me to e-mail it to you?'

'If you would. Thanks.'

'What's your interest, Kate? Is there a story in it for me?'

'I shouldn't think so. It's just that I'd met him at a mutual friend's funeral that morning and it was a bit of shock to see that he'd died himself so soon afterwards. I saw your name on the report in the *Mail* and wondered if you knew anything more about it.'

'You'd let me know if there *was* a story in it, wouldn't you?'

'Of course.'

The e-mail arrived a few minutes later. The first section of Bill's report was just as he had written it in the newspaper. But then there were two or three further paragraphs which Kate studied carefully.

While he was taking that final walk, Alec Malden had been seen by the owner of a narrow boat, Miss Ann Jones, who knew him by sight but not by name, and they had exchanged 'Good evening's. The only other evening stroller spotted (and remembered) by Miss Jones was a man in biker gear. She had only noticed him because he was wearing his visor down, which looked an uncomfortable way to take a walk, but doubtless was of no significance.

The towpath was muddy after the recent rain, and narrow, and slippery. There was a deep puddle straddling the path near where Alec Malden had been found and it was assumed that he had tried to avoid soaking his leather shoes by passing too near the edge of the path bordering the canal. The bank had been reinforced with a dry stone wall at this point. Footmarks in the mud showed that Alec Malden had slipped, and had then struck his head on rock projecting from the wall and fallen into the canal. Alec Malden could swim, but was assumed to be already unconscious on striking the water.

By the time the next passer-by found him, some fifteen minutes later, it was too late and he had drowned. Strenuous attempts had been made to revive him, but to no avail.

He had been divorced for about seven years and his wife had seen him only once in that time. She now lived in Derbyshire with her second husband. She could add nothing to the story.

Another accident, Kate told herself.

Well, and so it could have been. But who was the biker with his visor down? Admittedly one saw odd people when one was out walking or jogging, and this one wasn't as out of the ordinary as some. But she felt that she'd heard about a motorcyclist before. Wasn't it Camilla who had suggested that contract killers might ride motorbikes in order to make a quick getaway? But this wasn't a contract killing. Alec Malden hadn't been shot. And if the Fosters' killer had really escaped on a motorbike, no one had told her so, or even put it in the newspaper.

But this man could have parked his bike in Aristotle Lane,

followed Alec Malden along the towpath, then pushed him into the canal when no one was looking, and held him down until he drowned. It must have been dusk when it happened. The towpath was overgrown and winding. No one need have seen. A large leather gauntlet over Malden's mouth and he couldn't even have screamed out for help.

How did he know that Malden would be going for a walk?

Because it was his daily habit to do so, and usually in the same direction.

In that case, the murder was planned. Someone knew Malden, knew his habits, and the route he was likely to take. And paid the biker to kill him.

But why?

Kate turned the two flyers over again so that she could see the notes that Jeremy and Owen had written. There was nothing potentially lethal in the care of Camilla's house plants, surely? But what about Owen Grigg? And Sooz Hailey?

Kate pulled out an A4 pad and started to draw a spider's web. Sooz in the middle. Lines radiating to Alec – yes, at Jeremy's funeral; to Jeremy – at his house and at the funeral; *and to the Fosters*. Yes. Sooz had been visiting Jeremy on the morning the Fosters tripped back and forth with their good humour and their desperate curiosity. The Fosters met Sooz and the Fosters died the following day. Jeremy knew Sooz and *he* died. Alec Malden met her at Jeremy's funeral (had he known her before? He hadn't indicated as much) and now Alec was dead.

It had never before occurred to Kate that the buying and selling of paper – ordinary paper, the sort you used for printing books – could be a dangerous occupation.

She was missing something. She returned to her diagram.

She drew lines down from 'Jeremy' and added 'Bartlemas College' and 'The Concrete Onion'. Now she could fill in the names of Harry Joiner and Goldy Silverman and draw little stalks to link them to the others they knew. She linked Owen Grigg to Sooz Hailey, added Estelle Livingstone and Crispen Southmore. She might as well add her own name, she thought, if she was putting all these in. As she wrote 'Kate Ivory' and the spokes that joined her own name to the others in the diagram, she realised that she was the one person who had met them all.

Well, that makes sense, she reflected. You're the one drawing the diagram! You should be more interested in the people you *haven't* met.

Jester?

She added the name 'Jester' in the top right-hand corner and joined it to 'Jeremy'.

What about linking Jeremy and Owen Grigg? The green flyer came from the printing works, so either Jeremy had been there to see Grigg, or else Grigg had come to Agatha Street to see Jeremy. Why? She didn't know. And why pick up the flyer? She tapped it on the desk. She used such things as bookmarks; perhaps Grigg or Jeremy had done the same. Grigg could have given Jeremy something with this stuck in as a marker.

But what was it all about?

She still had the key to Jeremy's house. She could go and have another look round to see if there was a clue. She had learned all sorts of mingled facts and gossip since Jeremy's death, but she still seemed no nearer knowing what it was that Jester and his friends were *doing*.

Even in his 'Jester' file Jeremy was cagey about it. He had suspected drugs, but then been assured that the packet he brought back from Bordeaux contained nothing like that. She felt too edgy to settle down to reading the rest of the file just yet; she fancied action rather than study. And anyway, she had promised him she'd look after his plants. They probably needed watering again by now. She took the key and went next door.

Jeremy's house had started to smell of emptiness and abandon. The air was stale and cold. She wondered whether to switch the heating on, but wasn't sure who would pay the fuel bill. She filled the small watering can at the cold tap and started on a tour of the rooms, drenching plants as she went.

She stood again in front of Jeremy's bookshelves with their load of crashingly dull texts. But as she stared at them it came to her that 'monetary' referred to money. And presumably not just money in the abstract, but the real thing, coins and notes that could buy the things that Jeremy (and Kate, too, if she was honest with herself) wanted.

And presumably the people that Jeremy met, and investigated for Jester, were also money people. Bankers, perhaps? European bankers.

Were they planning a major bank raid?

A definite possibility.

But why involve Owen Grigg?

Why would they need a printer?

It was time to return to her own house. She wanted to follow this line of thought to its conclusion. She could well be on to something. And she must return to the Jester file. It might yet hold secrets and revelations. Alec Malden's death had over-shadowed it for a while, but now it was time to get back to it.

Would they have any further use for me once I had delivered the package back to England? wrote Jeremy Wells.

I had already queried the legality of the object and had my wrist slapped for my trouble, although they did provide the false passport. I think Red might have met Blue himself if they hadn't wanted to muddy the chain linking Chamalières to Oxford. And Jester knew the value of binding us into his operation so that we couldn't escape. He didn't want anyone running to their friends, to their family, or to the police. But sitting in that café, I had time to think. And again, on the plane, and sitting in the coach back to Oxford. I didn't want to be part of it. Up till then I hadn't done anything strictly illegal. What I had found out about Blue and passed on to Jester wasn't very nice, and I wouldn't want it to be generally bandied about Oxford that I had spied on him, but I didn't think the police would come visiting me in Agatha Street about it.

The worst moment was when Laura and Edward Foster invited me round for a drink that evening – I didn't want them to know I'd been away, so I accepted – and in walked the woman from the plane. Kate Ivory. I needn't have worried, as it turned out, because she hadn't recognised me. But I was edgy, and imagining things, and I thought she had, and that it amused her to pretend she hadn't.

But what if she had known who I was? It brought it right home to me then, just what I was risking. This, bringing some illicit 'item' from France to England, was different from what I had done before. I thought about opening the packet and seeing what was in it, but I believe by then I had guessed what it might be. I knew what was happening at Chamalières, after all, and it was easy enough for me to fill in the blanks in the story from my imagination. What I did next was stupid, but it was the only thing that occurred to me at the time.

I was out of the house early the next morning, slipping out through the back way, and I went to see Red, as I had been instructed. It wasn't even eight o'clock and the office staff hadn't yet clocked on, so he was alone in his office. I spoke to him about Jester's plans, tried to convince him that we should oppose them, but he laughed at me. And so I delivered the packet into his own hands, just as Jester had told me to.

And then I came straight home. Well, I didn't want to be there when he opened the packet and tried out the contents. He'd have to wait for Stoker, I imagined, but then they'd see straight away that there had been a substitution. As I'd thought, the package had contained an optical disk, which I'd replaced with a blank Zip disk of my own. They were the about the same size and weight and I hoped it would fool Red for long enough for me to get away.

It didn't take long for them to send someone after me. Tara came round later that morning, and that's when things really started to go wrong. That girl has a very piercing, vulgar voice, and I hadn't reckoned on the Fosters' overwhelming curiosity. Laura couldn't see a tall, striking redhead enter my house without following, with some excuse or other, to see who she was. Edward followed Laura, of course, as Edward always did.

I shouldn't have let them in. I thought, stupidly, that their presence might defuse the situation. Tara wouldn't be able to continue her diatribe with them there.

But Tara had thrown the package and its contents – my Zip disk – on the table and was shrieking at me about it as

Laura followed me into the house.

An awful silence descended on the room. Of course, Laura and Edward couldn't have known exactly what it was all about, but I was sure that any ideas they might have would be prattled all over the neighbourhood in no time. I persuaded them to leave. I told Tara that I had already disposed of the original disk and that there was no way I could give it to her. She threatened me, but I didn't believe her threats. What could she do?

I soon found out.

She must have reported back to Jester about the Fosters. I don't know how he persuaded them to come to their gate when the killer arrived in Agatha Street. I can imagine that it was a phone call from Tara from her mobile. Any sort of message that implied that Tara would discuss my private business with them would have the Fosters running to the door.

They paid heavily enough for their nosiness.

Then I had to get rid of the disk, but for real this time.

I had the idea that I was being watched. It would be a logical thing for them to do, so I asked an acquaintance (*Acquaintance, indeed!* thought Kate) to take it to the one man in this town that I can trust. I shall have to go to the police eventually, but for the moment the disk will be safe. Perhaps I should have destroyed it, but it gives me a bargaining counter if things get nasty.

Now I shall visit Jester. I haven't got his full address, but I did pick up one or two clues when we met in Brussels and I'm sure I'll be able to find it. I have to do it, although it's probably a very stupid act on my part. And that is why I am writing this account of what has happened. I want some record, however inconclusive, to be left behind for someone to find.

When I get back – *if* I get back – I'll write down the rest of it.

Kate needed to talk over what she had learned with someone. Roz was always a good bet, especially if you needed someone with expertise in the off-beat. Kate phoned her mother.

But Roz had installed an answering machine, apparently, and it informed her that Roz Ivory was not available to take her call, although she would consider phoning back if Kate cared to leave her name and phone number.

Oh, really, Roz!

Paul Taylor, her policeman friend, was another possibility, but she and Paul hadn't been on friendly terms for a long time, since before she took up with George.

Then there was, of course, George. Should she phone him? He had offered any help she might need in the unfortunate circumstances of the Fosters' death. And George would have knowledge, and contacts, that would answer many of her queries. She thought for several minutes, weighing up the pros and cons. She dialled his number.

There was no reply, and she realised that the sense of relief she felt was an indication of something that might be important. She knew the relationship was over, really she did, it was just that she thought she never need break the bond between them completely. She was fooling herself. She and George were finished.

The phone rang.

She looked at it. George was so vividly in her thoughts that she felt it must be him. Or Roz, perhaps, phoning her back.

She picked up the receiver.

'Kate? It's Emma here.'

The sense of anticlimax was so acute that Kate nearly laughed. Then she remembered that Emma, too, was going through a bad time with her own relationship.

'How are you, Emma? Have you spoken to Sam yet?'

'No. I was hoping that you'd have arranged to meet him by now. You did promise, after all.'

'I'm sure I didn't.'

'We talked about it, don't you recall? And you were going to ring up Sam and arrange to meet him for a drink, or lunch, and you were going to get him to explain everything that's been happening.'

And whether he still loves you. And if he's been unfaithful. And what he was doing with a purple vibrator. Yeah, yeah, Emma. 'I don't remember any firm commitment on my part,' she said.

'I thought you were my friend.'

'I was. I am.'

There was a silence.

'Where is he now? Is he at work or at home?' asked Kate finally, giving in.

'At work. Do you have his number?'

'Very probably,' said Kate crisply. Luckily Emma was useless at double entendres. 'I'll ring him straight away.'

'Thank you, Kate.'

What have I let myself in for, wondered Kate, dialling Sam's number.

'Sam? Kate here.'

'Hallo, Kate.' Sam sounded cautious.

'It's ages since we had a really good conversation,' said

Kate brightly, as though it was the sort of thing that she and Sam did all the time. 'How about meeting me for a drink after work?'

'Emma's put you up to this.'

'Emma? Good Lord, no!' She had to admit she didn't sound convincing even to herself. 'Are you free this evening?'

'I'm afraid I'm busy all this week,' said Sam.

'Then how about next Monday?'

'If I say no, you're going to take me through the days of the week until I say yes, aren't you?'

'You've got it. Which would you prefer, lunch or a drink after work?'

'Let's make it lunch.'

'It gives us a time limit, certainly. Where would you like to meet? I'm paying, of course.'

She heard in the pause that Sam was considering a very expensive restaurant, but then, since he was Sam and a kind and good-natured man, he suggested a bright, noisy and quite cheap establishment just five minutes' walk from where he worked.

'Ten to one, Monday,' confirmed Kate, just so that they were both clear, and Sam couldn't say he'd got the day or place wrong.

'I look forward to it,' said Sam wearily, and rang off.

Kate wrote it down in her diary, to give herself no excuse to forget it, either.

Now, she thought, back to the important question of Jeremy Wells and his involvement in illegal acts. But before she could find her place in the Jester file, the phone rang again.

'Kate? Estelle here.'

'Hallo, Estelle.'

'You answered the phone remarkably quickly. You weren't sitting at your desk, then?'

'No. I was taking a short break,' said Kate, conveniently forgetting that she hadn't touched the latest chapter of *Spitfire Sweethearts* at all that day. 'How are you, Estelle? I hope you enjoyed our trip to the printers.'

'Very much, thank you. And Owen and I have planned a delightful evening together this weekend.'

'Well done.'

'Did you like him? What did you think of him?'

'Delightful. Charming. Fanciable. Rich. What more does one need?'

'There's no need to be so sharp, Kate.'

'Sorry.'

'Is there something wrong? You sound preoccupied.'

Kate hesitated. She and Estelle didn't usually talk about anything except work. 'There's been another death,' she said.

'Who was it this time?' She sounded as though she was blaming Kate for the occurrence.

'His name was Alec Malden. He worked at Bartlemas College and he was a friend of Jeremy's.'

'The neighbour who died in an accident?'

'That's the one.'

'This must be upsetting for you, Kate. It isn't putting you off your work, is it?'

'Perhaps just a little.'

'You should get away. It obviously isn't healthy where you are. How did Alec Malden die?'

'He drowned. It was an accident and it's not catching, either.'

'It would still do you good to get out of Oxford. You can

207

take your laptop with you. It needn't hold up your work.'

'I'll think about it.'

'Pour yourself a glass of wine. Relax for the rest of the day.'

'Estelle,' said Kate impulsively, before her agent could hang up. 'You don't think there was something odd going on at Grigg's, do you?'

'What do you mean?'

'There was an odd atmosphere – of excitement, of celebration.'

'You're thinking of the red-headed girl.'

'And the people with her in the office.' She was finding it impossible to talk to Estelle about the contents of Jeremy's file. Estelle lived in a different world and she would think that Kate was mad if she brought it up.

'I tell you what I did notice,' said Estelle, who was, after all, no fool. 'The man – was his name Inman? – who was told to take the plate back to where he found it, well, it didn't look to me as though it contained the pages of a book.'

'What did it have on it?'

'I don't know. It was a colour plate, I believe, rather than black and white. It's possible it could have been a book. After all, they're not all a standard size and shape, are they?'

'You don't think they're producing pornography, do you?'

There was a pause. 'It's referred to as erotica, I believe, and several leading publishers have a specialised imprint that includes, well, erotic material.'

'I was thinking of something less acceptable.'

'Something illegal?'

'Possibly.'

'And you'd like me to ask Owen Grigg when I see him?'

'I don't want to ruin your evening. You can hardly accept his caviar and vintage champagne and then ask him if he's a secret pornographer.'

'I'll see what I can manage.'

'Thanks, Estelle.'

When she had hung up, Kate remembered another of her sensible friends. She rang Camilla.

'Are you busy? Do you think I could come round?' she asked.

'I'm always busy. But come round anyway. You can explain what was happening in my house while I was away.'

'Oh, that.'

'I'll see you in ten minutes, shall I?'

Kate put the Jester file back into its folder, placed it in her handbag and walked round to Camilla's house.

17

Camilla was a fast reader, presumably from years of correcting mountains of girls' homework every evening. She skimmed through Jeremy's file, replaced it in the folder and said, 'You should take this straight to the police.'

'They'll think I'm mad. Or they'll think I invented it.'

'Weren't you interviewed by the police when the Fosters were murdered?'

'Yes, of course I was.'

'Well, contact the policeman you saw then. Do you have a note of his name?'

'A tired-looking constable, called, I think, Mundy, came round and was intensely bored by what I had to tell him which was, admittedly, absolutely nothing. His opinion of my intelligence and observational powers was precisely zero.'

'Even so, I think you should phone the police station and ask to speak to PC Mundy.'

'He'll think I'm making it up. He had a very low opinion of historical novelists, I could tell.'

'He'll think that this is a very dangerous gang of criminals who have already killed three people and who should be put in prison for a long, long time.'

'Four people,' said Kate.

Camilla raised her eyebrows.

'Alec Malden, a tutor at Bartlemas, drowned in the canal.'

'I saw it in the paper. The report said it was an accident.'

'They said that Jeremy's death was an accident, too. I might have believed it, but when I collected his belongings from Deyton Infirmary there was a slip of paper that persuaded me he was on his way to visit Jester.'

'You collected his belongings? Why?'

'I was in his house when the phone rang, and it seemed sensible to answer it, and then they assumed I was his wife or mother or someone close to him.'

'And you didn't disabuse them.'

'No.'

'I'd better get out the bottle of sauvignon blanc that's cooling in the fridge. Or would you like something stronger?'

'Wine would be lovely.'

Moments later they were sitting in bentwood chairs in Camilla's immaculate kitchen, their elbows on the pine table, the folder between them, wine glasses to hand.

'So,' began Camilla. 'After the Fosters were killed, Jeremy got nervous and asked you to help him to find somewhere to hide.'

'That's right.'

'Here.' She didn't even bother to make it a question.

'He's very good with plants. I didn't think you'd mind.'

' "Kate, there's a gang of international criminals after me, please find me a place to stay." And you brought him to my house.'

'What's wrong? Are your plants all dead?'

Camilla sighed. 'The plants are flourishing. I only hope this house isn't marked down by the gang as the hiding-place of someone who has betrayed them.'

'I don't believe he was seen. Not then. I think they may have followed him from the St Giles's Fair, though.'

'Don't worry about it. They'd have found him soon enough, anyway, you can be sure. From the tone of his account, I would say he was quite capable of phoning Jester to announce his arrival. And even before that he probably trampled all over their feet, looking for Jester's address.'

They drank their wine in silence for a moment.

'Now you'd better tell me the real reason why you don't want to go to the police,' said Camilla in her best headmistressy voice.

'I need to tell you the rest of the story, as I know it.'

'Wait a sec. I'll fetch the bottle. I can see I'm going to need it.'

When she had returned, Kate continued with her story.

'Jeremy Wells gave me a small packet to deliver to Alec Malden. Alec, apparently, was the only man he trusted.'

'These are the two people he mentions at the end of his narrative? You're the acquaintance and Alec Malden was the trusted friend?'

'Yes. I went to the college to deliver the disk, but Malden wasn't alone. The new Master of Bartlemas was in his room. Harry Joiner. Not my favourite man. He seemed more like a double glazing salesman than the Master of an Oxford college.'

'Snob,' said Camilla.

'Well, you haven't met him. I thought he and Alec Malden seemed very close, and to be honest, I didn't like their attitude.'

'What attitude?'

You couldn't get away with much when Camilla was listening to your story. 'They were laughing at me.'

'They weren't taking the drama seriously?'

'No. And they convinced me that Jeremy was off his head so

that I wouldn't take *him* seriously. They wouldn't want me to believe him in case I worked out what he'd been doing and went to the police about it. They didn't blow the whistle on him themselves, of course, because they fancied a share of the profit. They wanted Jeremy to take all the risks while they pocketed the cash. I thought Jeremy might be making a bad mistake about Malden. But what could I do? I was just the messenger, so I handed over the disk. I thought I was doing the right thing.'

'But it means that you're involved, too. Jeremy really shouldn't have done that. He sounds like a very self-centred man to me.'

'I expect he was. Well, we all are to a certain extent, aren't we?'

Camilla said something that sounded like 'Hmph'. She was the only person Kate knew who could get away with such a comment without sounding ridiculous. 'Is this why you don't want to go to the police?'

'Just for the moment. I'll go to see them eventually. I want to find out more about the gang and what they're doing, then the police won't be interested in me and what I was doing as a simple courier, will they?'

'You're incorrigible,' said Camilla, filling their glasses. 'Why did they kill Malden, do you think?'

'I don't know. I saw him again at Jeremy's funeral, at Bartlemas. And Sooz Hailey was there. I believe she's the one that Jeremy refers to as Tara—'

'So she's one of the gang?'

'She must be. I think she's very bright and quite ruthless. I overheard a snatch of conversation that made no sense at the time, but now I believe that it meant that Alec Malden was attempting to sell the disk on to Sooz in his turn.'

'How did he know whom to contact?'

'Jeremy must have told him about Sooz/Tara. He could even have e-mailed a copy of his Jester file to Malden.'

'He sounds naive enough, certainly.'

'Whoever met Alec Malden on the towpath must have taken the disk and then killed him, making it look like an accident.'

'This time a drowning. In Jeremy's case it was a road accident, wasn't it?'

'Yes. No other vehicle involved. No explanation of why he ran off the road.'

'And now *you* want to find out more about what they're doing. It sounds to me like a very dangerous plan indeed.'

'What's this place Chamalières? Do you know?' asked Kate, avoiding Camilla's prophecy of doom.

'I'll look it up. Meanwhile, why don't I get us something to eat?'

'Thanks.' Kate was just realising how hungry she was. Camilla was the sort of cook who removed something from the freezer and placed it in the microwave, but she was in no mood to complain about that.

Kate laid two places for them on the kitchen table and then finished drinking her second glass of wine. It made her feel pleasantly fuzzy, going down on an empty stomach.

'Here,' said Camilla a few minutes later. 'It's lasagne, I think. I hope you like spinach.'

'It looks lovely,' said Kate, and tucked in.

'There's fruit for dessert,' said Camilla when they had emptied their plates.

Kate took their dishes to the sink and fetched fruit plates

and knives. Camilla, she knew, was particular about that sort of thing. She chose herself an apple.

After they'd eaten, they did the minimal washing-up together and then Camilla went to consult one of her many reference books.

'Chamalières is a small town in the Auvergne region,' she said. 'It has a pretty park, an art gallery, and a watersports centre, and it would like to encourage us to travel there to enjoy our summer holidays.'

They looked at each other blankly.

'Does it have any industry?' asked Kate. 'A secret research establishment, perhaps? An arms factory?'

'Not according to this.'

'Jeremy thought they wanted to muddy the trail from Chamalières to Oxford. Maybe the disk was taken there from somewhere further away and was picked up by – what was the man's name? Blue? – from someone that Jeremy didn't know about. It might have passed through half a dozen hands for all we know, and come from any part of Europe. Or beyond.'

Camilla was silent for a moment. 'Shall I make us coffee?'

'Yes, please.'

They had reached an impasse and neither spoke while Camilla put the kettle on and spooned coffee into the cafetière.

'It means that we can't follow the trail,' she said eventually. 'If Jeremy didn't know where it came from, how are we to find out?'

'Tricky, I admit.'

'And dangerous. Go to the police, Kate.'

But Kate had started on her third glass of wine and wasn't inclined to consider danger or any other serious subject for the time being.

'I'll think about it,' she said. 'But I don't believe I'm in any danger.'

'I'd say that was an unwise assumption to make,' said Camilla. 'Would you like to stay here at my place for a few days?'

'No. I'll get back to Agatha Street. I'm quite safe there.'

18

Since there is little justice in this world, Kate woke early the next morning without the trace of a headache. It was a fine, crisp, autumn morning and she felt full of energy and unwilling to sit at a computer in a gloomy basement for an hour or two yet.

'A good day for a run,' she told herself. She had been less than regular with her running for the past months. She really ought to get back into the habit of going out four or five times a week. If she wasn't careful she'd start to put on weight. Then she looked at herself in the mirror in her trainers, leggings and T-shirt and felt smug. Even without the exercise, she was still in pretty good shape, she had to admit.

She made herself a coffee, ate a banana, then left the house. Where should she go? She could jog past Camilla's house and up the lane to Port Meadow where she could join the geese and ponies by the water. Or she could turn into the Fridesley Road and run into the town centre, through the parks and down to the river that way.

She decided on the city route.

She wasn't quite as fit as she had hoped. For the first fifteen minutes or so she had to concentrate on what she was doing. She forced herself to slow down, to keep a regular pace. Her breathing wasn't as easy as it used to be and she started to get a stitch in her side. *Watch it, Kate! You'll be slowing down to a walk in a minute.* But she made herself keep to a run, however gentle.

There had been plenty of traffic on the road into town, but once she turned on to the towpath by the canal she was alone with the morning mist and the occasional dog-walker. The only sound was that of her own feet on the path and the noise of her own heartbeat. And then, as she approached Folly Bridge, she became aware of an echo of her own footfall. She slowed down; the echo slowed, too. It must be something to do with the curve of the path and the buildings on the opposite bank bouncing the sound back to her.

With the sun burning away the mist, she could see that it was going to be a lovely day, and she left the canal, crossed the main road, and turned through tall gates into a meadow leading down to winding paths by the river. Here she had the place to herself. Once or twice she passed another runner and lifted a hand in greeting, but it was so peaceful and deserted that she could immerse herself in her own thoughts in the silence of the morning. The early joggers must have finished their sessions, she thought, and the latecomers haven't set out yet.

Her spirits had lifted with the exercise and she was just thinking that she was starting to enjoy her run after all (and deciding that she wasn't as unfit as she'd feared) when she became aware of the echoing footsteps behind her again. This time she could see no reason for the sound. It could only mean that there was someone running on the path behind her, and they were getting closer.

There was something else. Those weren't training shoes, but something much heavier. Unlikely as it seemed, it sounded as though the runner was wearing boots.

She wanted to turn round and see who it was, but she felt

there was something so neurotic, so 'girlie' about the impulse that she forced herself to keep facing forwards. She increased her pace, though. Now that she had warmed up, her legs obeyed the request without too much complaint.

She looked to left and right. Why was the park so isolated? Why weren't there crowds of people out enjoying the beautiful morning? But no. There were just the two of them, Kate and the man – it had to be a man, she felt. A man wearing boots for a morning run.

She crossed a small bridge, her feet thudding on the slats as she did so. She was moving fast now, and she willed herself to keep the pace up. It was amazing what you could achieve when you were afraid.

She turned left, aiming back towards the town. She wanted to get out on to an ordinary pavement, with ordinary shops where she could dodge inside and shout 'Help!' and hide in a crowd of ordinary people. Ahead of her now there stood an iron gate, and just a hundred yards or so beyond it, a wide road with cars and buses and hordes of lovely shoppers and tourists.

But the footsteps were gaining on her – and he sounded like a heavy man. She made an effort and increased her pace again. Her calves were hurting and her lungs bursting, but she was frightened now, and she could ignore the pain. Why hadn't she listened to Camilla? The Fosters were dead, killed by a gunman. Jeremy Wells and Alec Malden had died in 'accidents'. She had walked in where she wasn't wanted, had asked questions, and now it was her turn.

The gate was only a few paces away. But she would have to stop to navigate it for it was was designed to keep bicycles out of the green spaces and was awkward for pedestrians. She was pushing it open, safety only yards away, when her pursuer caught up with her.

What has he in store for me? thought Kate in a panic. Drowning? A road accident? What?

She screamed as loudly as she could, but the sound was lost in the morning air. She kicked backwards, meeting a solid body. Her trainers had made no impression on him, she was sure. She twisted half round and saw that he was wearing motorcycling gear, though not the leather she had imagined, but some thick, waterproof material. He had left his helmet behind, and now she attempted to jab her fingers in his eyes.

He caught hold of her hands and held them quite easily in one of his. He was still wearing leather gauntlets. *So he had been on a motorbike.* Even in the midst of the struggle she made a mental note.

She looked for unguarded skin that she could bite, but the other gauntleted hand covered her mouth. She could smell his sweat and knew that she must be sweating, too, and smelling of fear. But still she struggled. She wasn't going to give in easily.

Her back slammed into the metal railings next to the gate, and now he had her pinned against them, his face close to hers. He smelled of unbrushed teeth, and coffee, and cheap fried food. His head had been shaved recently, and was covered in a short, dark stubble. She could see the clear patches where his hair was thinning and receding. His features were blunt, his eyes dark brown, his teeth darkened with nicotine. It seemed really important that she should remember all this so that she could report it to the police. She pushed aside the thought that she might not survive to see a policeman.

Then the hand at her mouth was removed, but she had no

time to scream for help as he had her throat in his grip now. Even one-handed he had the strength to crush her windpipe. Her head was jammed against the iron railings which were digging into her back. She tried to kick again, but he held her pinned with his body and she made no impression on him.

Her throat was on fire and there were red spots clouding her view of his face. He grunted with the effort. It was the first sound he had made. Her own efforts to shout and scream were useless.

And then, through the drumming in her head, she heard a sound like the squabbling of starlings. And footsteps. The pressure on her throat eased slightly. She even managed to take in some breath.

The bird noises resolved themselves into voices, foreign voices, calling out in alarm. Her attacker pushed closer and covered her face with his.

He's pretending we're lovers, protested Kate, struggling hard. She managed to emit only faint mewing, which probably, she thought wretchedly, sounded like encouragement and even sexual pleasure.

'Excuse me, please,' said a polite male voice behind the man's shoulder. 'I do not think the young lady wishes your attentions.'

Released suddenly, she saw that there must have been eight or ten of them – too many for her attacker to deal with, in any case. She felt her knees buckling, and slid to a kneeling position on the ground.

She tried to shout 'Stop him!' but her throat was still on fire and she found herself weeping with the frustration of trying to speak.

It was too late, in any case. The man had pushed his way

past the group and escaped through the gate and into the road beyond.

'Are you OK?' a young woman asked Kate anxiously.

'I am now,' she answered, shaking.

Two young men pulled her gently to her feet. She rubbed the tears away with her fist.

She looked round the arc of concerned faces. She had never been so pleased to see a group of Japanese tourists in her life.

'Thank you so much.' *I think you saved my life.*

'Shall we find you a taxi? You need to go home to rest, I think,' said the first young man.

'That would be very kind.'

And she allowed herself to be led a little way up the street while they found her a taxi, and then helped her inside it, and told the taxi driver to take care of her, and all waved to her as it turned into the High Street.

'Where do you want to go?' asked the driver, looking round at her curiously.

Kate gave him Camilla's address. She had a five pound note in her pocket, so she could pay for the taxi without asking for funds from her friend. But she didn't fancy going back to Agatha Street just yet. Not without an escort, anyway.

19

Camilla didn't say 'I told you so'. She did look very worried when Kate sat at her kitchen table, still shaking. Even her teeth were chattering.

'Hot, sweet tea,' muttered Camilla, and put the kettle on.

She came back to the table and stared at Kate. 'I think you should have a warm bath. Wouldn't that be a good idea? I could lend you some clothes,' she added doubtfully. She was at least two sizes larger than Kate.

'Tea,' said Kate through blue lips. 'Please.'

'And toast,' decided Camilla. She took a packet of bread from an earthenware container and jammed three slices into the toaster.

After two cups of sweet tea and a slice of toast and marmalade, it was true that Kate felt a little better. Not much better, but a little.

'And you won't argue about talking to the police this time, will you?'

'Do you think I could have a shower first, and borrow some clothes?' said Kate, putting off the inevitable.

'Of course. But I shall phone your Constable Mundy while you're in the shower.'

'Yes. Of course.'

Camilla was right. She couldn't put it off any longer.

* * *

It was about an hour later that she sat in Camilla's sitting room, facing Constable Mundy across the coffee table. She felt at a slight disadvantage in oversized, matronly clothes, but they were a lot better than the leggings and sweaty T-shirt that she had discarded on the bathroom floor. Camilla was sitting next to her on the sofa, for moral support. No one would bully her with Camilla present, Kate felt, and was grateful to have her there.

PC Mundy looked no more pleased to see Kate than he had the first time they had met.

'You've remembered something and wish to tell me about it, do you, Miss Ivory?'

'She's been attacked and nearly killed in the park!' exclaimed Camilla angrily.

Constable Mundy turned to look at her. 'Then she'd better tell me all about it. Unless, that is, she would prefer to talk to a female officer.'

'You'll do, now you're here,' said Kate.

She told her story, finding that she got more and more upset as she went on, the feelings of helplessness and terror reawakened by her narrative.

'I've jotted down what I remembered of his appearance,' she said at the end. 'Just in case I forgot any of the details.' She handed over the sheet of A4 that Camilla had provided her with earlier.

' "Five foot ten or eleven," ' read out Constable Mundy. ' "Stocky build. Maybe fourteen stone, but all muscle. Hair, black stubble. Studs. Eyes, dark brown. Diet, junk food." How do you know that?'

'His smell,' said Kate. 'He smelled of the oil they use in fast-food places.'

'I'm not sure how useful that will be to us,' said Constable Mundy doubtfully. 'Eating junk food is not yet an arrestable offence.'

Kate tried to smile, but didn't do very well at it. Constable Mundy read through the rest of her notes, then said, 'Why do you think he attacked you? Were you carrying money or credit cards?'

'No, just a five pound note for emergencies in an inside pocket, a Kleenex and my front door key.'

'So the motive wasn't theft?'

'No.'

'And what were you wearing?'

'Leggings and a baggy T-shirt. Not very alluring, if you were thinking that the attack was sexual.'

'So why should a complete stranger – he *was* a complete stranger, was he? – attack you while you were out for your morning run?'

'It's a long story,' said Kate patiently. 'And I'd better start at the beginning – with the flight home from Bordeaux towards the end of August. That was the first time I saw the man in the wig.'

It looked to Kate as though PC Mundy closed his eyes for a moment, then opened them again and concentrated on her face. He had bright blue eyes, but she was afraid they were not shining with either intelligence or interest.

Nevertheless, she told her story.

When it seemed appropriate, she passed across her printout of Jeremy's Jester file. It look PC Mundy a lot longer to read than it had Camilla, but he didn't seem as impressed with it as she had.

'You're telling me that this account came from another

neighbour of yours, a man who died recently in a car accident.'

'Yes.'

'That must have been very upsetting for you.'

'Yes. But I am not so distraught that I am inventing things.'

'But it does seem a very fanciful story. Was Mr Wells a novelist, too, by any chance?'

'No. He was an economist. Very boring. Very dull. Quite lacking in imagination.'

'No need to go over the top,' he said mildly. 'Now, as I understand it, you were attacked while you were out jogging this morning. I can see marks on your neck and what looks like a bruise forming at the side of your mouth. I assume you want to press charges if we find the man responsible.'

'Yes, certainly.'

'In that case, I will take a statement from you. I will report back on the other story you've told me, and if anyone wishes to take it further I am sure they will contact you.'

He was going to lose her account of the international criminal gang somewhere between Camilla's house and the police station, she could hear it in his tone.

'I'll make my statement,' she said. 'But I want to be sure, too, that the rest of the story does get passed on to a senior officer.'

He had taken out a sheet of A4 with an official-looking heading, and a black biro.

'I don't suppose you took the names and addresses of the witnesses you described as coming to your rescue?'

'I'm afraid not. I was too shaken to think about it.'

'Pity,' he said. He started to write. His speed of writing was about equivalent to that of his reading. Kate waited a long time before he reached the end of the page and asked her to read it through, and then to sign it.

'Is that all?' she asked, as he got up to leave.

'For the moment, yes.'

'But what about going back to my house? Do you really think I'll be safe?'

'Perhaps your friend would accompany you if you are still feeling nervous. But I doubt whether your attacker will still be hanging around.'

But someone else might be.

But she recognised defeat and all she said was, 'Goodbye,' and, 'Thank you.'

When he had left, Camilla said doubtfully, 'I suppose I could come back to your place with you. At least you could pick up some clothes and a toothbrush. Then you can come back and stay here for a few days.'

'You really think that no one will be watching?'

'I agree with PC Mundy that your attacker will be long gone by now.'

'Let's hope that no one else has taken his place yet.'

'We could dodge about a bit if you think it's necessary, just to make sure no one follows you.'

'You're right. It sounds ridiculous.'

As they walked round to Agatha Street, Camilla said, 'I don't know that it is so ridiculous,' as though she had been thinking about Kate's words. 'You know the thing that strikes me?'

'What's that?'

'They've killed four people to our knowledge, and they tried to kill you, too.'

'Or at least frighten me very badly.'

'So this must be quite an expensive operation. How much

do you pay for a contract killing these days?'

'I don't know!'

'Several thousand pounds, surely. Five thousand? Ten, maybe? That would be fifty thousand pounds' worth of killing. Twenty-five thousand at the very least, though perhaps they get a special rate for quantity.'

'Camilla! Do you have to think of it so cold-bloodedly?'

'I'm sure your Jester will have done his sums. It seems to me that they must be playing for very high stakes – millions, maybe – in order to take that kind of incidental expense in their stride.'

'So what sort of crime are we talking about?'

'I don't know. But I think that you might well find you have official visitors who are rather senior to our PC Mundy.'

'You think he'll really pass the Jester file on?'

'He could see he was dealing with a sadly deranged woman who wouldn't let it drop until someone had looked into it.'

'Good. I hope I made him feel nervous. He was certainly getting up my nose.'

Camilla was following her own line of thought. 'I can't believe that all this has been happening without someone in a law enforcement agency getting wind of it.'

'I do hope you're right.'

'I bet there are squads of policemen all over Europe, hunting down this gang. And your information is just the final piece of the jigsaw that will enable them to wrap the whole thing up.'

'I don't think life works like that.'

When they'd packed a small bag with enough of Kate's gear to keep her going for a week, they dodged round the back streets of Fridesley, taking short cuts through gardens and narrow, hidden lanes, to get back to Camilla's house.

'You can stay here for a couple of days,' said Camilla seriously when they were inside.

'What about Susanna?'

'Who?'

'My cat.'

'Oh, for goodness' sake! I'll feed her, or Roz can. It's the least of our worries. And then we should find somewhere really safe for you to stay until it's all over.'

'But with men of the calibre of Constable Mundy on the case, that might take years! I don't want to be out of things for that long. And anyway, I have a book to write.'

'You can do that anywhere. You've got a laptop, haven't you?'

'It's getting a little elderly.'

'Never mind. It's only word processing. You don't need anything state of the art for that, do you?'

Kate felt control of her life slipping away from her. 'It wasn't *that* serious an attack on my life, was it?'

'Maybe not. But that makes it all the more likely that next time he will return with his motorbike and a gun, the way he did for the Fosters.'

'You think it was the same man?'

'Don't you?'

'Perhaps.' And then there was the night of the St Giles's Fair. There had been young men in the pub who looked very like the one who had attacked her that morning. But he's a type, she told herself. Beefy build, no neck and a round, shaven head. Black biker gear, chains and studs. He probably kept a Rottweiler at home as a pet, got drunk with his mates on Saturday nights and beat up any passing member of an ethnic minority he happened to meet on his way home.

'You can work at my place,' said Camilla. 'You can sleep in the spare room and have the dining room as an office. If you need any reference books, I'll pick them up for you. Just keep your head down, that's all I ask.'

'And what about Roz, and my other friends?'

'Ring Roz, tell her where you are. The others will just have to wait.'

Kate had to admit that she felt a certain sense of relief that she wouldn't have Emma breathing down her neck for the next few days, though now she thought about it, wasn't she meeting Sam for lunch on Monday?

20

Fabian West had no intention of meeting Tel Carter face to face. He knew that such people existed – indeed he made use of Tel when it was necessary for him to do so – but that didn't mean the man had to come to Clay House and tramp his great booted feet across Fabian's carefully chosen rugs.

On the other hand, he was finding it frustrating speaking to the man on the mobile phone. Tel was not articulate and he had a tendency to shout when he was worked up, which was the case this morning.

'The whole affair sounds remarkably inept,' said Fabian distastefully.

'You what?'

'You bungled it,' said Fabian, then, just to make his meaning clear to the bullet-headed moron, he shouted in his turn: 'You fucked up, Stud.'

'You asked me to make it look like an accident,' said Tel accusingly. 'I'd have done you a professional job if you'd let me.'

'We don't want too many professional jobs occurring in one short suburban street,' explained Fabian patiently. 'People might start to wonder. They might even start to make connections and come up with something approaching the right answer.'

'You what?'

'Leave it for a day or two. We may have scared the woman

233

off. She might stop poking her nose into our business. If she doesn't, Stud, I'll get back to you and next time you have my permission to do a proper, professional job. But not until I give you the word.'

'What about my money?'

'You've had half the fee. You get the rest when the job is completed. You know that's the way we work.'

There was a grunt at the other end of the phone.

'Be patient. There's bound to be more work for you in the near future. But for the moment, leave well alone.'

He rang off and sighed. It was purgatory to have to deal with men like that, but he knew it was necessary. Tel Carter, from Reading, didn't know where Fabian West lived, or what he looked like. They were most unlikely ever to meet one another socially, thought Fabian, smiling. Tel Carter, whom he called Stud for reasons to do with personal decoration rather than sexual prowess (which didn't interest Fabian), couldn't shop him to the police even if he wanted to.

Kate Ivory, on the other hand, was quite a different matter. The woman had appeared from out of nowhere, and now seemed to be wherever she wasn't wanted. The Fosters, or Nosy Parkers as he had called them to his associates, had been taken out because they had seen just a little more than they should have done. They were stupid people, but very, very talkative, and he couldn't let them go gossiping around the place about who and what they had seen in Sancho's house that morning. Their deaths had been brutal and simplistic. But for Kate Ivory he would have to think of something more appropriate.

He rang the bell to call in his manservant.

'I'll eat in half an hour,' he said. 'Do we still have some of the pâté left? Yes? Good. And a green salad. Thank you.'

The pâté was the most delicate shade of pinkish brown and smelled of bay leaves and sun-warmed flesh. To get himself in the mood for its enjoyment, Fabian put on one of Monteverdi's more overtly erotic madrigals and poured himself a glass of chilled, very dry sherry.

21

For the rest of the day Kate did everything that Camilla expected of her. She sat quietly in the dining room, working on her new book. She prepared a light but nutritious meal for them both and even offered to wash up the dishes afterwards. She drank only one small glass of dry white wine and did not become loud or opinionated.

She rang Roz but found her still away from her phone. She went to bed early, accepting a couple of paracetamol from Camilla for the pain in her throat.

But when she woke the next morning she felt restless. She wanted to be away and doing something, not sitting quietly in Camilla's dining room. She couldn't face another day of work; her curiosity refused to stay battened down any longer.

There had been no word from the police station and she was glad that she had printed off the second copy of the Jester file while she had the chance.

In the afternoon, when Camilla had retired to her own office in the Amy Robsart School for Girls (Sunday was the only time she could get any work done, she said), Kate decided to go out herself. It couldn't hurt, could it? There wouldn't be anyone watching Camilla's house, and in any case she would put on her most anonymous clothes. It was a cool day and she could even wear an unflattering fleece hat pulled right down over her forehead. Navy blue was the most unassuming colour she could think of and she found a pair of trousers and top in that colour and put them on. Then she walked out into the Fridesley Road and took a bus into town. No one would look for her among the passengers, she was quite sure, since normally she walked into town.

She left the bus near the council offices and walked up to Carfax and then down the High Street. Oxford on a Sunday was as crowded as ever, and still packed with tourists, in spite of the unwelcoming weather.

She turned off into a narrow cobbled lane and entered Bartlemas College through its elegantly arched lodge. She didn't think Harry Joiner would be praying in the college chapel, somehow, even though Bartlemas was a Christian foundation and this happened to be a Sunday, but she hoped she'd find him at home in the Master's Lodging, preferably on his own. There were a number of questions she would like to put to him and she didn't think he'd want her to do that in public.

She walked through the college, crossing Pesant Quad and passing the Tower of Grace, then pushed open the gate into the delightful garden that was set aside for the use of the Master and his guests. A small, perfect lawn was flanked by a border of perennials which, even so late in the season, were softly colourful. In the springtime the fruit trees would foam with blossom, bluebells would mass around their ankles and song-birds would trill in their branches. Oh, the wonderful privileges of the senior academics! thought Kate enviously, nodding in approval at a lichen-spattered stone cupid who was aiming his arrow at one of the Master's windows.

The Master's Lodging, for such an august establishment as Bartlemas College, was not exactly what one would expect.

Instead of something graceful, dating from the eighteenth century perhaps, this house was a late example of a *cottage ornée*. It had been designed and built in the first quarter of the twentieth century by a Master with an over-developed sense of whimsy, who had perhaps taken the books of J.M. Barrie and Kenneth Grahame too much to heart. Its walls were of stone, its windows mullioned, and its roof was steeply pitched and thatched, with other leaded and mullioned windows peeping out of the thatch, rather like shy woodland mammals. As though to offset this impression, the door was painted black and sported a ferocious brass knocker garnished with bulbous eyes, a leering mouth and pointed teeth. It was probably very old and valuable and was possibly associated with all sorts of interesting stories from past centuries, but it was also uncompromisingly ugly and she could quite understand the impulse which had prompted someone to import it into this relentlessly charming setting. She lifted it and then allowed it to fall with an impressive thud.

Harry Joiner answered the door himself. She didn't know whether this was because the servants were given the afternoon off on Sundays, or whether the college had slimmed down the Master's expense account so that he had to behave like any normal servantless householder.

'What are you doing here?' he asked.

'May I come in?' Kate refused to be insulted by his lack of enthusiasm at seeing her.

'I'd rather you didn't.'

'Then we shall have to conduct our business on the doorstep.' She raised her voice a notch or two. 'Something has been puzzling me. What was it that I delivered from Jeremy Wells to Alec Malden that the pair of you found so interesting that you had to steal it?'

'Come in,' he said, interrupting, and held the door just wide enough for her to enter the house.

The interior, luckily, had avoided the cloying prettiness of the exterior and featured much dark, polished wood, white chrysanthemums in blue and white pottery jugs, and leather furniture.

'Sit down,' said Harry Joiner, indicating one of the leather armchairs. Kate sat, leaning back on a dark-red velvet cushion. 'You're not expecting tea, are you?'

'Just the answers to my questions,' said Kate.

Joiner was not looking as sleek and healthy as he had the last time she had seen him. His high colour had faded, leaving his skin blotchy, and there were lines and shadows about his eyes that she hadn't noticed before. 'What's brought this on?' he asked.

'Four murders,' said Kate.

'Four?'

'Don't pretend you don't understand me. First there were the Fosters, then Jeremy had an unexplained accident in his car, then Alec Malden was drowned. Do you really expect me to believe that they weren't all killed by whoever they – and you – were mixed up with? And I was attacked, too,' she added. 'I'd probably be dead if a gang of Japanese tourists hadn't happened to be passing.'

At this, Joiner leant back suddenly and his face appeared to deflate. He looked old.

'Yes,' she said, pressing home her advantage. 'They've attacked me, so why shouldn't you be next? They must have worked out that you and Alec Malden were working together?'

'No!'

'But you were. It was obvious when I met you first in

Malden's room and again at Jeremy's funeral. And if I saw it, then Sooz Hailey must have noticed it, too. Jeremy sent a computer disk to Alec for safe-keeping. He sent it to Alec Malden because he was the one person in the world he trusted, but Alec knew how to exploit it and you and he set out to make money for yourselves.'

'Even if what you say is true, why are you so sure that I'm involved?'

'When I came to Malden's room, the two of you struck me as very friendly – as friendly as two conspirators. You were in on some joke together that the rest of us had missed.'

Joiner smiled. It was a slight, wintry smile that lifted the corners of his mouth and didn't touch his eyes. 'I can assure you of one thing, Kate. If you are right in thinking that Alec and I were in some kind of conspiracy together – and I'm not admitting that we *were*, mind you – then *I* would have been in charge. It would have been my idea, not Alec's, even if he was the one that Jeremy confided in.' *Arrogant bastard*, thought Kate. 'You don't know what this is about yet, do you?' He sounded more like his old complacent self.

'I'm starting to get a good idea,' said Kate with more confidence than she felt. 'I saw Jeremy Wells on the flight from Bordeaux to Gatwick in August. I noticed him,' she said severely, 'because he was wearing a wig—'

'Stupid man!'

'Yes, perhaps. But he was frightened and people do stupid things when they're afraid.'

Joiner lowered his eyes briefly as though remembering a time when he, too, was scared. 'Well? Is that all?' he said impatiently.

'No. I know that he had met someone – he was too discreet

to give away his name – in a café in Bordeaux, and this man had travelled from Chamalières, bringing a disk with him.'

Joiner was looking wary. Kate allowed a silence to develop between them. Wasn't that how you encouraged people to talk?

'And that's all you know?' asked Joiner softly.

'I know that Jeremy wanted to get out of whatever it was you were all involved with. He was on his way to Worcestershire to see the Jester to talk to him about it.' She was exaggerating her knowledge here, but she thought that Joiner knew little more than she did about what Jeremy was up to.

'And what about Sooz Hailey?' she asked. 'I saw her at Grigg's printing works as well as at the funeral. What has *she* got to do with it all?'

'But without Sooz the whole enterprise would be impossible,' said Joiner. 'Didn't you realise that?'

'I know she was supplying the paper, wasn't she?'

Paper. Anyone could buy paper if they needed it, surely? A trip down to W.H. Smith's and you were well away.

Joiner was laughing at her again.

'And why was she so angry?' Kate continued.

'I think perhaps Alec overplayed his hand,' said Joiner. 'I told him to ask 10K for the disk. We were going to split it fifty-fifty: I wasn't greedy. But Alec was, and he must have asked for more.'

'Perhaps the gang wanted to teach him a lesson. They reckoned the disk was theirs in the first place and they didn't see why they should pay for it at all.' And according to Camilla, 10K would buy you at least one killing, if not two.

'And have you worked out the significance of Chamalières yet?' asked Joiner, moving to take back the initiative.

'Little town in the Auvergne,' said Kate, remembering

what her friend had told her. 'Small park, large centre for watersports—'

'And a printing works,' said Joiner, watching her.

'Like Owen Grigg's.' Why would they need *two* printing works?

'Similar, perhaps. But there's more to it than that.'

At that moment the telephone rang, and Harry Joiner answered it. He spoke briefly and then replaced the receiver.

'I have to leave, and so do you.'

'Was that the leader of the gang?' asked Kate.

'Don't be so melodramatic. It was the tutor for women students. I have to meet her in five minutes and our talk will have nothing at all to do with Chamalières.'

He opened the door for Kate. 'You'll need to undertake a little further research, Kate, if you wish to discover what has been going on under your eyes. But first I'd remember what happened to that other nosy woman, Laura Foster, if I were you.'

'Was it you who phoned the Fosters and imitated, I don't know, Jeremy perhaps? to get them to come out of the house when the killer arrived at their gate?'

'I'm not a member of your so-called "gang", Kate. I've never worked for them, or been paid by them.' It sounded as though he was making a statement to the police, but Kate thought it was probably true, nevertheless.

They left the house together and passed through the gate into Pesant Quad. Joiner said, 'The lodge is in *that* direction,' pointing to his left, and he turned towards a building on his right.

'Goodbye,' he said. 'I don't imagine we'll meet again.'

Kate watched the jaunty figure disappear through the door,

then walked out through the lodge. She returned to Camilla's house in thoughtful mood. What had she learned from Joiner? Not a lot. The Fosters had died because they were nosy and had seen or heard something that worried the gang. She was fairly sure now that Joiner had had nothing to do with their death. Jeremy had tried to free himself from Jester's gang and had been killed, too. Joiner and Malden had attempted to sell the optical disk back to Jester, and Malden had been killed, presumably at the moment when he had expected to be handed a thick envelope full of twenty-pound notes. Why had they left Joiner alone? Either because the death of Malden was enough to frighten him off for good, or because they didn't know of his involvement (which seemed unlikely), or because they were coming for him when he least expected it.

On the other hand, Kate admitted, sitting in the Fridesley bus, perhaps it was because he was too high-profile. There had been too many fatal accidents recently in Oxford, and they wouldn't want to take a chance that the police would ignore yet another. 'Head of Oxford College slain' would be an eye-catching headline, and not just in the local paper. It might attract so much attention that all four deaths – no, it would be *five* by then – would be linked together. It was too risky, and Joiner wouldn't trouble them any more in any case.

She, on the other hand, was obviously of such low-grade importance that the gang believed they could attack and kill her in a public place with impunity. It was not a comforting thought.

22

Next morning at breakfast, Kate said, 'Hasn't the new term started yet?'

'You forget that I am headmistress of a private school,' said Camilla. 'Our terms are shorter—'

'And your fees are higher.'

'Our results are pretty nifty, too,' said Camilla smugly. 'But you're right in a way. Although the term hasn't started yet, I do have to go into school again today. I have meetings with my staff and a load of paperwork to get through. Will you be all right on your own?'

'Don't worry. I'll be sitting in your dining room, beavering away at the novel.' She paused. 'Except for lunch time, when I'm meeting Sam Dolby.'

'Do you have to?' She heard the disapproval in Camilla's voice.

'This is not a romantic assignation. His wife has been begging me to talk to him for her. Why they can't have their own marital conversations I'm not quite sure, but since I have been dragged into it I'll have to see it through.'

'You think that because you're feeling guilty at leaving Sam's brother. It really isn't necessary. You and George were destined to break up at some time. Everyone could see that.'

'Possibly. But I'll still have to meet Sam. Emma's a friend, after all.'

'You'll be safe enough in his company. Can you persuade him to see you home afterwards?'

'He'd be mystified and a little nervous if I asked him to!'

Camilla laughed, which broke the tension. Then the phone rang.

'Hallo. Camilla Rogers speaking.' Camilla was back in headmistress mode. Kate heard the soft murmur of a male voice at the other end of the line.

'Why do you wish to know?' asked Camilla sharply. 'Who is that?' There was a pause and then she said, 'Wait one moment. I'm writing down your name and that of your organisation.'

She handed the phone to Kate, saying, 'It's someone called Jon – that's without an h – Kenrick. He says he works for something called Ensis.' She made it sound as though Kenrick's veracity was doubtful.

'Ensis? Oh, you mean NCIS. Aren't they the ones who want to read our e-mails?'

'Why on earth would they want to do that?' said Camilla.

'To make sure we're not child pornographers. They're very aggressive crime-fighters. Here, give me the phone. I'd better talk to the man. Perhaps they're taking my story seriously at last,' said Kate, taking the receiver from Camilla. 'Hallo, Mr Kenrick. Kate Ivory speaking.'

'Miss Ivory, I've been speaking to an officer in the Thames Valley Police. I believe you handed a document to their Constable Mundy.'

'The Jester file,' agreed Kate.

'And you'd found this on a computer belonging to Jeremy Wells?'

'That's right.' She sensed that she might be in trouble for

being in Jeremy's study, let alone for hacking into his computer. She wanted to say that it was all right, she had the key to his house, and she was sure Jeremy wouldn't mind that she'd guessed his password and hacked into his computer, but perhaps it made her sound too much on the defensive.

'I'd like to come and talk to you about it,' said Kenrick, who had a pleasant voice, rather deep, and a classless, probably educated, accent. He didn't sound at all interested in how she had acquired the file.

'Where was it you said you were from?' asked Kate, knowing perfectly well what he had said to Camilla.

A pause, then, 'I'm with the National Criminal Intelligence Service,' he said.

'Yes?'

'We're interested in stopping major crimes before they're committed, and in picking up the main players in organised crime,' he said. It sounded as though he was quoting from a press release.

'So PC Mundy did take me seriously, after all.'

'I believe he passed your folder on to his superior officer, but without any great enthusiasm. That's why it's taken a couple of days to get to me. But I can assure you that a number of people now are very interested in its contents – and about what happened to you subsequently. Can we talk?'

'Aren't you in London?' she asked.

'At the moment I am. But I could come down to Oxford and we could talk over lunch.'

'You'd better make it a little later. I have someone else to see this lunchtime and I can't get out of it. How about two thirty? Do you want to come here to Camilla Rogers's house or would you rather meet somewhere neutral?'

'Miss Rogers's house sounds very suitable for a private conversation.'

'Yes, she is pretty impressive, isn't she? Two thirty, then,' said Kate, resolving to be at least five minutes late. It was always possible that someone *would* follow her when she left Sam Dolby and she might need protection. The National Criminal Intelligence Service sounded brainy rather than tough, but even if Kenrick were short and puny his presence alone would surely be sufficiently off-putting to anyone who wished to attack her.

And she really did have to talk to Sam. She didn't like to think that the future of his and Emma's marriage might depend on her powers of conciliation, but she had been forced into acting as mediator, so she had better do her best. Then she put all her problems out of her head, at least for the time being, and concentrated on her book.

The restaurant was already crowded and noisy when Kate arrived. She saw Sam sitting over to one side, his back firmly against the wall as though in preparation for an argument.

'Hallo, Sam. I'm so glad you could meet me.' Kate spoke as mildly as she knew how as she took the seat opposite him.

'Yes, well, that's all right,' mumbled Sam. He had ordered a bottle of wine and was well down his first glass. Kate accepted a glass for herself, just to be sociable, but drank it very slowly. Alcohol took the edge off her concentration, and she mustn't forget that she was meeting Kenrick immediately after lunch. She didn't want to breathe alcohol fumes all over him and give him the wrong impression.

'Shall we order?' asked Sam, obviously eager to be getting the lunch over and done with.

'I'd better take a swift glance at the menu,' replied Kate, skimming down the list of dishes. Something light, she decided. Fish. A green salad. Sam ordered, copying her choice as though he had little interest in the food, then buried his head in his wine glass again. He was looking quite smart, for Sam, in sports jacket and grey trousers, his beard and hair recently trimmed.

'The thing is, Sam,' said Kate, keeping all hint of blame out of her voice, 'Emma thinks you must have grown tired of her now that she's pregnant yet again. She sees herself as large and unattractive and she believes you've found some young and slender woman – one of your students, most likely – and are having a torrid affair with her.'

Sam swallowed too much wine and choked into his napkin.

'Me?' he said eventually. 'That's ridiculous!'

'That's what I told her,' said Kate sweetly, 'but she wouldn't listen to me. She's convinced you've got another woman on the side – one with whom you play exciting sexual games.'

Sam stared at her with the expression of a man who has never before heard the words 'exciting', 'sexual' and 'games' put together in a single phrase.

'No,' said Kate, watching his face. 'I knew that couldn't be the answer.'

They were interrupted by a white-aproned waiter who placed plates of fish and bowls of salad on their table, registered their choice of dressings, provided them with what they asked for and then disappeared again. The service here was brisk, observed Kate, presumably because they shifted a large number of customers every lunchtime.

'I've never . . .' Sam was saying, embarrassed.

'Don't worry, Sam. I know you've never,' soothed Kate. It

was quite obvious to an objective observer that Sam and Emma never looked outside their marriage for alternative partners. 'Only I do have to go back to Emma and give her some kind of explanation. And she is an intelligent woman, even when pregnant, so we'd better make it credible. You see, our second thought is that you're into something criminal.'

'You're saying that Emma thinks I'm a criminal?'

'If I'm strictly honest, I'm the one who believes you've got yourself involved in something illegal. Emma's sticking with the love-rat theory for the time being.'

Sam groaned. Kate had never heard a man groan before and it was a sad sound. 'Where is all this coming from?' he asked. Kate felt he was about to ask, 'What have I done to deserve it?' but he managed to avoid it.

'Well, as with so much else,' she said, 'it started with my return flight from Bordeaux to Gatwick. First there was the man in the wig, then there was you, obviously trying to avoid me, looking embarrassed, and dropping clanking bags on the ground.'

'I wasn't wearing a wig!'

'Forget that bit. It's part of a different story. At least, I think it is. Have you heard of Chamalières?'

'Who's he?'

'Not who, but where,' explained Kate cryptically. 'And if you haven't heard of it you can't really help me with the other half of the story. No, what was worrying Emma and me was where you were getting the money from.'

'What money?'

'The money to buy the minibus.'

'It's not quite that big. And it's secondhand,' said Sam sheepishly. 'And a friend is doing me a favour on the price.'

'I told Emma that was the most likely explanation. It's good to hear it confirmed, though. Well, we're really getting this sorted out, aren't we, Sam?'

Sam looked as though he might allow himself to relax a little. He finished his second glass of wine while Kate still sipped at her first. Then he poured himself a third glass. He pointed the bottle in Kate's direction but she indicated that she didn't need any more. They chewed fish and healthy green salad leaves in companionable silence. Kate let a few minutes pass. Sam had laid his knife and fork neatly together on his plate when she asked: 'And the other little thing that Emma was wondering about was how and why you acquired the purple vibrator.'

Sam, having concluded for a while there that he was off the hook, looked stricken again. 'Vibrator?' he asked.

'Purple plastic, battery-driven, AA batteries extra,' said Kate, using her imagination.

'What's a— '

'No, Sam. Not even you can pretend not to know what I'm talking about.'

The waiter had joined them again, scooping up empty plates and dishes, handing back the menus, asking whether they would like desserts. Kate was tempted to order a blackcurrant sorbet just to tease Sam, but in the end opted for a simple coffee. Sam ordered the same as though incapable of making an independent decision.

'I should finish the wine, if you'd like to,' said Kate kindly. 'I shan't be drinking any more.'

Sam did as she suggested.

'It is true that we're a bit strapped for cash,' he said when the waiter had served their coffee.

'And?'

'And I found a way of supplementing my income. It's simple. It doesn't take up too much of my time. And it is legal.'

'But you're not going to tell me any more about it?'

Sam had drained the wine and now hoovered up his coffee while Kate was still waiting for hers to cool.

'Just because it's legal doesn't mean I want everyone to know about it. And now I really do have to get back to the office,' he said. 'Waiter!'

'It's my shout,' Kate reminded him. 'I invited you, remember?'

'Can't we go Dutch?'

'No,' said Kate, knowing how modest the bill would be, even including Sam's bottle of wine.

'Kate, you will reassure Emma that everything's all right, won't you?'

'I'll do my best.'

'She knows I'd never look at another woman.'

'Emma might believe that, but I'm afraid I wouldn't believe it of any man,' said Kate. 'I'd accept that you at any rate wouldn't get any further than looking, though.'

'I really do have to leave,' said Sam, not looking as grateful for this testimonial as Kate had expected him to.

'You get back to the office. I'll ring Emma when I get home.' Even to Sam she wasn't giving away that she was staying at Camilla's for the time being, she noticed.

She made her way back to Fridesley by taking the most crowded route, slipping in and out of shops to throw off anyone who might be following her. She felt slightly ridiculous to be doing this, but the fact that some élite London law enforcement agency was taking an interest in what had happened to her made her take it more seriously herself. Constable Mundy had made her think she was imagining the whole thing.

It was two twenty when she arrived at Camilla's house. She had ten minutes before Jon Kenrick was due to arrive, so she phoned Emma, as she had promised Sam.

'Well?' asked Emma. 'What did he say?'

'He said he had taken on some extra work to supplement his income, and that this work wasn't illegal. He said he wasn't having an affair, or even looking at another woman. I think you should trust him, Emma, and stop worrying.'

'And you believed everything he said?'

'Yes.' Sam had always had that effect on her. She didn't think he had the sort of mind that would know how to be devious. 'And you know I'm not easily taken in,' she added.

'You are rather cynical,' said Emma, which wasn't what Kate was meaning at all. 'And what about the . . .' Emma paused delicately.

'He didn't actually explain its presence in his sports bag,' conceded Kate. 'But I think he was just as horrified that it had found its way there as you were. Perhaps a friend borrowed his sports bag to go to the gym, and just happened to leave it behind by mistake.'

'That does not sound like a convincing story.'

No, thought Kate, but it was the best I could come up with on the spur of the moment.

'I think you should give him the benefit of the doubt,' said Kate. 'And I really have to go now, Emma. I'm expecting someone to call to see me in a couple of minutes.'

23

'We need your help,' said Jon Kenrick.

As an opener it had a certain appeal, Kate conceded.

They were in the sitting room, drinking coffee. Jon Kenrick was tall, broad-shouldered, dark-haired, blue-eyed and fit-looking. He might have been handsome if someone hadn't broken his nose at some time in the past. He was barely into his forties, Kate reckoned, and looked as though he had spent some years in the police force, or some equally disciplined employment, before joining NCIS.

'Of course, I would like to co-operate with the police, and with you,' said Kate.

'I sense a "but" coming here,' said Kenrick.

'But I need to know what's happening. What is it I've fallen into? I've read Jeremy's file and it tells me some things, but *I don't understand what's going on.*'

'But surely you understood about the disk they persuaded Blue into copying for them at Chamalières?'

'That's the part where you all lose me. I looked it up. It's a pleasant French town, somewhere in the Auvergne, and it's hoping to attract more tourism. Harry Joiner said it contained a printing works, but I still don't see the relevance of that. We have printing works here in England, surely.'

'Who's Harry Joiner?' Kenrick spoke sharply.

'He's the Master of Bartlemas College.'

'An academic?'

'Not your typical academic, more a retired captain of industry. I think he realised what Jeremy was mixed up in and wanted a smallish slice of the money. Perhaps he's bored with college life and needs some excitement. Certainly he was in Alec Malden's room when I delivered the disk.'

Kenrick looked a question.

'Jeremy said it was the outline and sample chapters for his book, and at the time I believed him. He sent me to Alec Malden, also at Bartlemas College. He thought he could trust him, and that Malden was his friend, but I believe Malden and Joiner went straight to Jester or some other member of the gang, and tried to sell the disk themselves.'

'How would they know who to approach?'

'I wondered about that. At first I thought Jeremy must have told them himself – after all, he was in confessional mood during those last few days. But now I wonder whether Joiner didn't already have wind of what was going on.' *And I wish I did.* 'He and Malden were in the same field as Jeremy, so they would have known more about it than I do, certainly. Now, I think you should explain.'

Kenrick leant forward a little in his chair, like an enthusiastic schoolteacher. 'The printing works at Chamalières is one of eleven national centres where the new European bank notes will be produced,' he said, as though this explained everything. He must have noticed Kate's blank look, for he carried on, speaking carefully, as though to someone very ignorant.

'By January 2002, it is hoped that some thirteen billion bank notes will have been printed in readiness for the launch of the Euro. They started printing last year, and they're still working flat out to have them all finished in time.'

'That's a lot of banknotes,' said Kate, trying to look intelligent.

'But still very probably not nearly enough. And there have been difficulties in producing even this number. Workers have been objecting to the compulsory overtime they have had to undertake. Just think about it: eleven countries simultaneously getting rid of their old currency and replacing it with the Euro. Shops, banks, businesses – they're all going to need the new notes.'

'You think that Jester and his gang are going to help fill the shortfall,' said Kate, guessing at last where this exposition was leading.

'Yes. As I'm sure Jester knows, the best time to flood the market with forged notes is when new notes are being introduced. Of course the ECB – that's the European Central Bank – has incorporated all the latest security features into the new notes, but two factors will work in Jester's favour and make it difficult for us: the shortage of notes, and their unfamiliarity. If the paper isn't quite crisp enough, the embossing not quite right, people won't pick it up straight away because they haven't had time to get used to the real thing. Just think about it: you've been prepared by publicity, by photographs of coins and notes, but this is the first time you've actually seen and handled them. You go on your first shopping trip of the New Year and it's as though you've arrived in a foreign country.'

'You have to read your money before you can pay for your purchases,' said Kate, remembering her recent trip to France.

'Right. And a few million of them will be good fakes. So we need to get our hands on Jester and his gang *and* the banknotes before the launch date,' said Kenrick.

'Did you say embossing?' asked Kate thoughtfully.

'Yes?'

'The Heidelberg press.' The lovable thing from outer space with arms and legs and other protuberances.

'Where did you see a Heidelberg press?'

'At Owen Grigg's printing works. He said it was used for embossing the covers of paperback books. Is it important?'

'There are more modern machines for that particular job. And yes, it could be very important.'

'I bet the modern machines aren't as pretty as the Heidelberg press. Have you ever seen one?'

'Yes,' said Kenrick repressively.

'So you think Owen Grigg is one of the gang? I was sure there was something smarmy about him. And Sooz Hailey.'

'You've met her?'

'A couple of times. But she's only a paper rep.'

'But she's a rep for a company that sells specialist papers for printing bank notes.'

Kate let this sink in. 'Would this company sell them to Grigg? Aren't they old-fashioned and completely trustworthy?'

'I believe she's a very persuasive young lady. And perhaps Grigg thought up a valid excuse for ordering the paper. Or Hailey somehow diverted part of a legitimate order. We'll have to find out how it was done. But don't worry, we will. We have people working on every aspect of Jester's operation.'

Kate had a vision of hundreds of police officers hunched over computer screens, following the trail left by Jeremy Wells, Owen Grigg, Sooz Hailey, Alec Malden and the rest of the people she had written into her diagram. What an amateur she was at this game!

'And you've definitely got Owen Grigg down for one of the gang?' she said.

'Ah, yes, we do know about him,' said Kenrick guardedly. 'We'd come across him before. Red Pale. Whatever that may mean.'

'It's the sign that William Caxton hung outside the very first English printing works,' said Kate helpfully. There were times when being a writer with a rag-bag mind came in useful.

'You do realise that all I'm telling you is strictly confidential, don't you?'

'I wasn't planning on chatting about it in Mrs Clack's shop.'

'Good,' said Kenrick as though he understood the significance of her remark.

'There must be quite a few of them in this gang,' said Kate thoughtfully. 'Which means that there's a lot of money at stake.'

'As I said, they're dealing in millions.'

'And you're in charge of the operation to catch them?'

'There are three different agencies involved. As well as ourselves, there's Thames Valley, and the City of London Police.'

'Why do the police need you as well?'

'We collect information and make sure it gets to the people who can make best use of it.'

'And what put you on to Jester?'

'The usual. It was a tip-off.'

'By Jeremy Wells?'

'I don't know. We've been working on this one for months, so I doubt whether his was the first tip-off we received. But he could have given us a call, too, more recently. In fact, after reading his Jester file, I think it's more than likely.'

'Do you think they found out? Is that why they killed him?'

'We're sure they don't know we're on to them. They're an

arrogant crowd and they've been getting a little careless recently.'

Kate noticed that he didn't contradict her when she mentioned that Jeremy had been killed.

'What do they do with the forged money once they've printed it? How do you get rid of that many notes?' Visions of white packages stacked on pallets in Grigg's printing works came back to her.

'They have someone in charge of distribution. They call him, rather unimaginatively I thought, "Feet". He's a petty criminal himself, with a prison record, and many connections to criminals, petty and otherwise, throughout Europe.'

'But why should people take forged currency from him?'

'Because he sells it at a fraction of its face value.'

'And the disk – the one I took to Alec Malden? Did that contain the designs for the notes? Owen Grigg told us that the plates were etched using computer disks.'

'Of course. Disque Bleu works for the ECB, on the new currency project. He's involved in producing the Euro at Chamalières and elsewhere, so has access to the optical disk containing art work to produce the blocks.'

'They must have a platemaker on their payroll,' mused Kate.

'There are up to seventeen plates used for the colour separation for work of this standard. And yes, we do know who their expert platemaker is.'

At this point Kenrick looked as though he had had enough of Kate's questions, so she put in quickly: 'And I want to know who Jester is. And who killed the Fosters.'

Kenrick might have answered, or not, but at that moment there was a ring at the front door. Kate sat rigidly in her chair. Kenrick gestured to her to stay there, and moved to the hallway.

A few seconds later, Kate heard the door open and a woman's voice say, 'This is Camilla Rogers's house, isn't it? Who on earth are you?'

Kate rose from the chair and went out to join Kenrick.

'Hallo, Roz,' she said. 'Don't worry, it's my mother,' she said to Kenrick. Now that she could see him in action she noted that he did in fact look tough as well as intelligent.

Roz followed them into the sitting room. And then Kate noticed that her mother wasn't alone. She had brought a man with her.

'I'm not interrupting anything, am I?' said Roz, seeing the coffee cups on the table.

'We were talking,' said Kate, hoping that her mother would get the message and leave again as soon as possible. She didn't want to have to explain in front of Roz's companion what was going on.

'And aren't you going to introduce me to your friend?' Roz spoke sarcastically. She could be infuriating at times, as Kate well knew.

'This is Ion Kenrick,' she said, and then looked pointedly at the man who had followed Roz into the room.

'Barry Frazer,' said Roz. 'Meet my daughter, Kate.'

Barry Frazer was younger than her mother by at least eight years, Kate reckoned. Of course, Roz was in very good nick and didn't really look her age, but there was still an obvious difference between them.

'If you're thinking how shocking it is that Barry's younger than me, you're being very old-fashioned, Kate.'

So Roz had embroiled herself in a new relationship. But it wasn't just his age she didn't like, Kate thought. His tan was a little too smooth, his hair a shade too fair, his gaze just a little too shifty. Or was she being unfair – or jealous?

'Where did you meet?' she asked.

'Now, would you allow *me* to question *you* like that about a new friend of yours?' And Roz sat down, making herself entirely at home in Camilla's sitting room. Barry followed her example. 'Aren't you going to offer us some coffee, too?'

'I have to get back to London soon,' said Kenrick.

'Don't take any notice of us, you just finish your talk with Kate,' said Roz.

At this point, Barry spoke for the first time. His eyes were cornflower blue, exactly matching the colour of his shirt. He had a soft voice with an estuary accent. 'I do believe Mr Kenrick is a law enforcement officer, Roz. Perhaps his business with Kate is private. Or confidential, maybe.'

'Not another policeman!' exclaimed Roz. 'But that would explain why you want us out of here, certainly,' she said to Kate.

'Come on, Roz,' said Barry. 'We should be going. We'll visit with your lovely daughter another time. Nice meeting you, Kate. Goodbye, Kenrick.'

He shook hands with them both. Manicured hands, too, Kate noticed. He was even wearing clear nail varnish. She followed them out to the door. Roz paused at the front door.

'You have worked out by now what Sam Dolby's doing, haven't you?' she said.

'No. What?'

'We'll talk about it next time we meet,' said Roz, and kissed her daughter's cheek.

Kate watched them leave. Barry was driving a large car, she saw. She didn't recognise the make, but she could see that it was very new, very shiny, very expensive. *Only drug dealers drive cars like that.* She really did hope she was wrong.

'I'm sorry about that,' she said when she returned to the sitting room. 'It seemed easier to let them assume you were in the police if it was going to get rid of them. I'm afraid my mother can be quite impossible at times.'

'Probably just a phase,' he said. 'Do you know anything about Barry Frazer?'

'No. That's the first I've seen of him. She did mention that there was a new man in her life, but she didn't even tell me his name before today. Why? Do you know him?'

'I'm not sure. Probably not under that name. But if he's who I think he is, I suggest you try to persuade your mother to drop him.'

'She won't listen to a word I say.'

'Well, I could be mistaken about him.'

But Kate had been unable to comprehend what her mother could see in the man and she was quite prepared to believe he was a criminal. She pushed the thought out of her head. She had to concentrate on what Kenrick was telling her. And she had to keep alert, too, because the man hadn't come all this way to see her without wanting something from her in return.

'Let's get back to Jester,' she said. 'And do you know who killed the Fosters?'

'After reading your Jester file we at least know *why* they were killed,' he said. 'It was a contract killing, of course, and professionally done. Nobody saw anything that could connect the killing to a particular person; it was too quick. He arrived, fired the shots and was away. The whole thing took seconds, not even minutes.'

'But he must have killed Jeremy and Alec Malden, as well.'

'He might have done. Or Jester could have used three different people for the three separate occasions. But on the whole we think the murders were committed by a man from Reading. He's someone we know, though we haven't got the evidence to accuse him of murder. Not yet. He uses a motorbike and he fits the description of the man who attacked you at the weekend as well, by the way.'

Kate put her hand to her throat. The bruising had still been there when she looked in the bathroom mirror that morning and it wouldn't fade for several days yet.

Kenrick went on. 'The problem is going to be making the connections between the different members of the gang in terms of evidence that will stand up at their trial.'

'There is something,' said Kate slowly. 'It's in my study. Sitting in my in-tray.'

'Yes?'

'Jeremy and Grigg wrote notes on the same scrap paper. It was a pale-green flyer for a correspondence college.'

'That doesn't mean anything. Thousands of them might have been distributed.'

'No, they weren't. That's the point. Grigg happened to mention it: the flyer was never used. It was a sample that the client failed to approve. The college chose a different design. The green ones with the hideous logo didn't leave the printing works. So Jeremy must have been there, or else Grigg must have visited Jeremy.'

'Perhaps we should go straight round to your own house now,' said Kenrick. 'And then I can explain what it is we want from you while we're on our way.'

'I wondered when you were going to get to that.'

Kate took their coffee cups out to the kitchen, then she

picked up her jacket and they set off on the short walk to Agatha Street.

'You see, I think that Carter will have another attempt at killing you,' said Kenrick calmly.

Kate tried not to show the alarm she felt at his words. 'Who is Carter?'

'The man I was telling you about. Terence Carter, known as Tel, lives in Reading and is available for hire for killing people. It'll cost you a few grand, of course. But if a man like Jester finds that someone's in his way, he calls up Tel Carter.'

'I'm in the way?'

'You've been a lot nosier than the Fosters, from what I can make out. And look how ruthlessly he dealt with them.'

'You didn't answer when I asked you if you knew who Jester was.'

'We know some things about him. We believe he's an unusually large man. Fat, if you like. And tall. We don't know his real name, though. And we certainly have nothing on him that would stand up in court. He's been too careful to stay clear of the other members of the gang. If they've ever met face to face we don't know about it. He's been bankrolling the project, of course, and it must have taken a very large investment to do that. Jester is a man of wealth and position. Even if we knew his identity the police couldn't just drag him into the station on a whim.'

'I hope they couldn't do that to anyone!' said Kate tartly. Kenrick smiled slightly at her vehemence.

After a moment's silence she said, 'I think he lives in Worcestershire. I believe Jeremy was on his way to see him when he died.'

'How do you know that?'

'Just a hunch.' When she knew Kenrick a little better she would tell him about collecting Jeremy's belongings from the Deyton hospital, and finding the scrap of bloodstained paper. Not yet, though.

They had reached the corner of Agatha Street. As they approached number 10, Kate again became aware that hers was the odd one out. Number 8 was empty now, and so was number 12. Her house was still occupied, but for how long? Three people dead. What was in store for her? She had to stop herself from crouching with her arms protecting her head as they reached her gate.

'I was hoping you'd let Tel attack you again,' said Jon Kenrick in a matter-of-fact voice.

And then all three houses would be empty.

'Why on earth should I do that?' She had her door key out ready to open the door, but now she paused and stared at him.

'Let's go and look at these flyers of yours, shall we? We can discuss my plan afterwards.'

So she turned the key and they walked into the house. It had the stillness that comes from lying empty for a while. She didn't feel like going in: perhaps she was frightened of what she might find. *Superstitious nonsense*, she told herself. She bent over and picked up the post to put the moment off. There was nothing interesting; it was mostly junk mail. Time to move on.

'Down here,' she said, leading the way down the stairs to her study.

She crossed the room and picked up the in-tray. And there they were, just as she had said, two green flyers, each with its handwritten note.

'We'll have to check with the correspondence college,' said

Kenrick. 'It shouldn't be difficult. We have their address here. But if what you say is correct, this could be important.'

'Good. But why do I have to go through a second attack by your Tel Carter then?'

'Because we haven't tied him in with the others. And we've never managed to get him for the murders we're sure he's committed. You'd like to put the Fosters' murderer in prison, wouldn't you? And Mr Wells's?'

'Yes. But that's *your* job, not mine.'

'And you could assist us. There's nothing to be frightened of. You wouldn't be in any danger. We'd be here. You'd be quite safe. We'd bring in the heavy mob to protect you.'

Kate recognised that this was meant to be humorous. She didn't feel like laughing.

'We'd find a woman officer who looked something like you. Give her a blonde wig. Dress her in your clothes.'

'Is it really necessary?' She didn't like the idea of a strange woman dressing up as her. It gave her an odd feeling, as though her life might split in two at this point and she would never be able to get back into her own half again.

'Yes, I think it is necessary.'

'Oh, very well.' She couldn't get out of it, not if she wanted to live at peace with herself.

She was rewarded by one of Jon Kenrick's beautiful smiles.

'What do you want me to do?' she asked.

'If you show me the way to the kitchen, I'll make us both a cup of tea,' said Kenrick.

I bet they send them on training courses to teach them how to win over susceptible women, thought Kate. But she showed him the way to the tea bags anyway.

Before he left, Kenrick gave her his mobile phone number,

just in case she remembered any other vital detail. Some time during the evening her conscience got the better of her and she rang him to tell him about the scrap of paper she had found in Jeremy's 'effects'.

Kenrick didn't take her to task for keeping it to herself, but made her read out the fragments of words carefully while he wrote them down.

'Is it useful, do you think?' she asked.

'Could be.'

24

It was quite simple, thought Kate, to put yourself firmly in the firing line. There was nothing to it!

After all that had happened, here she was, on a sunny Wednesday morning, walking openly through Oxford. Her head was bare, her bright blonde hair in full view. She had refused to wear her lightest or brightest clothing for Kenrick, however.

'You might just as well paint a target on my back,' she had said when he picked out a white jacket from her wardrobe.

'The chest is a more likely area to aim for,' he said seriously.

Thank you, Jon Kenrick.

'Just walk down St Aldate's,' he had said. 'Then go into the police station.'

'Do you want me to run a zig-zag course, crouching as I go?'

'We really don't believe that anyone will attack you in broad daylight in the centre of Oxford. It would be too difficult for them to escape afterwards, so close to the police station and through the heavy traffic.' He had realised that it was her nerves talking, of course.

'What do you want me to say when I go into the police station? Will they be expecting me? Do they know what I'm doing?'

'It's better if as few people as possible know that.'

'Well?'

'Tell them anything. Tell them your car's been stolen.'

'But it's sitting outside my house.'

'Drive it round to Miss Rogers's house, park it in her driveway, and *then* report it stolen.'

She had wanted to ask why she couldn't just say she was with Jon Kenrick, and please could they pour her a stiff drink to calm her nerves, but perhaps Kenrick wasn't known to the sergeant on the desk at St Aldate's. Was he even who he said he was? Had she asked to see any identification when he first appeared on Camilla's doorstep? She didn't think so.

'And are you so sure that I'll be followed?'

'I told you. This is a big operation. I expect someone's been looking out for you since Sunday.'

And so she had to believe him, and do what he said, although she felt horribly vulnerable as she walked down that long, wide street. There could be snipers on every roof. One of them could be aiming at the centre of her back at this very moment. Or would it be her head? Kenrick had thought that the chest was most likely, though, and he was a reliable man, she was sure. The sort of man you felt could take your life over and reorder it for you so that it worked better, and more smoothly. Not that she needed someone like that in her life. For a moment she thought of George. It would be nice to have him at her side at this very minute, she had to admit.

And then she had arrived at the police station, and had walked in through the doors, and felt safe at last.

When she came out again a while later, having reported her car as stolen, she was vaguely aware that she wasn't alone. She just hoped that it was Kenrick's people who were following her home, protecting her, as well as the Jester's.

The phone rang just after she entered her house. She rushed

to answer it and felt a sense of anti-climax when it turned out to be Estelle.

'I'll ring you back,' she said. 'I'm a bit busy at the moment.'

Of course, this wasn't strictly true. Everything had been organised without her help. She was just the decoy, the bait, the stalking horse, whatever passive object you wanted to call her.

And was Estelle's phone call as innocent as she assumed? If she had let Estelle speak, would she have suggested that Kate walk to her gate in precisely thirty seconds' time, just as a man on a motorbike, with murder in his mind, drove past? She told herself briskly that if indeed Estelle had become so embroiled with Owen Grigg that she wanted to lure Kate to her death, she would ring back again very shortly.

The phone refused to ring.

Kate had nothing much to do. There were men from an armed unit inside her house, hidden in her back garden and presumably hiding, too, in cars or vans up and down Agatha Street. Kenrick and the police officer who was to take Kate's place were in her sitting room, drinking endless cups of tea, speaking to colleagues on their radios, irritating the hell out of Kate.

Nothing was going to happen. She knew it. She was off the hook. Well, no. She couldn't really believe that. Once he realised that his plan hadn't worked Kenrick would just smile and look at her appealingly and ask her to go through the whole rigmarole again. Just one more time. She could hear him already. He would suggest that she could walk back to the police station tomorrow and tell them that her car had reappeared.

The minutes, and then the hours, dragged on. She thought about getting on with some work, but couldn't settle down to anything useful. She wished the whole dark-blue crowd of them would *go* and just leave her alone.

And then, as the brightness was leaving the sky, the phone rang a second time.

'Hallo?' Kate answered, with Kenrick listening on the extension that one of his colleagues had installed that morning.

'It's Camilla here. Can you come round to my place straight away?'

She might have been taken in if she hadn't been expecting something similar. 'Not Camilla,' she mouthed silently at Kenrick.

'What's up?' she asked. It was presumably all right to sound startled.

'I can't explain now. Just come!'

The caller broke the connection.

'Are you sure that wasn't your friend?' asked Kenrick urgently.

'She didn't say very much, but I really think it wasn't Camilla. It was a good imitation, but it's not easy to sound like a headmistress unless you've had a lot of practice.'

'Right,' said Kenrick. 'Is everyone ready?'

'What happens now?' asked Kate, though they had already been through the routine several times.

'Get down to your study and stay there,' said Kenrick crisply. 'I don't want to explain to that mother of yours that you've been injured and that I'm to blame.'

A policewoman in a blonde wig and the jacket that Kate had worn that morning was stepping forward. Kate knew that she was wearing body armour, but even so, this was dangerous.

'Go,' said Kenrick. 'Don't come out until I give you permission.'

And so Kate went down to her study.

It was just like the day when the Fosters died. In her study it was completely silent. It was almost as if she could hear a couple of dozen police men and women holding their breath. But this time, unlike the day when the Fosters died, since she wasn't wearing ear plugs or her headphones, she heard the rattle of the automatic weapon.

That could have been me.

She just hoped that the policewoman was unharmed.

Kenrick came to fetch her about ten minutes later. 'We've got him,' he said.

'What about Kelly?' She remembered the officer's name.

'She's fine. One of the Thames Valley men spoiled Carter's aim. Kelly's a bit bruised, but nothing serious.'

'Do you know who was impersonating Camilla?' Kate found herself incensed at the idea that one of her friends had been used in this way.

'No. But Jester could buy a fortyish actress to do the job for fifty quid, don't you think? I imagine he pulled the same trick to get the Fosters out of their house, too.'

He was looking towards the door, as though wishing to be away.

'What happens now?' asked Kate.

'It's already started. We're picking up the other members of the gang.'

'And Jester? Could you trace his address from the words on the torn paper?'

'We worked it out eventually.'

'I should have given it to you earlier, shouldn't I?'

Kenrick didn't reply.

25

'What do you mean, you were hoping this man would attack you?'

Roz sounded more like someone's mother than she usually did. 'Why on earth did you let them persuade you to do such a thing!'

'Really, they told me I was in no danger.'

'And you were foolish enough to believe them?'

'I'm all right, aren't I? And they've rounded up the gang and arrested them.'

'I'm sure they could have done that without your help.'

'Apparently they couldn't. They told me my help was invaluable.'

Roz was at Kate's house, prowling round the sitting room, setting Kate's nerves on edge.

'Why don't you pour yourself a whisky?' she suggested.

'Will you have one too?'

'Yes,' she said, more to keep her mother company than because she really wanted a drink.

Roz came back from the kitchen with two very large whiskies.

'And now you're going to tell me about Sam Dolby,' said Kate, more to keep her mother off the subject of Tel Carter and Jester's forgery operation than because she really wanted to know the answer. In truth, the Dolbys had faded from her mind during the past couple of days. Her head was too full of the excitement and terror of trapping the Fosters' killer.

'It's obvious,' said Roz, sitting on the edge of her chair as though poised for flight at any moment.

'Go on,' said Kate resignedly.

'There are countries, believe it or not – Catholic, or Puritan, or formerly Communist – where goods like contraceptives, or aids to interesting sex—'

'Viagra?' suggested Kate.

'Quite probably.'

'And purple—'

'Yes. Those, too, are forbidden. And since it is impossible to stamp out profit and the march of capitalism, there is a lucrative trade in their surreptitious import into these countries.'

'What was Sam's part in this? I can't imagine him as the brains behind any such scheme.'

'He was just a courier, I imagine. You can't ring up one of the standard companies and ask them to transport cartons of multi-coloured, textured condoms, or boxes of penis rings, to the airport, can you?'

'So there's a small factory somewhere in Oxford, turning these things out—'

'Just a warehouse, I should think. Or a garage, even. The foreign buyers e-mail an order, Sam picks it up and drives it to the airport, disguised as hand luggage. Each consignment would be quite small, you see. And Sam passes it on to the person who's going to smuggle it abroad.'

'Why doesn't the smuggler pick it up themselves?'

'Gatwick's a long way away. Perhaps the smuggler is a simple peasant who doesn't drive a car.'

'Are you sure about all this? Sam wouldn't be paid much money, surely?'

'Fifty quid a trip, plus petrol? It would soon mount up.'

'You're making it up.'

'Would I mislead you like that?'

'Quite probably.'

'Well, you think of a better explanation of his behaviour, then.'

Kate was silent for a couple of minutes while she considered the problem.

'I can't think why he didn't talk to Emma about it,' said Roz.

'I don't think she would have approved. She has a puritanical streak in her, that woman. I think she really believes that sex is just for procreation.'

'Silly girl.'

'I wonder what the things were that clanked when he dropped them,' said Kate.

'Perhaps you should suggest to your friend Emma that she and Sam explore their possibilities together.'

It was inevitable that Estelle would ring her the next day.

'I'm sorry I didn't ring you back,' said Kate.

'That doesn't matter now. Did you see the news last night?'

'Yes.'

'They raided Owen's printing works. What on earth is it all about? Do you know what's happened to Owen?'

'I know he's been arrested.'

'It said on the news that several different locations had been raided by the police, twenty or more arrests had been made and thousands of pieces of paper had been removed for forensic examination. Tell me what you know, Kate.'

Kate had been warned by Kenrick not to speak to people about what she knew, so she prevaricated.

'Could they have been printing pornography, do you think?' she said.

'That's not illegal, is it?'

'Some of it is.'

'You never really trusted him, did you?'

'There was something strangely unlikeable about him, certainly, as far as I was concerned.'

'I shall have to listen to your opinion next time I meet someone lovely,' said Estelle.

'What an excellent idea.' *And you might listen to my opinion on literary matters, too*. But even Kate wouldn't dare to say that to Estelle Livingstone.

George rang, sounding concerned. It was good to hear him and to know that he still cared about her wellbeing. But this time Kate wasn't tempted to invite him back into her life.

As she listened to his familiar voice she knew that he was just a friend, no longer a lover.

Emma was the next to phone.

'I think things are going to be all right with Sam,' she told Kate. It was just as well that Emma hadn't bothered to watch the news and had no idea of the danger that Kate had been put into.

'I'm glad to hear it,' she said.

'He promised me he'd never looked at another woman.'

'So you managed to have a proper conversation.'

'We did. Though it was on the short side because Tris is running a temperature and I had to change his pyjamas because they were simply soaked with perspiration, and then I had to find clean sheets and change his bed, but I think Sam and I understand one another.'

'That's the most important thing, isn't it?' said Kate, deciding it would be inadvisable to ask the current whereabouts of the purple object that had caused all the trouble. And anyway, Jon Kenrick had taken a note of her address and phone number, so with any luck she wouldn't need to ask to borrow it in the future.

26

The day after Owen Grigg started to co-operate with the police, Kenrick and a large number of police arrived at Clay House, Lower Grooms. They found it empty. Even the manservant had left. The garages were empty. Both cars had gone.

The house was tidy – quite unusually so. There were no drawers with their contents spilled on the carpet, no splashes of water from a hasty shower in the bathroom, no unwashed cup or glass in the kitchen. One wardrobe was filled with suits in all shades of grey, the other contained tweed garments suitable for a country gentleman. They were cut to fit a very broad man, and a tall one. There were shelves of percale shirts in delicate tones of dove and lavender, others of tattersall check. There was a drawer of matched and paired black silk socks, another of woollen ones in heathery shades. There were linen handkerchiefs and freshly ironed underclothes. Everything had been either recently laundered or else was hanging in plastic covers as though just returned from the dry cleaners.

All the furniture was solid, and dated from the early nine-teenth century. Curtains were of velvet or silk, sofas covered in leather. There were a couple of pleasant watercolour landscapes on one bedroom wall, but otherwise it looked as though all the pictures in the house had been removed. Mr West had left no cuff links or other jewellery. There was a computer in his study, but the hard disk had been wiped. There were no floppy disks at all. No notebooks, no diaries.

They searched the house thoroughly but found no evidence that would link Fabian West to the rest of the counterfeiting gang. In fact, there was nothing at all of a personal nature in the house, nor was there any trace of Mr West's business activities, whether criminal or legitimate.

They returned to the sitting room, which, with its owner missing, resembled a stage set, but whether for a tragedy or a farce was difficult to tell.

There was a CD playing on the stereo which had been set to repeat endlessly the same track. It was something classical, and nothing that anyone recognised. A constable was asked to remove it. He noticed that it was part of a boxed set of Verdi's *Falstaff*, conducted by John Eliot Gardiner, but he was unaware that it was the delightful final fugue that he had interrupted, nor did he translate (however roughly) the Italian of Boito:

> Everything in the world is a joke.
> Man is born a Jester,
> And in his head
> Reason always falters.
> We are nothing but fools!
> Every woman and man laughs
> At every other.
> But he laughs best
> Who has the last laugh.
>
> *Ma ride ben chi ride*
> *La risata final.*

Headline hopes that you have enjoyed reading OXFORD DOUBLE. We now invite you to sample Veronica Stallwood's next Kate Ivory mystery, OXFORD PROOF, available soon in hardback.

1

'Kate? I have some lovely news for you.'

Kate Ivory put down the mug of coffee she had been drinking and gave the phone call her full attention. Estelle Livingston, her agent, was on the line, sounding unusually enthusiastic.

'Lovely news?' Kate's head was full of plans for selling her house and moving away from Fridesley and it took an effort to realise what Estelle was talking about. 'About my book, do you mean?' She had been hoping to leave thoughts of work to one side for a few weeks.

'That last novel of yours . . .'

'*Spitfire Sweethearts*,' prompted Kate helpfully.

'That's the one,' said Estelle.

'Set in World War Two,' Kate added, as much for her own benefit as Estelle's. It was amazing the way the plot of a book disappeared from her memory once it had been printed out, consigned to a Jiffy bag and posted to her agent.

'Stop interrupting,' said Estelle, returning to her customary sharp style. 'I'm trying to tell you that now Fergusson's have accepted *Spitfire Sweethearts*, you've completed the two-book contract we had with them, and we can be more ambitious with your next book.'

Kate moved the coffee cup a couple of inches to the left so that she could read the details of a house for sale in Fridesley Lane. How much were they asking for it? she wondered. She really needed to move: Agatha Street was getting her down since the recent tragedies. And the street was changing. Familiar peeling paintwork and rusty fences had been replaced, while the tussocky, overgrown front gardens had been transformed by low-maintenance coloured gravel and miniature Japanese maples. Young professional couples, too busy for a conventional marriage and children, had taken over from large, noisy families like the Venns, whose messy lives had spilled on to the street and in through Kate's back door.

'You're not paying attention,' snapped Estelle.

'Really, I am.' Kate turned her mind from weeping cherry trees back to the contract for her next book. 'You haven't mentioned whether Fergusson's have offered a decent advance this time.'

'I've been trying to tell you. I'm not talking about Fergusson's. This is a much better proposition. I've been showing your outline to three or four top editors *and one of them has made an offer*. You're going up-market – at last!'

'I am?' Kate looked down at yesterday's washed-out T-shirt and the jeans she'd meant to consign to Oxfam. Definitely not up-market. She quickly imagined herself into a smart black suit and crimson silk top to project the right classy image to her agent.

'I have an offer from Foreword,' continued Estelle.

Kate added a string of real pearls and a pair of black pumps from Charles Jourdain. On reflection, she removed the pearls and replaced them with flame-printed scarf in finely-pleated silk.

'They like what they've seen of your work and they believe you have a future with them.'

Kate repressed the urge to jump up and down with pleasure, and tried hard to sound cool and sophisticated. 'They're the people who really know how to market their authors, aren't they? They sell *millions* of books?'

'And they're talking about a three-book contract,' crowed Estelle, unable to conceal her own jubilation.

'How much?' asked Kate, voicing the serious novelist's primary concern.

Estelle gave her a figure which was more than double Kate's expectation.

'And you'll like your new editor. A delightful young man.'

Kate hoped this didn't mean that Estelle was about to embark on another unsuitable liaison. She had a penchant for delightful young men and when the relationship broke up – as Estelle's relationships invariably did – Kate might well find herself with a cancelled contract, looking for a new publisher.

'He's one of the bright new generation,' continued Estelle, 'but with a real love of books and good writing.'

'You mean you want me to watch my spelling?'

'He'll be more interested in your style and original use of language. But he does love your natural gift for storytelling. And now you'll be able to go deeper with the psychology of your characters and their motivation. Neil and I think that Fergusson's demand for historical romances has been holding you back. But with Foreword you'll be able to let your true talent shine out.'

'He sounds like the ideal editor. Does he have a surname?'

'Orson. Neil Orson.'

Neil Orson would have enjoyed hearing Estelle's description of him, and would have agreed with every word of it. It would have been no surprise that she was delighted to have netted him as editor for her young protégée, Kate Ivory. (Kate, as she passed through her thirties, would have been equally pleased at the epithet 'young', but Neil wasn't to know that.)

While Estelle was speaking to Kate on the phone, Neil had bolted himself into the *en suite* bathroom that was one of the perks of his new job at Foreword, and was staring at his face in the mirror. The bathroom was tiny – in fact he could hardly turn round in it, let alone swing some innocent small feline – but he was the only editor to have such a luxury, and he felt sure it was because he had been marked down for early promotion.

What was concerning him at this moment was not the originality (or otherwise) of Kate Ivory's prose, or even the accuracy of her spelling, but rather the exact stage of development reached by the small boil in front of his left ear. If he squeezed it now, would it crumple up and die, or would it explode into angry red life so that Roland Ives would stare at it during their meeting? At the moment it was quite inconspicuous (or so he thought) and it was probably safer to leave it alone, but it was itching slightly, and the yellow, pus-filled point was protruding in a way that told him it was almost certainly ripe for squeezing.

His dilemma was solved by the abrupt ringing of his telephone. He unbolted the bathroom door and returned to his desk.

'Yes?' He looked with approval at the receiver in his hand: it was the colour and texture of a Granny Smith apple and matched precisely the wall-to-wall Wilton. He would have liked polished wooden boards and an antique rug, but he could see that it would not be practicable on the fifth floor of a modern office block. It was a pity, too, that they hadn't given him a corner office, which boasted windows on two sides, but at least he wasn't consigned to one of the claustrophobic boxes in the centre of the building, which had no windows at all and were strictly for losers, he considered.

The office was nearly perfect. He frowned at the 'nearly', but it was only imperfect in the sense of incomplete. He had brought one or two things from home, and had his eye on one or two more that he would purchase when he could take an afternoon off. Where other people personalised their office or work station with a spider plant in a plastic pot, a whimsical fluffy toy and a couple of wacky cards pinned to a partition, Neil had a shelf with two heavy glass vases in smoke-blue, shaped like large raindrops. On the wall he had hung an original Rainer Kleemann, with that same smoke-blue predominating. He had thought about a pale chair from Rolf Benz to seat his visitors on, but he hated to think of what might happen to it in the casual ambience of a publishing office. And how many of his visitors would recognise its designer's name without prompting?

'Mr Neil Orson?' a voice was repeating in his ear.

'Yes.'

'This is Tracey from the Customer Services department at your bank,' the voice continued. Tracey had an ingratiating tone and a mild Midlands accent.

'I don't need another pension plan,' said Neil, preparing to replace the receiver.

'Oh, no! It's nothing like that!' trilled Tracey, sounding almost like a real human being. 'I'm not *selling*, Mr Orson, I'm trying to *give* you something.'

One part of Neil's brain told him that the likelihood of his bank's giving anything away to one of its customers was small, but another, more primitive, part (remembering perhaps the deprivations of his youth) put in quickly, 'What are you offering?'

'A small number of highly valued customers have been carefully selected to receive completely free for the next six months our Accident and Sickness Cash Plan,' Tracey recited, apparently reading from a prepared script.

'How much?' he interrupted.

'I'm sorry?'

'How much will you pay me to break my leg or catch pneumonia? That's what you're talking about, isn't it?'

'Benefits are related to the customer's income, averaged over the previous six months. In your own case this would result in a payment in the region of five hundred pounds per day of incapacity, as certified by your own GP.'

'And you're giving me all this free of charge?'

'For the first six months, yes. Only after that period would you pay our low monthly premiums which would be deducted from your account by direct debit.' As Neil hesitated she added, 'And you may cancel your cover at any time during the first six months and pay absolutely nothing.'

'You're telling me I can't lose.'

'Exactly that, Mr Orson.' For a moment it sounded as though she might have departed from the script.

'Then you'd better sign me up,' said Neil. 'Just send on the bumf.'

'Fine. Just one more—'

'Isn't that all? I have to leave for a meeting in a few minutes.'

'For your own protection, I should just like to run through a few simple questions in accordance with our security procedure.

Can you give me the number of your current account?' As Neil hesitated, she added, 'You'll find it printed on your debit card, Mr Orson.'

'Oh, yes,' and he fished in his pocket and gave her the number.

'Right. And you have just the Visa credit card?'

'Platinum,' confirmed Neil. 'And the Mastercard, of course.'

'And I see you have an agreed overdraft facility of—'

'Five thousand pounds,' put in Neil proudly.

'That's correct. Now, I'd like your full name, please.'

'Neil Geoffrey Orson.'

'Date of birth?'

'Fourteenth March, nineteen sixty-nine.'

'And, finally, if you could give me your mother's maiden name.'

'Budleigh.'

There was two-beat pause. 'I didn't quite catch the name. How are you spelling that?'

Neil obediently spelled it out for her.

'Thank you so much for your co-operation, Mr Orson. Your Accident and Sickness Cash Plan cover will start immediately, though the paperwork may take a week or two to complete and send on by post.'

Neil replaced the apple-green receiver. It was almost worth falling under a bus to get five hundred a day, though it might be prudent to read through the policy's small print before doing so.

He might have wondered why Tracey, if she had his details in front of her, had needed to ask the spelling of his mother's maiden name. But he had the meeting with Roland in three minutes, and he only just had time to pick up his document case and take the lift to the top floor. It didn't do to keep the managing director waiting.

Oxford Shadows

Veronica Stallwood

When the flying bombs terrorised London in 1944, anxious mothers sent their children away to the peace of the countryside to escape the danger. Oxford and its surrounding villages appeared to be havens of safety, but dangers other than bombs menaced some unlucky children – and for ten-year-old Chris Barnes, the result was death.

Over fifty years later, novelist Kate Ivory, searching for wartime love stories as material for her latest historical romance, uncovers Chris's tragic tale. Amongst the piles of old papers in the attic of the house she shares with her partner, George, she finds the child's diary and drawings, and, in an old newspaper, a haunting photograph of a face she cannot forget. But one thing remains unclear – why he died so young.

Never able to resist a mystery, Kate determines to find the truth, but the knowledge comes at a price – the boy's death appears to implicate George's family – and Kate is faced with an impossible choice . . .

'Novelist Kate Ivory snoops with intelligence, wit and some nice insights' *The Times*

'Stallwood is in the top rank of crime writers' *Daily Telegraph*

'One of the cleverest of the year's crop [with] a flesh-and-brains heroine' *Observer*

0 7472 6844 4

headline

Shades of Murder

Ann Granger

In 1889 the late Cora Oakley's husband William was put on trial for her murder. The case was dismissed, but Oakley fled the country, never to be heard of again.

Over a hundred years later, the only remaining members of the Oakley family are two elderly sisters who, after years of struggling to maintain their dilapidated ancestral home, have decided to sell up. But then Jan, a young Polish man who says he is William Oakley's great-grandson, comes to visit, and claims half the profits from the sale of the house. When Jan is found dead, poisoned by the same substance used to kill his great-grandmother, it seems that the shadow of murder has returned to haunt the Oakley family once again, and Superintendent Markby must look back at the events of a century ago to find the killer . . .

'You'll soon be addicted' *Woman and Home*

'Ann Granger has brought the traditional English village crime-story up to date, in setting, sophistication and every other aspect of fiction writing . . . sheer, unadulterated bliss' *Birmingham Post*

'A good feel for understated humour, a nice ear for dialogue' *The Times*

0 7472 6803 7

headline

Written in Blood

Caroline Graham

It is clear to the more realistic members of the Midsomer Worthy's Writers' Circle that asking best-selling author Max Jennings to talk to them is a little ambitious. Less clear are the reasons for secretary Gerald Hadleigh's fierce objections to seeing the man – a face from his past – again. But, astonishingly, Jennings accepts the invitation and before the night is out, Gerald is dead.

Summoned to investigate, Chief Inspector Barnaby finds that Gerald's solitary life was as much of a mystery to his well-heeled neighbours as his violent death. The key is surely their illustrious guest speaker – but where is he now?

Now part of the major television drama series, *Midsomer Murders*, starring John Nettles as Chief Inspector Barnaby.

'Plenty of horror spiked by humour, all twirling in a staggering *danse macabre*' *The Sunday Times*

'Very funny, with a brilliant cast of eccentrics' *Yorkshire Post*

'Enlivened by a very sardonic wit and turn of phrase, the narrative drive never falters . . . a most impressive performance' *Birmingham Post*

0 7472 4664 5

headline

Stronger than Death

Manda Scott

Sometimes tragedies come in waves. First Eric, irrepressible, indestructible, climbing alone. Second Joey, choking, drunk – though not much more than usual – the night after his great triumph. But then there was the statistician, overdosing on Flatliners he thought were something else. Three's a series, not a coincidence: three men dead, three colleagues with a shared past. A past also shared by the one person Kellen Stewart would trust with her life, pathologist Lee Adams. Suspect number one.

'Scott's writing is powerful and subtle, her characters have depth, the plot is impeccable and original, and the shiver-count high. Her first two novels were impressive; *Stronger than Death* propels her into the front rank of British crime writers' Marcel Berlins, *The Times*

0 7472 5881 3

headline

Now you can buy any of these other
books by **Veronica Stallwood** from your
bookshop or *direct from her publisher*.

FREE P&P AND UK DELIVERY
(Overseas and Ireland £3.50 per book)

Deathspell	£5.99
Death and the Oxford Box	£5.99
Oxford Exit	£5.99
Oxford Mourning	£5.99
Oxford Fall	£5.99
Oxford Knot	£5.99
Oxford Blue	£5.99
The Rainbow Sign	£5.99
Oxford Shift	£5.99

TO ORDER SIMPLY CALL THIS NUMBER

01235 400 414

or e-mail <u>orders@bookpoint.co.uk</u>

Prices and availability subject to change without notice.